But his appreciation vanished within seconds as he turned to Casey. A frown tugged at his handsome lips. "Elvis jumpsuit? Elvis conventions? Why do I have the feeling I've been left in the dark about this project?"

"Left in the dark? Alex." A nervous laugh escaped her withering voice. "I told you Heather likes to entertain." Alex moved toward Casey, purpose in his steps. He reminded her of a Rottweiler who'd had its bone taken away. "Didn't I?"

"What's going on here?" he asked, his voice low and hard.

Casey swallowed. *Here it comes.* She braced herself, ready for him to express his dissatisfaction.

"Casey…what haven't you told me?" he said into her ear, his tone menacing. The feel of his warm breath against her skin sent her senses reeling. A wave of desire washed over her like a sudden summer storm, weakening her knees.

www.blackvelvetseductions.com

Review of Sherry James first book in the Studs for Hire series.

Studs for Hire - Woman on Top

Sherry James has an awesome read on her hands with *Studs for Hire*. Ms. James hooks the readers from the first page and keeps them hooked until the end. *Studs for Hire* has everything a reader wants and so much more. Sydnie and Trevor offset each other well, and with the fabulous twist in the story, will have readers begging for more. Ms. James has the reader laughing and crying with this emotion-packed romance. Ms. James has wowed this reviewer with the laughter and romance of *Studs for Hire*. This is a must have romance story. I cannot wait to see what Ms. James comes up with next.

Fallen Angel Reviews

Sherry James

Studs for Hire
Woman in Charge

ISBN 978-0-9774682-9-4

Published 2007
Printed by Black Velvet Seductions Publishing
Company in the United States of America

Visit us at:
www.blackvelvetseductions.com

Dedication

For Wyatt and Hannah
Two of the many blessings in my life.

And as always, for Mike.
My hero.

Special thanks to Kari Schwarz—*official staff for Sherry James, Romance Novelist*, AKA babysitter extraordinaire!

Acknowledgment

I've been an Elvis Presley fan since I was a kid, and when I started plotting this book a few years ago I knew I wanted to somehow include Elvis in the storyline. My original vision however, was that his role would be a minor one. Then I started writing the book and it didn't take me long to discover that the King of Rock 'n' Roll was going to play a bigger part in the story than I imagined. It was fun to revisit my youth and pull out my Elvis LPs, books and clippings that I had collected years ago, and add a few new items as well. Although I never had the privilege of meeting Elvis or seeing him in concert, I know that he had a special way of captivating people. And just like all those years ago when he captivated me as a kid, he did it all over again as I wrote *Woman in Charge*. Along the road of this creative journey I saw that this book was really becoming my fun, but respectful tribute to Elvis for the humanitarian he was, and all that he accomplished in such a short lifetime. I hope you feel I've done him just.

Thanks, Elvis, for all the music, movies and memories.

Chapter One

His plane was late.

October rain dumped from the gray Nebraska sky, turning the airport runway into a temporary lake, delaying incoming and outgoing air traffic.

Casey Burrows' hair was a mess. Her suit was damp, and her pantyhose sported a runner after she'd scraped her leg against her car door when she'd slipped on the wet asphalt. She'd pulled a muscle when she fell, and if that wasn't enough, her purse hit the ground and sent her favorite lipstick spiraling down a storm drain.

What else could go wrong today? Her nerves were damned near close to being shot—all because one man, a man she didn't even know, who at this very moment circled high in the sky on a delayed airplane, held her future in his hands.

Drumming her manicured fingernails on her folded arms, Casey resumed pacing the carpet of Omaha's Eppley airport and tried to conjure up positive thoughts.

Positive thoughts? She needed more than positive thoughts to get her through the balance of this disastrous day. A Casey emergency always called for at least a pound of dark chocolate, or a pitcher of strawberry margaritas. Hell, why not both? This day from hell deserved drastic measures. Besides, everybody knew strawberries and chocolate went together.

Unfortunately, she had neither at her disposal. She was on her own.

Casey inhaled. Exhaled. Inhaled. Exhaled. So much rode on Alex. Her future, her friends' futures, and the future of their company, Studs for Hire, all hinged on this one man's answer. Two simple words, yes or no, never held more power as far as she was concerned.

Casey stopped her pacing, gazed out over the empty runway and checked her watch and the arrival board for the hundredth time. Time ticked away, mocking her.

Taking a calming breath, she shook her arms and wiggled her fingers in an effort to ease her tension. It didn't work. She shook her arms again, this time a little harder. It was bad enough she'd let her nerves get the better of her in the first place—breaking her steadfast rule to always be cool and collected in any situation.

Today, however, proved too much and had tested every self-control skill she possessed. And now, thanks to the addition of Alex Roy's flight delay, her nerves teetered on the edge.

Yet, every minute Casey *didn't* have to face the high-dollar Denver architect, was one more minute of spared humiliation. One more minute of blessed relief.

"Heather. I ought to wring your neck for putting me in this situation," Casey grumbled under her breath. She turned, ready to wear another round in the carpet with her Jimmy Choos when she noticed an elderly gentleman sitting to her immediate right. He stared, a huge smile lighting up his face.

"Got an imaginary friend there, sweetie?" he asked with a voice that sounded like a rusty door hinge.

Wonderful. Grandpa thought she was cracked because she was thinking out loud. She sighed, so ready for this long day to be over. But out of sheer respect for the elder man, she gave him a smile and turned away.

"Makes no difference to me if you have imaginary friends, sweetie. You're hot."

Casey spun around, her mouth gaping open in shock. Words failed her.

"I'd love to see what's under that red suit of yours," he said with a growl. Puckering his lips, he blew her a kiss.

Casey's temper flared. Okay. This pervert was an exception to the rule when it came to respecting one's elders. He didn't deserve any respect, regardless of how old he was. Casey took a step back, increasing the distance between her and Mr. Love Machine sitting contentedly in one of the black vinyl seats. He grinned wider, revealing crooked and tobacco stained teeth.

Joy. Casey groaned under her breath. Just what she needed to plunge her day completely into the toilet— being the object of the plaid polyester king's desires.

And hey, didn't people know fashions changed each year? Didn't they know they couldn't keep the same suit for thirty-plus, moth-filled years and expect it to still be in style? Sure, fashion trends recycled every so many decades, but there were limits. Certain articles of clothing should never be resurrected. The polyester leisure suit topped the list.

The old man winked and patted the empty seat beside him. *Skippidy-do-dah.* Time to resume her pacing on *the other side* of the waiting area.

But what the hell. She could be ornery, too, and give the guy the thrill he was desperate for. Giving him a

quick wink, she hurried off, afraid to find out if he got
overly excited and suffered a heart attack or stroke.

Casey glanced up at the arrival board. Flight fourteen-
ninety-two from Denver was now minutes from landing.
The rain had stopped, and her life was moments away
from potential ruin. The next few hours with Alex, if
he gave her that long, would help determine her future.
Studs for Hire was Omaha's latest and most unique
construction and handyman company. Because they
were so new, they couldn't afford the blow of a job gone
wrong. One unhappy wealthy and influential client and
the phones would stop ringing, the jobs would cease,
and the bank account would dwindle to zero.

Casey was determined not to let that happen. Letting
down her friends wasn't an option. The three women
despised the corporate scene. As far as they were
concerned, the corporate world was still dominated by
men who believed the only job in an office for a woman
was fetching coffee and polishing desktops with their
backsides. No way was Casey going to be responsible
for sending them all back to that misery.

Besides, being the boss in a business where the women
were in charge held a certain rush. Throw in employees
who were buff and sexy construction men, and you had
a girl's dream job come true. No way would she let it all
slip through her fingers just because a high-and-mighty
architect refused to do the job she had to offer.

But if he did refuse... She didn't want to think about
it. No Alex Roy meant no job at the Gridmore mansion.
No job at the Gridmore mansion meant no money, no
publicity, and no future clients from among Omaha's
wealthiest citizens. Heather Gridmore knew practically
everybody who was anybody in Omaha, and if Casey

could satisfy the wealthy widow's eclectic tastes, the whole city would know about it.

Talk about pressure personified. Casey took a deep breath. She could do this. With her business experience, charm, and a dash of sex appeal thrown in if necessary, she'd convince Alex he'd be a fool to turn down the job.

Her biggest challenge, of course, was assuring Alex that Heather's remodeling ideas weren't…cuckoo. If she broke the news to him with tact, and assured him he'd be well paid for his services, he shouldn't care what he designed—even if it wasn't exactly his *forte.*

"Waiting for someone, sweetie?" a cagey voice asked. Casey jumped, unaware her polyester admirer now stood only inches away to her left. What was he? A hungry vulture and she his prey? His eyes gleamed with silent suggestions and expectations, making her realize her spate of orneriness earlier had been a bad idea.

Wonderful. She couldn't just roll her eyes and walk away again. No doubt he'd follow and try some other lewd tactic. Her best course was to stand her ground and hope the guy could take a blatant hint.

"As a matter of a fact, I am waiting for someone," she said as politely as she could muster.

"A man? Course these days you could be waiting for a woman. It's not like in my generation when men only lusted after women, not each other."

"Yes, well, times change. As do fashions." She lifted an eyebrow, hoping he was sharp enough to catch *all* of her hints.

"True. Women show a lot more skin these days. That's one change I have embraced." He assessed her form-fitting, short skirted red business suit again with appreciation.

Casey shook her head. The guy had no clue she was referring to *his* fashion sins. Some battles couldn't be won, and right now she didn't care. Alex's plane had landed and taxied down the runway toward the gate.

"Something about those big planes," he said excitedly. "The size, the power, the shape." He wiggled his bushy eyebrows, suggesting more than Casey wanted to ever contemplate.

"Don't go there, old man," she said, a hard edge to her voice. Fudge. She didn't know what was worse— waiting for the man that could ruin her business with one word, or putting up with a dirty old codger who had nothing better to do then harass women in the airport.

Casey returned her gaze to the plane approaching. Rough plaid polyester pushed up against her and she gasped, stumbling backward.

"That's going too far. Back off or I'm calling security." She searched the terminal for the presence of uniformed personnel, but saw none. What was the deal? Normally you couldn't walk ten feet and a security guard was lurking, watching every move.

"You've got fire, sweetie. I like that." He winked.

"You haven't begun to see my fire, mister," Casey seethed. "I suggest you leave me alone."

The man growled in his throat and wiggled his eyebrows a second nauseating time. What was it with old men and their eyebrows, anyway? They always looked like they had untrimmed hedges on their foreheads.

Casey glanced over the man's matching plaid fedora hat at the bank of windows overlooking the runway. The plane was now parked at the gate. Here was her chance to escape without making a scene. Right now she'd gladly take the man who could ruin her professional life over this sex-crazed old fool.

"Please excuse me, my husband is on that plane. He'll be joining me soon," she fibbed, and hurried away before the man could utter a word around his floppy dentures.

Casey smoothed her skirt and attempted to fluff her rain flattened hair, hoping she didn't look as stressed as she felt. Meeting Alex Roy as a blonde bimbo wouldn't do much for her cause.

Slowly, passengers disembarked and filtered through the long passageway leading from the plane. Many were greeted by loved ones and friends. A few, by the presence of a laptop case hooked over their suit-clad shoulders proved they were in Omaha on business.

As the number of passengers who filled the terminal increased, and there was still no sign of a man who could be Alex, Casey's stomach clenched.

What if she had the wrong flight? What if she'd missed him? What if he'd changed his mind and decided not to take the job after all? Casey pressed her fingertips to her forehead, hoping for relief from the headache threatening to explode inside her brain.

Damn. If Alex wasn't on that plane, Heather Gridmore would have a fit. If Studs lost the biggest potential client they'd had to date, before the job even got off the ground, they'd all be drowning their sorrows in calories and fat grams.

Where was he? The man had first class tickets. He should have been one of the first passengers off the plane.   Maybe she *had* missed him? She'd never met Alex, but she'd seen him and his high-dollar log homes featured in several magazines. Surely he didn't look that different from his photo?

Turning, she scanned the seating area where only a handful of passengers still lingered. She saw no one who looked even remotely like Alex's picture.

Glancing at her watch, she let out a frustrated sigh. Heather was expecting them in a half-hour. How was she going to explain to the wealthy widow her prize architect was nowhere to be found?

But if he was here, Casey was missing out on valuable time. She needed every single minute to prepare Alex for Heather's plan for the mansion. With time slipping away, proving to him that he hadn't been duped, that this really wasn't a hokey job he'd accepted, wasn't going to be easy. She'd have to rely on every ounce of business savvy she possessed.

To put it bluntly, she had a minuscule number of minutes to save her ass.

A thought struck Casey. If he wasn't here, her ass was sort of saved, at least temporarily. After all, it wasn't her fault he'd missed his flight, or had a change in plans, or a change of mind. She'd done her part by making contact with Alex, well, mostly his secretary, and she had made the arrangements to get him to Omaha and to Heather's. No way could Heather find fault with Casey.

At least not yet.

Casey would simply have to find a way to pacify Heather until she could reach Alex, find out why he hadn't showed, and make new arrangements. Stuff happened. Plans changed. Emergencies struck. Heather would have to live with it.

"Husband stand you up?"

Casey's shoulders stiffened. Her temper sparked. Not the old man again. Elder or not, the guy had overstayed his welcome. It was time to tell him to get lost once and for all.

"I don't see where that's any of your business," she said through clenched teeth.

"Well, it is if you were lying about a husband in order to get rid of me. I'm telling you, I can be a lot of fun. Give me a chance, sweetie."

A sharp pain pierced Casey's backside. She jumped and shrieked. The old codger had pinched her on the butt.

"Look here, buster." She pointed a trembling finger at his nose. "I have a right mind to slug you one where it counts." Who knew a ninety-year old man could think so indecently, let alone have the energy to act indecently? And where the hell was security when a girl needed them?

"What's going on here?" a hard-edged male voice asked from behind her.

Casey spun around, anger pulsing through every inch of her five foot, eight inch frame. *Finally* someone was being noble and getting involved, even if it was after she'd been made to look like the bad guy. "Grandpa here was getting his jollies by pinching me."

"Me? Pinch you? Sweet lady, you are sorely mistaken," the old man said dramatically. "I was walking by and stumbled into you. I apologize if you were given the wrong impression. My old legs aren't as steady as they used to be."

"Stumbled? That's a lie and you know it." Casey leered at the old man, her hands fisted at her sides. "You're a dirty senior citizen and should be locked away."

"Whoa. Hold on," the stranger said. He placed a firm hold on Casey's shoulder, silently commanding her to take a few steps back. "The lady is right, old man. I saw you pinch her. I suggest you apologize."

"Bullshit. I won't do it." The old man stomped a foot in protest. He jerked his bent body into motion and hobbled off into a new crowd of passengers gathering at another gate.

"Hey." Casey moved to follow but the stranger didn't relinquish his hold. "What are you doing? He's getting away."

"Ah, let him go."

"Let him go?" Casey threw up her hands in frustration. "The man has been harassing me for the past twenty minutes and you're telling me to let him go? He needs to be reported."

"I agree. But most likely, in his mind he doesn't know he's in the wrong. And with his advanced age, what real harm can he do?"

Casey bit her bottom lip and considered the stranger's words as she watched the old man sit down by himself on the other side of the terminal. He looked so alone, so lost. "True, but it still doesn't make it right."

"I know. But what are the cops going to do? They'd probably just tell him to knock it off, give him a ride home, and that would be the end of it anyway."

Casey planted her hands on her hips, not thoroughly convinced she should let the matter go. "Whose side are you on?"

"Well, I'm not really taking sides. I just think reporting him would be making a mountain out of a mole hill and—"

"Let me tell you something." Casey poked her index finger into his firm chest. "The man wiggled his eyebrows, blew me kisses, and followed me around the terminal like a panting dog. I reached my breaking point when he pinched my..." She twisted and pointed to the assaulted spot on her backside.

The stranger shifted his weight onto one hip. He quirked an eyebrow and looked at the offended spot. A grin tugged at the corner of his lips. "I have to admit, he's got great taste."

Casey stilled. Recognition hit her like another unwelcome pinch on the posterior. She knew that voice. Their one conversation on a static-filled cell line had been brief, but she'd know that whiskey smooth voice anywhere.

And now, too late, she recognized that lazy, sexy smile from a photo she'd seen in a magazine article.

Oh boy.

"Alex Roy," he said, holding out his hand for her to take. "I bet you're Casey Burrows? Right?"

Boy, oh boy. It was him. Embarrassment heated her cheeks. This was one helluva a first impression—him finding her in a tussle with an old man, and now with her butt cocked out for the world to see. Really, could this day get any worse?

Casey snapped herself into a straight position and lifted her chin, stepping into her professional mode. Sliding her hand into his, his lean fingers wrapped around hers perfectly. Alex's grip was strong and firm, yet gentle. And Casey could feel a slight roughness to his skin, confirming he didn't just design log homes, but had a hand in the actual building process of his creations as well.

Oh, sweet tangerine. The man *was* to die for. Tall, dark-haired, broad shouldered and with deep, soul-filled brown eyes, he was a delectable delight. He was better-looking up close and personal than in the picture she'd seen. Now she fully understood why Heather had been so insistent upon hiring Alex. Pure intelligent and talented hunk through and through, he was not only the perfect architect for the job, but the perfect addition to Studs for Hire. He was a master design himself.

Once word got around Omaha that Alex was working exclusively with Studs, the phone wouldn't stop ringing. Maybe she'd have to figure out a way to thank Heather for being so insistent.

"Nice to finally meet you, Alex," she said around the zings of awareness pulsing through her veins. "I was beginning to wonder if you were on this flight or not."

"Sorry. If I'd gotten off the plane sooner I could have saved you from being *harassed*." He winked.

"Yes, you could have," she teased. "But I do want to thank you for *ultimately* coming to my rescue. No one else did."

"Most people these days feel it's safer not to get involved."

"I guess it's true what they say. The days of chivalry are dead."

"Maybe."

Casey saw a darkness cloud his eyes and got the feeling he agreed with her statement more than he wanted to let on. "So, what were you doing on the plane for so long? Napping?" she asked, hoping to ease the tension in his eyes.

"Uh, no." He chuckled. His laugh was deep and sensual. Casey found herself liking the sound, maybe a little more than she should. "I don't like to sleep on planes," he continued. "At least if I'm awake, I feel like I have some semblance of control in a totally out-of-my control situation."

Casey smiled. "I can relate. I love to travel, but flying isn't exactly my favorite part of the trip. Knowing my safe arrival is in the hands of someone I've never met bothers me."

"Yeah. If something goes wrong, I'm powerless to stop it. I know nothing about airplanes."

Casey nodded her head in agreement. "It's a control issue."

"Guess so." Alex shrugged. "I can't help it. I'm serious about my business. I'm very hands on in both my professional and personal life."

And so was Casey. Being that way came from practically raising four younger brothers and sisters by herself. But that didn't stop her from worrying if she and Alex, two control freaks, could work together without locking horns and facing major challenges? For the job, they'd have to, or else end up in a disaster she didn't even want to contemplate.

She filed away her apprehensions, forcing the butterflies in her stomach to take a hike.

"So," she said, getting back on track. "If you weren't sleeping, what were you doing? Wooing a flight attendant?"

"Hardly." He laughed again and the sound soothed her nerves. "I was talking with the pilot. He's thinking about building a log home."

"Ah, a potential client. Your reputation precedes you. Impressive."

He shook his head. "Not really. I guess he recognized me from an article."

"The one in last month's *Timber Home Living*?"

"I don't know. Maybe." He shrugged as if it didn't

really matter to him in the least.

"Publicity is good for business. Get plenty of publicity and you'll never want for clients."

"I prefer my homes to speak for themselves."

"Absolutely," Casey agreed, a new round of worry and dread coating her words. Heather's design was certainly going to speak for itself. There was no doubt the mansion was going to be one-of-a-kind. And in a class by itself.

That is, if they ever made it that far.

* * * *

Casey glanced at her watch as she and Alex stood outside the front door of Heather's colossal home. They'd arrived with two minutes to spare. Heather might be impulsive, and oftentimes deserving of the dumb blonde label, even though her hair color changed with the wind, but she was a stickler for punctuality. If you wanted to stay on Heather's good side and continue to be invited into her circle, you were never late. For anything.

This was one time Casey thought being late might be a wise move. With Alex's flight delay, his luggage being momentarily lost, she'd had no time to brief him on the plans for the Gridmore mansion.

Well, there was the drive from the airport to Heather's home in the Happy Hallow area. However, telling Alex the truth while trapped in a speeding car zigzagging through Friday five o'clock traffic, with her nerves already fried, wasn't exactly prime spill-your-guts time. Wrecking her brand new Mazda Six with in-transit stickers still stuck to the windows, would play hell on her insurance.

So, now here they stood. Casey steeled her shoulders

and pushed the doorbell. Even through the heavy oak door, she heard the muted chimes tolling the moment of truth. Crawling under one of the large landscape boulders decorating the yard sounded like a good idea at the moment.

"This place is huge," Alex said, breaking the quiet of the fall evening. The rain had stopped, but a heavy dampness clung to everything like carpenter's glue. "I can't believe she wants to add on." His strong hands splayed over his hips, pulling back his waist-length bomber jacket. As he studied the exterior of the house, Casey couldn't help noticing the broad chest hidden beneath his jacket and flannel shirt.

According to what she'd read about Alex, he was a no nonsense kind of guy, practical and down-to-earth. His basic, durable wardrobe reflected that personality. But it wouldn't matter if he wore a space suit for his clothing of choice. Alex Roy would still look sexy as sin.

His gaze landed on Casey and her pulse picked up another notch. A strand of his coffee brown hair fell over his forehead and she fought the urge to brush it aside. Yeah. He was sexy all right—with a capital S.

"What for?" he asked.

"Hmm?"

"Why does she want to add on?" Alex stared at her, a question furrowing his brow.

Crap. Why did he have to ask that question now when she felt like a drowned rat and her confidence was in the toilet? Casey pulled up the lapels of her black trench coat, giving her hands something to do, and her mind time to figure out how to answer. Never in her life had she felt so out of sorts. Maybe she was coming down with something—like terminal idiot syndrome.

"Heather likes to entertain…a lot." There, that wasn't a lie, or stretching the truth. Heather loved to party, and when she did, it was a five-star event.

The brass door latch clicked. Casey sucked in a breath. At least for the moment she was saved from answering any more of Alex's questions. In a matter of minutes the truth would come out and short-circuit her plans, her business, and her future.

Chapter Two

"Casey, sweetie!" Heather Gridmore said as she swung the door wide. Her green-eyed gaze landed on Alex within two-seconds flat of opening the door.

Casey groaned under her breath. *Here we go.*

As expected, Heather was dressed to the nines. When it came to fashion, the young, wealthy widow never missed a beat. And today was no exception. With her barely anything there black heels, short black skirt and sheer, loose fitting black top that conveniently exposed one tan shoulder, one that Casey noticed Alex admiring, she looked ready for a night on the town, not a business meeting.

"Heather, it's good to see you again," Casey said, putting her business facade firmly in place.

"Oh, and you're Alex," Heather cooed, not waiting for an introduction.

"In the flesh," he said.

Heather wasted no time in slipping her arm through Alex's and pulling him into the house. In an instant Casey found herself left out on the cold, damp doorstep. To say this job was going to be a challenge was an understatement, and her business sense told her she better get control of the situation now, or she never would.

"Welcome to Omaha, Alex," Heather said with a voice seductive enough to charm a cobra. "And welcome to my home. I'm thrilled to have you here."

I bet you are, Casey thought as she moved up beside Alex on his left.

"It's a pleasure," he said.

"I hope you had a good flight." Heather stopped in the middle of the massive grand foyer and waved her hand. A man dressed impeccably in a black tuxedo appeared out of the shadows and moved toward them. He walked as if he had a golf club rammed up his back, but he proceeded to take their coats without making a sound and disappeared into the shadows of the house again.

"Yeah. It was all right." Alex said, tugging at the collar of his navy and red checked flannel shirt.

"Oh, yum. Flannel," Heather crooned as she brushed her hand up and down the length of Alex's arm. "It's so warm, cozy, and rugged. I love rugged," she growled.

Casey rolled her eyes. Apparently Heather was in no mood for subtlety tonight. Once Heather made up her mind she wanted something, she didn't stop until she got it, regardless of the cost.

Time to throw a wrench in the little seduction scheme Heather had going. "Your late husband must have worn flannel a lot then," Casey said.

"Hecky didn't care for flannel." She stuck her pert nose in the air and sniffed.

"That's right. I remember now. Hector preferred polyester blended fabrics."

Alex threw Casey a confused look. "Late husband?"

"Heather is a widow. I guess I forgot to mention it."

Alex quirked a brow, the irritated look on his face hinting that she'd neglected to tell him much of anything. Well, he hadn't asked, either, Casey thought silently.

"I'm sorry, Heather. I didn't know," Alex said with compassion in his voice.

"Really, you didn't know?" she asked. "His accident was reported in all the newspapers. He made national headlines."

"Accident?"

"Yes." She flipped her long hair over her shoulder. "He died while lounging on a deck chair at the Happy Hallow Golf Club."

"Heart attack?"

"Oh, no. He was hit by a runaway golf cart. Another member had a few too many before heading out onto the course. He had a blood alcohol level of point zero five. Anyway, he was so confused as to where he was, he lost control, and wham!" Heather slapped her hands together. "That was it. I don't know how he thought he was going to play eighteen holes in such a condition."

Casey watched Alex's expression go blank, obviously at a loss for words. Heather had a habit of effecting people that way.

"That's him over there," Heather said, pride in her voice. "The last portrait on the right."

The three of them walked over to the portrait where it hung under a small light. The balding, elderly man leered down at them with a scowl that made him look more like Ebenezer Scrooge than the philanthropist he was. A shrewd businessman, Casey knew he relished playing the part of a curmudgeon, when in actuality he possessed a heart of gold.

The sensation of Hector watching them from beyond the grave zipped down Casey's spine. Hector had worked hard and played hard during his life, and had always treated his friends and loyal employees with respect and compassion. But if anyone messed with two of his most prized possessions: his wife and his house, there was hell to pay.

"*He* was your husband?" Alex asked with disbelief.

"I know what you're thinking." Heather placed flawlessly manicured fingertips on her slim hips. "I've heard it all. Sure, he *was* old enough to be my grandfather. But Hecky and I loved each other. Our age difference didn't matter to us."

"Of course, Heather. I think what took Alex by surprise is that you were married to the founder of the famous Gangsters Pizza. Weren't you, Alex?"

"Uh. Yeah. I had no idea you were married to *that* Hector Gridmore." Alex cut Casey a glare, then turned and walked around the foyer, appearing to study the details of the architecture.

The place really was dreary. And why Hector liked it so, was beyond Casey. The dark paneled walls matched the equally dark gray marble tiles covering the floor. A dimly lit chandelier hung in the center, and a wide staircase swept around the east perimeter of the room.

"Your home is really amazing, Heather," Alex said. "It looks like it's straight out of one of those gothic novels my aunt used to read."

"I know. Isn't it appalling?" Heather mumbled. "I'm so tired of living in a mausoleum."

"That's why we're here," Casey said, anxious to get this over with so she had an excuse to indulge in the chocolate and strawberry margaritas she'd fantasized about earlier. "We'll have your home brightened up and updated in no time."

"It's so exciting." Heather clapped her hands in excitement, her Flamingo pink nails glowing like neon orbs in the dimly lit room. "Alex, I just know with your expertise, you'll make this place perfect for my Elvis conventions."

Slowly, Alex turned around, his eyes narrowed in question. "Elvis conventions?"

Oh. Shit. Casey cringed.

"Excuse me, Mrs. Gridmore." The man who'd taken their coats earlier stood at the edge of the foyer. "I'm sorry to interrupt, but you have an important phone call."

"Take a message, Joey."

Joey? The butler who looked like he'd swallowed lemons for breakfast that morning was named Joey? Casey sighed. Leave it to Heather.

"Normally I would, ma'am, but it's in regards to that Elvis jumpsuit coming up for auction next week."

Heather squealed. "Oh, at last, I've been waiting months for this. Excuse me. I *have* to take this call. Casey, fill Alex in on all we've talked about so far, will you?"

"Sure."

Heather trotted toward the door, her heels clicking on the marble. There was no missing the appreciative gleam in Alex's eyes as he watched that personally trained butt of Heather's sashay out of sight. But his appreciation vanished within seconds as he turned to Casey. A frown tugged at his handsome lips. "Elvis jumpsuit? Elvis conventions? Why do I have the feeling I've been left in the dark about this project?"

"Left in the dark? Alex." A nervous laugh escaped

her withering voice. "I told you Heather likes to entertain." Alex moved toward Casey, purpose in his steps. He reminded her of a Rottweiler who'd had its bone taken away. "Didn't I?"

"What's going on here?" he asked, his voice low and hard.

Casey swallowed. *Here it comes.* She braced herself, ready for him to express his dissatisfaction.

"Casey...what haven't you told me?" he said into her ear, his tone menacing. The feel of his warm breath against her skin sent her senses reeling. A wave of desire washed over her like a sudden summer storm, weakening her knees.

Dangerous, a tiny fragment of her brain whispered. *Very dangerous.* Casey stepped back, putting some much needed distance between her and this man who smelled like spice and fresh mountain air.

"What's going on here is exactly what I told your secretary over the phone," Casey said, her business facade firmly in place. "Heather wants to remodel the existing house and add on." She shrugged, trying to act as if this was no big deal and that he was overreacting. Alex scowled. He wasn't buying it.

"Remodel it how? For some reason I'm getting the feeling her idea of remodeling isn't up my alley."

"I admit Heather is a bit...unusual."

"Unusual?" He gritted his teeth. His eyes darkened.

"Eccentric is a better word, maybe?"

The sound of Heather's heels clicking on the marble announced her return. Alex turned away.

"Oh! I've been waiting months for that suit to be authenticated," Heather said excitedly. "It's a genuine Elvis. I have to have it."

"So you're an Elvis collector?" he asked.

"A very serious collector. I've amassed nearly a thousand items so far. That's why I want to add on. Did Casey tell you my ideas? I've got everything figured out just how I want it."

"No. Unfortunately Casey hasn't filled me in, yet." He turned his gaze to Casey and there was no missing he was more than a little unhappy.

"Alex's plane was late," Casey said in her own defense. "We didn't have time for me to go into detail."

"*Detail*," he mocked. Casey winced. Would this rotten day never end?

"Well, you're here now," Heather squealed. "And I'll be happy to tell you all my ideas." Heather wrapped her arms through Alex's and led him down the hallway and into a large room on the right.

The room sported a heavy masculine decor, and Casey remembered from working for Hector that this room had been his office away from the office. Now it overflowed with Elvis memorabilia. Everything from records and photos, to clothes, shoes, newspapers and magazines covered every available space.

"I see you weren't kidding when you said...serious," Alex said.

"I never kid about Elvis. He's one of my passions. I want to add on a special room to showcase my collection. Of course you'll need to factor in temperature and humidity control, all that archival stuff."

"Of course." Alex unhitched himself from Heather and shoved his hands into his jeans pockets. Slowly he made his way around the room, perusing the vast collection.

Casey watched as Alex stopped and studied a life-sized

cardboard cutout photo of Elvis. Dressed in his famous black leather outfit, and complete with the sexy sneer that made women's hearts palpitate, Elvis looked delicious. And so did the architect standing next to him, she thought. Unfortunately the sneer on Alex's face at the moment didn't exactly exude the sex appeal that the King's did. To be frank, Alex looked pissed. Not a positive sign.

"I also want to remodel the entire house to reflect an Elvis theme," Heather continued. "It'll be so cool. I thought I'd name each room after a different Elvis song. For my bedroom I like the *Burning Love* suite. I can see it all decked out in red and gold, can't you? It needs to be really hot and wild."

Heather's bedroom wasn't the only thing going to be hot. By the tight set of Alex's jaw, and the tinge of red coloring his cheeks, Casey figured he was well on his way to getting hot under the collar.

Time to get him out of here before things got really ugly and Casey found herself short one architect, and one very big job.

"Sounds like you know exactly what you want, Heather," Alex said with calmness Casey sure as hell didn't feel.

"I've always known what I want." She leveled a sultry gaze on Alex and ran her tongue along her bottom lip.

Okay. Now it was really time to go. "We've taken enough of your time, Heather. We should get going. I'm sure you have plans for tonight."

Alex turned his gaze on Casey. "It's been a long day. And I can see Casey and I have a lot to discuss."

Ouch. That didn't sound good.

"We'll talk more tomorrow, right?" Heather asked.

"I'm anxious to get started. Every square inch of this house reminds me of Hector's morbid side. I can't handle it anymore. I'm far too young to live like this. And I'm feeling cramped. I need more space."

"I'm afraid—"

"Alex and I'll kick around some ideas tonight and be in touch," Casey interrupted. She circled the room and took him by the arm. "I'm sure we'll come up with something that will show off your Elvis collection without compromising taste and style. We'll call you."

"We?" Alex asked, as she ushered him out of the room. They grabbed their coats from Joey as Casey pushed Alex out the door.

"Yes. We."

* * * *

"We? Kick around ideas?" Alex grumbled under his breath. Casey gave him a tight smile, squeezed his arm and hurried him down the steps and away from the Gridmore house. For a tall and slender gal she was pretty darn strong. He liked that.

He didn't, however, like the remodeling ideas Heather had dropped on him like a bomb. This whole deal was starting to feel like one big peck of trouble, and a major headache he sure as hell didn't need.

Fog had settled on the October night, surrounding them as they stepped onto the damp blacktopped driveway. Casey hurried toward her car, not relinquishing her hold on his arm. Obviously she wanted to get him as far away from Heather as possible. For that he was grateful, but the real reason she pushed him along was what bothered him the most. She didn't want him saying no to the job. At least not in front of her star client.

He could see it coming. She'd beg and plead with him

to take the job, but she was in for a helluva surprise. No way was he going to say yes to building a shrine to Elvis.

At last they reached the car. She let her hand fall away and the sudden loss of her touch left him with a surprising emptiness. Not a good way to be feeling right now. This was no time to let his libido get the better of him. His reputation was on the line.

He leaned against the driver's side door and crossed his arms. "Just what do you mean by kick around ideas?" he asked again. He wouldn't let her skirt the issue forever.

"Omaha has a great French restaurant down in the Old Market. Sound good to you? I hope you're hungry because the food is to die for." She dropped her gaze to her purse and dug for her car keys.

"You're changing the subject, Casey."

"Food is always a good subject. One of my favorites, actually."

"One of mine, too. But you're avoiding my question. I want an answer."

"Alex, Alex." She smiled sweetly and smoothed the collar of his leather jacket. "There's no need to get testy. The weather really isn't conducive to an outdoor conversation. We'll discuss matters at the restaurant."

She was so close the delicate scent of her perfume wafted gently around him on the evening air. The soft glow of the antique street lamps lining the crescent shaped driveway reflected through the fog and onto her blond hair, creating a halo effect.

Alex seriously doubted Casey was an angel. Well, maybe. She did look like one with more curves to her than a racetrack. Any man worth his salt would drool over this babe. However, looks and what was on the inside were two totally different issues. He'd seen plenty of gorgeous women who harbored major ugly streaks on the inside—including one woman who had personally taken him to the cleaners.

As for what Casey's insides looked like, he wasn't sure. He'd only known her for a few hours, not near enough time to make that kind of determination. Although he'd been burnt to a crisp by a scheming woman, Alex considered himself a fair guy. He preferred to give a woman the benefit of the doubt before he handed down a verdict. And in spite of the craziness of the job Casey was offering him, he was willing to give her a chance and hear her out—that is if he could get her to talk.

"I'd rather discuss it here," he said. Casey slid her hand down the length of his arm. Unexpected bolts of awareness warmed his flesh, even through the layers of leather and flannel. Damn. "And I'm not testy. Yet. But if you keep avoiding my question, I can't make any promises."

Forcing himself to retain his resolve, he stepped away, breaking the contact. Man, he needed some space, but they weren't going anywhere until she fessed up. He'd be damned if he'd let himself be blindsided a second time in his career, but he had to admit, she'd piqued his interest. The curious side of his brain wanted answers. And he wanted them now, before she tried to snooker him into taking the job.

"Tell me what's going on here?" he asked again. "Kick around what ideas?"

"Alex, the weather." She pulled her collar up against the elements and shivered. "Let's at least go someplace warm and dry."

She was a determined woman. For that he'd give her credit. But he'd already wasted an entire day on this crazy endeavor. And wasting time wasn't a luxury he could afford.

"What kind of joke are you trying to pull?" he asked, determined to make her come clean.

"Joke?"

"Yeah, joke."

"There's no joke."

Alex's heart stopped in his chest. Casey's face was as sincere as a heartbeat. Either she was one hell of an actress, or she was genuinely telling the truth.

"You mean Heather's serious about this?" He spread his arms and glanced at the mansion looming tall and encompassing behind her. It was an amazing house, architecturally speaking. "She really wants to turn this place into a Graceland?"

"I wouldn't go that far. But yes, she does want to redo many of the rooms with an Elvis theme."

"Why?"

"You saw her collection. She's a fan."

"A fan? Heather wasn't even born yet when he died."

"What difference does that make? She can still have a love and appreciation for his music. I'm a Marilyn Monroe fan myself."

Alex eyed Casey. Yeah, he could see why she'd be a fan of one of the greatest sex symbols to ever live. In fact, Casey even looked a little like Marilyn in a modern, updated sort of way.

"Okay, so I watch John Wayne movies but—"

"So, that means you'll do it?" Casey smiled.

"I didn't say that." Even in the dim light Alex could see her excitement fade as fast as a deflating balloon.

"But you said okay."

"I said okay to the fact that Heather can be an Elvis

fan as much as you are a Monroe fan. Not okay to this crazy remodeling plan of hers. What she's proposing is insane. Obsessive, even."

And Heather's bank account no doubt reflected the blow of her obsession. Alex had spied the 1975, Elvis Las Vegas Hilton menu from the Showroom where he'd performed, and an original Sun Records 45 RPM of Elvis' *Good Rockin' Tonight*. Both rare and pricey items.

"But you said yourself you're a John Wayne fan."

"I said I like to watch his movies. That doesn't mean I want to turn my home into a shrine to the man." He shook his head and uneasiness dropped into his stomach like a lead weight. "I can't be a part of this."

"Can't, or won't?" Casey placed her hands on her hips causing the collar of her black trench coat to open and reveal the slender expanse of her throat. Against his better judgment he let his gaze travel the length of that exquisite path down, down, and down.

Oh, yeah. He didn't need to see her standing there in nothing but her birthday suit to know what lay beneath. He had an imagination.

And he was a man. Certain things were instinctive.

"Are you through ogling?" she asked, her voice tight.

Shit. Alex raked his fingers through his damp hair. A light mist now fell around them and he hadn't even noticed. And what was worse, she'd caught him in the act of blatantly checking out her attributes. What the hell was the matter with him?

"Typical," Casey mumbled.

"What's typical?" Alex knew he was asking for trouble here, but for some reason he couldn't seem to help himself. Much to his chagrin, he was curious to know what made Casey Burrows tick.

"You. Men. Always letting a certain part of their anatomy do the thinking for them instead of their real brains."

Alex's temper hitched up a notch at her slam of the male species, but she did have a point. Sort of. Well, maybe in a lot of ways. Especially after her ordeal with the old man in the airport.

If only she wasn't so damned delectable standing there, the mist clinging to her clothes and skin. How could he help but ogle? Under the light her face took on a luminous glow, glistening as though diamonds had been sprinkled on her skin.

Where the hell did that come from? He never thought about women in romancey terms and clichés. Trading in his T square for a chance to lick those "diamonds" off those sexy lips was mighty tempting, though.

"Hello? Alex? Here?" She waved a hand in front of his face.

Damn. He was becoming more demented by the minute. "Ah, sorry. I was thinking." He shrugged and hoped he could get himself out of this mess without making matters worse.

"Well, why don't we do our thinking together, and someplace dry? I've been soaked enough for one day."

"Thinking together?" he teased, unable to resist. "Your place or mine?" He winked. What the hell. She already believed he had nothing but sex on the brain— he might as well make the most of the situation. Besides, he was going to be in Omaha less than twenty-four hours. First thing tomorrow he was heading back to Denver. How much trouble could he get into in this short span of time?

"As tempting as that might be, that isn't the kind of

thinking I had in mind."

"Tempting? Why, Miss Burrows, you like me enough, even with my limited brain capacity, to be tempted? I'm flattered."

"You should be."

Alex chuckled at her self-assuredness. She had spunk. Yeah, he liked that. Too damn much.

Chapter Three

"Hello," an aggravated voice answered on the other end of the line.

"What did you find out? Did your disguise work?" she asked, anxious to get the scoop on all he'd seen and heard at the airport.

"Sugar, you're way too anxious. I haven't even had time to get all this makeup off yet. My pores are screaming for air."

"Your pores can wait. I want to know what happened. Did it work?" She paced the ugly paisley carpeting covering her bedroom floor.

"The disguise worked like I said it would. Casey saw me exactly as I wanted—a dirty old man. Hey, you didn't tell me she could get so feisty. I like a woman with fire. Maybe you could set us up sometime?"

"Stop, Rory. Get your mind back on business. What did you find out?"

"Not much, really."

"What? Surely they talked."

"Not a whole lot. His plane was late and then he was detained on board talking to the pilot about building a house."

"You didn't learn anything about Alex's personal life,

like if he's in relationship—serious or casual, or about his current financial state?"

"Cripes. Not asking for much are you? They talked for five, maybe ten, minutes in the airport surrounded by hordes of people. And they'd just met. It wasn't a place conducive to a personal history revelation."

"Dammit, Rory. Didn't you learn anything at all?"

"He doesn't particularly like to fly. Is that helpful?"

She sighed in frustration. "Anything else?"

"There is one thing." A long pause hummed on the line.

"Well, what is it? I don't have all night to play guessing games."

"He's very gallant."

"Gallant? What's that supposed to mean?"

"I was having a little fun, playing up the part of the dirty old man pretty good." He laughed.

"And?" she asked through clenched teeth.

"Oh, I got a little too friendly for Casey's taste and Alex came to her rescue."

"What did he do?"

"He insisted I apologize. I didn't, of course, because I was putting on the ruse I'd stumbled, that I didn't pinch her butt like she claimed."

"You pinched her butt?"

He whistled. "Damn nice one, too. Firm, toned. Perfect contour for my hand."

"You can tell all that from one pinch?"

"You bet, sugar. When it comes to women there are just certain things men know. Our instincts are as sharp as a hawk's."

"Are your instincts telling you now I'm having doubts about donating my annual ten-thousand dollar contribution to your Theatre of the Arts Foundation next year? Hmm?"

"You wouldn't. We need that money. Think of the kids."

"Sounds to me like you wouldn't want to risk losing it, now would you?"

"No," he said flatly.

"I didn't think so."

"What do you want me to do now?"

"Don't leave town any time soon. I don't know when or how, but I'm sure I'll need your dramatic services again. I want you to be on call."

"On call? But I scored tickets to the Nebraska and Texas A & M game next weekend. Me and a group of the guys are planning on driving down to Texas. We're all set for this huge tailgate party."

"All right, you don't have to beg. Go. But after that, hang close."

"Okay. Okay. Whatever you say. Look, I've got to go. I've got to get these false eyebrows off, they itch like crazy." The sound on the line switched from Rory's voice to a dull hum, telling her he'd disconnected.

She pushed the button on her phone, ending the call. Things were in motion. Maybe not quite how she'd envisioned, but moving along, nevertheless. As long as her end goal was realized, she didn't care how she got there.

* * * *

Casey zipped her car into the driveway of her town house and cut the engine. The delicious aroma of the Chinese takeout they had decided to pick up, instead of going to the French restaurant, filled the interior. The wonderful smells of Mongolian Beef and Sweet n' Sour made it a little bit easier to focus on the food rather than the grumpy man sitting beside her, but not much. Since they'd left Heather's, Alex had been quiet and reserved, as if he pondered serious answers to serious questions.

Stealing a glance at him, she noted his striking profile. Strong jaw, high cheekbones, full lips. Alex Roy was all male, no doubt about it. And in spite of his current mood, he was still the handsomest, most tantalizing man she'd ever met. If she managed to convince him to stay, this had potential to be one scrumptious job.

"Nice place," Alex said, his voice mixing nicely with the steady thrum of the rain on the roof of her car. "Have you lived here long?"

"A while."

"Looks pretty big. Any roommates?"

"One."

"Oh."

Casey smiled at the flicker of disappointment in his voice. Even though he was trying hard not to be, she was confident he was interested. Over the years she'd dated enough men to recognize all the signs of attraction.

She stole another glance at Alex out of the corner of her eye and caught him admiring her legs in spite of the unsightly runner. Why in the hell hadn't she thought to ditch the hose while waiting for his plane?

But by the gleam in his eyes, the runner was irrelevant. The man was definitely interested. If she played this right, she'd have no problem convincing him to stay in Omaha for the Gridmore job.

"Shall we go in? I'm starving," she said, anxious to get things hashed out between them so they could move on to the fun of talking design.

"Sure."

"Why don't you grab your suitcase? You need to get out of your damp clothes."

"Sounds great."

Together they scooped up the bags of takeout, a bottle of wine and Alex's suitcase. The rain, now falling in a steady downpour again, re-soaked them both by the time they made the short dash from the car to her front door. Once inside they temporarily deposited their dinner on an entry table and shed their coats.

"Here, let me take that," Casey said as she hung Alex's bomber jacket in the closet before removing her own. Standing there in his checkered flannel shirt and a pair of faded blue jeans spotted with rain, he reminded her more of a lumberjack then an architect. The look suited him.

She was one lucky girl. One hundred percent male perfection stood in her foyer. *Yummy.*

A steady pounding broke the silence as four furry feet bounded down the wood laminate hallway, bringing the direction of her reckless thoughts back around one-hundred and eighty degrees.

"Brudy, there you are," she said. "I was beginning to wonder." The Golden Retriever slid to a halt on the slick floor, sat on his haunches, and lifted a paw. Casey knelt down, accepted his offering and said silent thanks for the distraction the dog provided. He barked twice before racing back down the long hallway.

"Nice homecoming," Alex chuckled.

"It's an evening ritual." Casey stood. "By the way, he likes you."

"He didn't even notice me. How can you tell he likes

me?"

"Oh, he noticed you all right. The fact he didn't bother you means he likes you."

"And if he didn't like me?"

"You'd be flat on your back and I'd be calling 911." She laughed.

"Uh-huh. Thanks for warning me before I set foot in your door. I might've been mauled to death."

"Nah. I wasn't worried." Casey picked up the bags of Chinese and headed for the kitchen. "I knew he'd like you."

"You knew?" Alex followed behind, bringing the bottle of wine and his suitcase. "How could you be so certain?"

Because I like you. Casey decided to keep that little piece of news to herself, and flipped on the kitchen light. She set about gathering plates and wine glasses. "Brudy and I have been together a long time. We know each other's tastes and quirks."

"Really?" he asked with disbelief.

"Not a pet owner, Alex?"

"Not since I was six. And then it was only for a short time."

"Parents say no?"

"No. They gave me a puppy for my birthday one year, but he ended up getting hit by a car a few days later."

"Oh, I'm so sorry." Casey set aside two plates and turned to him. "That must have been terrible."

"Yeah, it wasn't easy. Things happen, though, and life goes on." He shrugged and gave her a slight smile that didn't reach his eyes.

Casey's heart pinched. There was no missing the sadness the memory held for him. She'd had a number of pets while growing up and remembered all too well the heartbreak she endured when losing one of her beloved, furry friends.

But getting stuck on a morbid topic wasn't what she had in mind for this evening. Keeping things light, simple, and on business was paramount. No matter how much she wanted to rip that flannel shirt from his body.

"It's a bit chilly in here," she fibbed, hoping to distract herself from the outrageous direction her thoughts kept straying. Thanks to Alex, she actually felt like she needed to turn on the air conditioning. She hurried from the kitchen by another door that led directly into the dimly lit living room. Heading for the large stone fireplace on the left side of the room, she sat on the hearth and she set the flames to glowing within a matter of minutes.

Brudy nudged her arm as if to say he approved, then trotted over to the plush couch, jumped up onto the cushion and snuggled down into his usual spot.

Casey returned her attention to the fire, the flames adding to the already cozy atmosphere of her living room. If she wanted to sway Alex to her side she needed every advantage, and the proper atmosphere for a relaxed evening was crucial. Especially after the minor fiascos she'd faced at both the airport and at Heather's.

When it came to business, Casey preferred to always be professional, and to be in control. Several times today she'd lost some ground in that department, and now she deemed mixing in a dash of sex appeal a necessary tactic. The trick with relying on seduction in business was knowing how much to use, and when.

Although in Alex's case, she wasn't sure any type of sexual undertones were a good idea—for her sake. The guy had a knack for making her heart trip all over itself the way it was. Two little words from him would have her falling at his feet.

The flames leaped high and danced in the grate. That's how she felt—like those logs trapped in blazing heat.

"So, when do we eat?" Alex asked. "I'm starved myself."

Casey froze, certain she hadn't imagined the suggestive undertones in his words. Her nerves twitched.

"Right after you and I get out of these damp clothes." She stood, turned around and bumped into Alex.

"Oh!"

Alex steadied her on her two-inch heels, his firm and gentle hold exuding a suggestiveness she'd never experienced before. His gaze caught and held hers captive. Mesmerized, she watched as his dark eyes flickered between tinges of anger and desire. A dangerous combination, she knew, but she couldn't pull herself away.

He brushed a strand of damp hair from her face. "I've got nothing against spontaneous sex," he said, his voice low and seductive.

Warmth that had nothing to do with the fire behind her inflamed her skin. *Neither do I,* she wanted to shout. With mere inches separating them, Casey struggled to stay composed, to act the professional. Alex smelled of rain, leather...and man, turning composure into a foreign word. Her knees weakened.

And, ah hell, she couldn't breathe. How was she supposed to focus on business when she couldn't even take a normal breath around the man?

His gaze didn't waver and the glow of the fire added to the smoldering intensity brewing in the depths of his eyes. A low moan escaped Casey's throat. On its own accord, her body leaned into him as though drawn by some unknown force. A force she was powerless to stop.

It would be so easy to fall into bed with this man. So much time had passed since she'd been in an intimate relationship. She was ready. Needed it. Wanted it.

But then, she wanted and needed chocolate everyday, too, and she didn't let herself indulge in the pleasure. Well…more like her wardrobe didn't allow it. If she could limit her chocolate intake, she could limit her daily dose of Alex as well.

Yeah, right. What the heck for? Life was short. Didn't they always say you should eat dessert first anyway?

Casey reached out to touch him, dying to know the feel of the shadow of whiskers dusting his chin.

"Since we might be working together," Alex said, "we should probably abstain from such indulgences."

Casey's hand stilled in mid-air, his words hitting her as fast and hard as if he'd punched her in the stomach. Oops. She was getting way ahead of things here. She hadn't had a serious date in months. Maybe she was losing her touch when it came to men.

No. She was simply overacting due to a day that rivaled her worst nightmare. What she was dealing with here was a man full of ambivalence—one of the most dangerous types of men there was to get involved with. If she wasn't careful, he'd rev up her libido, screw up her hormones, and drive her insane.

And what was it he'd said moments before? *Might be working together? Might* was positive, but she had a feeling she still had a ways to go to convince him to stay. She took a deep breath. Alex Roy was going to be one major challenge for her control department.

"I never said anything about having sex," she said, feeling more off kilter around Alex than any other man before him. A muscle ticked at his jaw and she realized she'd said the words with more force than intended.

Way to play it cool, Case. So, she wasn't having the same effect on him as he was on her—a major blow to her already fragile relationship ego. She took a step back, frustrated and slightly embarrassed by the blunders she kept making around him.

He released his hold and let his hands fall to his sides.

Disappointed by the loss of his touch, Casey resisted the urge to grab his hands and put them back around her waist.

Brudy lifted his head from his resting spot on the couch and barked, breaking the awkward silence surrounding them.

"You can change your clothes in the spare bedroom," she said. "It's the third door on the right."

"Thanks," he said dryly. Alex widened the space between them. Picking up his suitcase, he headed up the stairs without saying another word.

Casey groaned. Again she wondered if this lousy day could get any worse.

* * * *

That was one helluva close call. Alex shook his head, silently reprimanding himself as he climbed the stairs. Another move like that one and he wouldn't have to worry about turning down the job. Casey would kick him all the way back to Denver. What the hell had he been thinking, letting his guard down like that?

He hadn't been thinking. That was the problem.

Alex stopped at the top of the stairs and saw only

three doors, all on the right. Casey had said the spare bedroom was the third room. He opened the door, flicked on the light and found the bedroom fashionably decorated, but obviously used very little. That's funny. Casey had said she had a roommate, but this room showed no evidence of regular use. This room was exactly what she'd called it, a spare bedroom—used only when company came, or as a place to stash out-of-season clothing.

She and her roommate must then share a bed, making their relationship far more than a co-habitation designed to save a few bucks each month. Alex didn't want to care whether Casey was involved or not, but he did.

"Cool it right now, Roy. You're not here for a woman. This is business." He tossed his small suitcase on the bed and pulled out a dry pair of jeans. After changing, he made his way to the bathroom and hung his jeans over the gold shower rod. Nabbing a towel, he rubbed the soft terry fabric over his head and worked most of the dampness from his hair.

The bathroom was as spic-n-span as the bedroom. If someone used this bath on a regular basis, they were a neat freak. Casey obviously had a master bath off her room. And again he found himself wondering what kind of relationship she had with her roommate. Must be pretty darn serious if they both shared a bed and a bathroom on a regular basis. Alex forced his mind away from that dangerous direction, but as he neared her bedroom door the impulse to take a peek inside nagged at him.

He stopped and stared at the honey oak-colored door. What would he find in there? The latest fashions? Expensive, intoxicating perfumes? Silky, mind-blowing lingerie? He'd bet all three. In spite of the mishap at the airport with the old man, he knew Casey had class and style. The fancy red number she'd worn today accentuated every dip, every curve of her luscious body and proved her tastes ran on the expensive side.

So did this house. With its vaulted ceiling, stone fireplace, and open staircase, this was no efficiency home. This was a high-dollar-a-month mortgage.

And she was high maintenance—with a capital m. But then, what woman wasn't.

A noise sounded on the other side of the door and Alex realized Casey must be inside changing her clothes. Stepping away he headed for the stairs, not wanting to get caught lollygagging at her door. That would make a good impression, he thought sarcastically. He'd already put his foot in his mouth, he didn't want her thinking he was a snoop and a pervert, too.

Sure, he'd love nothing more than to catch her in a few strategically placed pieces of silk, but this trip wasn't about pleasure, or putting his already fragile reputation on the line again. Over a mouthful of Chinese he'd stand strong and break the news he wasn't interested—in the job that is. True, he'd be interested in Casey if he let himself be, but he wouldn't. A woman only complicated a man's life and caused more trouble than the sex was usually worth. Alex had learned that piece of wisdom the hard way.

Keeping this meeting with Casey strictly on a business level was the right course to follow. Deal with the problem at hand, accept the outcome, and head home. No more slip-ups like earlier tonight. No matter how bad he'd like to have spontaneous sex with Casey, after he got done telling her thanks, but no thanks, *dessert* would be out of the question.

Alex paused halfway down the stairs and glanced out over the living room. Her dog lounged comfortably in his spot on the sofa, the fire blazed, and soft music hummed from the stereo.

Even though the room was decorated with sophistication and style, the deep rich colors of rust and sage fabrics on the furniture gave it warmth. The added extra touches of oversized pillows, thriving green plants, and several rustic paintings hanging on the walls all gave the room a comfortable touch. A touch that a man could appreciate and feel right at home with.

Did her roommate have a say in the decorating scheme, he wondered? A hint of jealousy filled his bones. He forced the thought away as fast as it had hit and finished his trek down the steps. Circling around the sofa he sat on the hearth with his back to the fire. The heat and comforts of the room felt good after being doused with a fall rain. Way too good.

The dog didn't bother moving from his spot, or bother even moving his head from the top of his paws. He puffed a sigh, and watched Alex with interest in his dark, soulful eyes.

Casey certainly was a woman of contrasts. With her fine clothes and sophistication, he'd never thought she'd prefer Terry Redlin paintings on her walls and a Golden Retriever on her couch. If asked, he would have said Thomas Kinkaid and a snow white Westie were her art and animal of choice.

When it came to understanding women, however, he didn't have the best track record—a trait he'd inherited from his father.

"Are you cold?" a voice asked from above. Alex looked

up to see Casey standing at the top of the stairs. He shot to his feet, more to keep his jaw from dropping than out of politeness. Dressed in an oversized chambray shirt with a white tank top beneath, and a pair of faded blue jeans hugging her hips, she looked like a sexy farm girl. Her now dry blond hair fell in soft waves around her face, giving her a sultry look.

Yep. Strictly business. You bet.

"I was," he said. She moved slowly down the steps, her left hand sliding along the smooth oak rail. "But...not anymore. The fire helped."

She smiled. Was that a *meet me later gaze* she just gave him? No, he had to be mistaken. He figured she'd be pissed as hell, not coming on to him.

She stepped off the last stair and walked over to where he stood. Even in the soft light of the room he saw her eyes were a deep, vibrant shade of green—almost shamrock green. How did he miss such a striking feature earlier?

"Fire will do that," she teased.

"Yeah. Fire will do that." Alex swallowed hard, knowing the heat encompassing every pore on his body was no longer from the artificial logs behind him. This sudden burst of heat was one-hundred percent Casey induced.

Strictly business. Man, he was in trouble here.

"Speaking of heat," he said, clearing his throat.

"Yes?"

"I bet our supper is none too warm by now."

"I've got it under control," she said over her shoulder as she headed for the kitchen. "I put it in the warming drawer before I went up to change. Our supper will be just right."

"A warming drawer. Nice touch."

"It is. It was a must have when I was designing this place." She handed him the set of wine glasses she'd taken out of the oak cupboards earlier, the bottle of wine and a corkscrew. She grabbed napkins and utensils and headed back to the living room.

"You designed this place?"

"Don't sound so surprised." Casey said over her shoulder.

"I'm not. Well, okay, I am. A little. I thought you were an accountant."

"That's me," Casey said as she set up their dinner on the glass-topped coffee table. "Accountant by degree, designer by desire."

"This place is…incredible. You did well."

"Wow, a compliment from Alex Roy. I feel special." She winked and Alex found himself laughing at her playful banter.

"I'm serious, Casey. You're good as what you do."

"Thanks." She smiled. "I can't take all of the credit, though. My business partner, Sydnie, and her family deserve a lot of it. Her dad and brothers also own a construction company. They did the framing and all the interior work well before we started Studs. But to hear such approval from a world famous architect like you means a lot. I'll be sure and pass on the kudos."

Alex chuckled as he set the wine and glasses down on the table. "I wouldn't go that far. One small profile in a magazine is a long way from being world famous."

"Yes, but it was that one article that led to the job with Heather Gridmore. She liked what she saw and insisted you were the man for her."

Alex wanted to ask, *in what way*, but held his tongue.

He might not be the most savvy when it came to what women secretly desired, but he'd been around long enough to know when a woman wanted more from him than blueprints.

"I hope you don't mind sitting on the floor while we eat?" Casey asked. "I thought it'd be kind of cozy on this damp night."

"Not at all. Kind of fitting since we're having Chinese."

"Yeah, I guess it is." Casey sat, her back against the sofa. Brudy put his head on her shoulder, obviously waiting for a handout. Alex joined Casey on the floor and hoped he didn't make a fool of himself by spilling wine or food all over her oatmeal-colored carpet.

"If it makes you feel more comfortable, you're welcome to take your boots off," she said. "After running around in killer heels all day, my toes are ready for a respite." Casey wiggled her stockinged covered toes and smiled.

"Sounds great." Alex removed his boots and got comfortable. They dove into their meal, making small talk as they ate. The food was good, the wine excellent, and the company divine. He hadn't felt this relaxed since he didn't know when.

Maybe coming to Nebraska hadn't been such a bad idea after all? A change of pace was a good thing now and then, but no matter how good, he couldn't afford to take another step in the wrong direction. Designing a hangout for a bunch of crazed Elvis fans wasn't the move he was searching for to rebuild his tarnished reputation.

Better get on with it.

Alex set down his fork and took a large sip of wine.

"Casey," he said, his reluctance clear even to his own ears. "We need to talk about this Gridmore job."

Chapter Four

Crap. Here it comes, Casey thought silently to herself. Alex was going to turn down the job. Her business instincts were never wrong, and they were stating loud and clear that he wanted no part in Heather's shrine to Elvis.

Casey, however, wasn't going to give up, at least not yet. So far she'd done little to convince him why he *should* take the job. Time to get with the program and save her tush.

"You're right, Alex. We do need to talk about Heather's house." Casey refilled their wine glasses, hoping Alex would take a few more sips and let the alcohol relax him enough to take the edge off the attitude he'd been sporting since Heather's. "I know her ideas are kind of…off the wall—"

"Kind of?" Alex arched a brow. "That's an understatement."

"Okay. So they are *really* off the wall. But I think if we put our heads together, we can pull this off with taste and style while still giving her what she wants."

"Pretty optimistic, aren't you?"

"Why shouldn't I be?"

"Casey, the woman wants to call her bedroom *Burnin'*

Love and deck it out in red velvet and gold lamé. How the hell do you propose to do that and keep it…tasteful?"

"I'm not sure yet. Like I said, I'm sure we can come up with something."

Alex shook his head. "I'm sorry, Casey. You're a…great gal, and I appreciate the offer, but I'm afraid I'm going to have to decline."

There it was. No beating around the bush for Alex. Just drop the bomb and be done with it. Yeah. Typical man, all right.

"Alex, give me a chance here," Casey said, trying to keep emotion out of her voice. Getting down on her knees and begging wasn't exactly what she had in mind. She'd try such a tactic only as a last resort if necessary. She did have some pride. "You can't just walk away."

"Yes, I can."

"You accepted the job already. We had a deal. You can't leave me hanging."

"Look. I regret this isn't going to work, but all I agreed to was to come and give the job due consideration. And since you weren't totally honest with me, I've given it all the consideration I'm going to."

Hmm. The man had a serious stubborn streak.

"Alex—"

"I'm sorry. My mind is made up." He shook his head. "You know, I should really be pissed at you." He raked his fingers through his hair.

"Pissed at me? Why?"

"Why? Because, I had no idea what I was walking into here. And that, darlin', was exactly the way you wanted it."

"That's not fair." Casey's temper flared.

"Isn't it? Tell me. Was it fair of you to lead me out

here under false pretenses?"

"I did no such thing. This is a legitimate job."

"All right. I'll give you that. It is a legitimate job. But what do you need me for? With your talent..." He raised his hands, indicating the room. "You sure as hell don't need me. You're capable of handling this job on your own."

"I appreciate your vote of confidence," she said sarcastically. "However, I need you more than you realize." And in more ways than one, Casey was discovering, but she wouldn't let the physical enter the picture.

"How's that?"

"I'm not an architect. I can't draw up blueprints for the addition."

"There's bound to be a local firm that can handle that end. This *is* Omaha."

"Yes, but Heather Gridmore wants you. No one else. In her mind, you are the only architect for the job. And when Heather makes up her mind, there's no changing it."

Alex raked his fingers through his hair. "Under normal circumstances I'd be flattered she insisted on me. Heather though, is far from normal. You have to admit her idea of remodeling leaves a lot to be desired. I can't do it."

He grabbed his work boots. Panic and anger hit Casey full throttle as she watched his fingers tie the long brown laces with speed and efficiency. God, obviously he couldn't get out of here fast enough.

"Alex, please." She reined in her urge to throw something and instead placed a hand on his arm. Maybe her touch would hold some sort of magic powerful enough to keep him from leaving. He stilled, his gaze aimed at her hand. "You can't back out on me. If you don't draw up the blueprints and help oversee this job, she'll cancel on me."

Without looking at her, he got to his feet, picked up his plate and headed for the kitchen.

"Didn't you hear what I said?" she asked, rushing after him. "If you aren't in on this job, I'm not either." Panic dumped on top of her frustration. Dammit. Apparently as far as he was concerned, there was no more discussing the issue. Boy, was he going to find out she didn't give up easily.

Casey stood in the door and leaned against the jamb. She studied his broad back as he placed his dishes in the sink and tried to think of something prophetic to say. The fabric of his shirt pulled taut as he set about turning on the faucet and was way too distracting for her to focus on anything but hard, lean muscles.

Dishes clattered against the sink as he put them into the sudsy water.

"Alex," she said, coming to her senses. "You walk out on this job, we both lose. Big time."

His shoulders slumped. He let his head fall forward and Casey worried if she'd pressed too hard. She pushed away from the door and walked over to him. With the lightest touch she placed a hand on his arm. His body stiffened.

"Look, I admit I didn't tell you about Heather's Elvis fetish. I'm sorry," she said softly. "But I knew if I did, you wouldn't take the job seriously. Regardless of what you think, this is a serious job. I didn't mislead you. I didn't make any false promises. And I didn't make this job out to be something it isn't."

His knuckles turned white as he squeezed the edge of the sink. "True, you didn't. You didn't exactly shoot straight with me though, either. It's not a major trip from Denver to Omaha, but this has been a total waste of my time. Time I can't afford to lose."

Casey winced. His accusation stung deep. Granted, they were still practically strangers, but it was nice to think that the hours they'd spent together meant at least a little something. That their paths had crossed for some profound reason, no matter how small.

Apparently not.

Alex grabbed a towel, dried his hands and hurried back out to the living room without so much as a glance in her direction. He picked up the remaining dishes.

"What are you doing?" she asked.

"Cleaning up. It's the least I can do for letting you down."

"I appreciate the thought. The dishes can wait, though. We need to settle this."

"Casey, as far as I'm concerned it is settled. First thing tomorrow I'm heading back to Denver. There's nothing more to discuss."

Casey stood, her mouth agape. Frustration vibrated through every follicle on her head, and she struggled to suppress a scream. After the day she'd had, she deserved a good scream.

Why did he have to be so stubborn and bullheaded?

And why did he have to look so sexy standing there with his sleeves rolled up and his hands full of dishes? If it wasn't for the fact he was making her life difficult at the moment, she'd be thinking he was the most perfect man in the world.

"Alex?" she sighed, ready to give it one more try. "Do

you realize how big a paying job this is? Heather is extremely wealthy. Money is immaterial to her. What she wants, she gets, regardless of the cost. I know. I used to write plenty of checks to cover her habits and whims."

"You worked for Heather?" His eyebrows rose in surprise.

"No and Yes. First, I worked for her husband. As you know, Hector was the founder and CEO of Gangsters' Pizza. I was his accountant for a few years, both on a business and personal level."

"And when he died? Did you quit?"

"No. I stayed and worked for Heather only long enough to help close the sale on the company after Hector's death. By then we'd started Studs for Hire, anyway."

"So that's why Heather hired you for this job. She knew she could trust you."

"That's…part of the reason, yes."

"And what's the other part?"

"You might say I had a knack for getting exactly what Heather wanted. I took care of arranging everything for her, from an L.A. based masseuse to fly out here once a month, to a New York fashion designer to create each season's fashions."

He let out a low whistle. "You weren't kidding when you said she had money."

"Money is one thing I never kid about," she said dryly. "And when Heather offered Studs the job, her only requirement was that I secure you for the project. She knew I could get you. And I did. The problem now, I see, is keeping you."

"Look, Casey." He shook his head. "I admit the money

is tempting, but it's not the only issue here. I'm working to establish my reputation in the timber home field. What Heather wants doesn't exactly fall into that category."

"So, expand your horizons. Be more versatile."

"It's not that simple." Alex headed back to the kitchen and deposited the remainder of the dishes in the sink. He turned around and braced his hands on the edge of the counter. "I have to consider my reputation. A failed job can be like a death sentence in this field. Screw up once and people don't want you designing their homes for fear it'll fall down around them."

"So, we're facing a similar peril, aren't we? The only difference is I'm screwed for sure because you won't do the job. You, on the other hand, only have the potential to screw up. It isn't a given."

"No. It is a given. I do this job, and I'll be a laughingstock. People will automatically assume I've screwed up when I haven't. "

"You don't know that. We pull this off with grace and style and you could be the most sought after architect in the world. You'll be revered as much as Frank Lloyd Wright."

"Yeah. You bet." Alex rolled down his sleeves and Casey knew he was ready to call it a night. Men. When they made up their minds about something, the conversation ended. They relished going into their caves and shutting women out until they were ready to reemerge—confident they had the answer, their way being the only way.

"My partners and I sunk just about everything we had into Studs. We can't afford to lose this deal. And if you go back to Denver, that's exactly what will happen.

Heather won't settle for anyone else. That's just the way she is. When her mind is made up, it's made up." Damn, she sounded desperate, pathetic even, but then she was.

"Casey," he sighed. "I'm sorry. I really am. I've got a valid reason for not doing this and you know it."

"Valid?" She crossed her arms in front of her. Her defenses firmly in place. Well, she had her own valid reasons *for* wanting to do this.

"Look. I'll call a cab and grab my things. I don't want to trouble you any more than I already have. Thanks for a great evening." He pushed away from the counter and strode toward the door. Without looking back he headed for the stairs to retrieve his suitcase.

So that was it? No good luck? No good-bye? No sorry I ruined your life? Casey covered her face with her hands and fought the impulse to throw a bona fide tantrum. So much for being in control.

* * * *

Ten minutes after Alex had left, Casey lounged on the couch in her favorite comfy, yet stylish scarlet-colored sweat outfit. A cold cloth covered her face, Brudy snuggled at her feet, and a half a glass of wine dangled dangerously in one hand over the edge of the couch.

What else could she do? Her stomach roiled, her head ached, and in general, her life sucked. The day had gone from bad to horrendous with each tick of the clock. And what was worse, Alex's leaving had brought back ugly memories of the night her father had walked out the door of their split-level home. He never came back, except to sign the divorce papers.

And it looked like she'd seen the last of her star architect, too. Casey let out a deep sigh. At age thirty-three, it seemed her life had become nothing but a series of disappointments.

She stole a glance at the mantel clock. Thank God in forty-eight minutes the day would be over. However, tomorrow didn't look promising, either. Breaking the news to Heather that Alex wanted no part in her Elvis-encrusted world, wasn't going to be pleasant.

Maybe she could persuade her dentist to do a root canal on a Saturday. Anything would be more appealing than telling Heather she wasn't going to get *exactly* what she wanted this time. When Heather didn't get her way, she made an Amazon warrior princess look like a chocolate cupcake.

"Chocolate." Casey bolted upright. "That's what I need, chocolate. Chocolate makes everything better." Setting down her wine glass, she padded to the kitchen in search of all the chocolate she could find.

By the time she'd searched all the cupboards and found none, panic took over. "I can't believe there's no chocolate in this house. There's always chocolate in this house. Brudy, have you been raiding the cupboards again?"

Brudy stood by her feet in anticipation of his own treat, his tail wagging his entire hind end from side-to-side. His tongue hung down to his knees.

"Gee, and I thought I was desperate for food." She reached for a biscuit from his doggie treat jar on the counter and the phone rang. The sound startled Casey. Glancing at the clock she was reminded again that it was well past eleven. She raced for the phone afraid something was wrong with a member of her family.

"Hello, mom?" she asked, without even bothering to check the caller ID.

"I've been called many things, but mom isn't one of

them," an all too familiar female voice replied.

Casey's stomach dropped. Holy crap. Heather. Honestly, what had she done to deserve this day? Her mind whirled. Did she dare hang up and hope Heather thought she'd dialed the wrong number?

"Casey? What's going on?"

Damn. So much for hanging up and pretending she hadn't called. "Uh, nothing. I guess I'm not really awake," she fibbed, throwing in a yawn for good measure. "I'm not used to getting calls this late."

"Is it late? I've no idea. I have to talk to you."

"Really? What about?" Casey clamped her eyes shut, crossed her fingers and toes, and hoped all Heather wanted to talk about at eleven thirty-one was the latest Elvis artifact she'd acquired.

"I'm concerned about Alex."

Shit. Her luck really was in the toilet today.

"Oh," she croaked. Gutless. Spineless. Let's see, what other adjective could she use to describe herself? Like a madwoman, Casey started combing her cupboards for another round of searching. Chocolate. She needed chocolate.

"He didn't seem very enthusiastic tonight about the remodel. I need some reassurance," Heather whined.

"Reassurance?" Casey searched faster, now digging through the hot pad drawer. There had to be some chocolate somewhere. Whenever she started a diet she hid all the chocolate in the house in places where she figured she'd forget. However, the concept didn't usually work—her willpower was never strong enough to allow time for forgetting.

Crap, why couldn't her willpower have held out at least once? She was desperate for a bag of M & M's or a

Hershey Bar.

"Yes. Reassurance," Heather said, now with irritation. "Is he excited about the job?"

"Ah, excited? Yeah, he's excited." She moved onto another cupboard, frantically pushing aside jars and cans of spaghetti sauce, applesauce, and pickles. Nothing.

"Are you sure? I'm pretty good at reading people's auras and stuff and I got the sense he's not. Casey, you wouldn't be lying to me, would you?" Heather asked, her tone cold enough to freeze the M & M's dancing in Casey's mind like sugar plums.

Her heart stopped. She couldn't breathe. Her roomy kitchen suddenly felt restrictive and suffocating. Brudy barked, knocking her out of her panic attack. Okay, she needed to get a grip, stop obsessing about chocolate and be that professional woman she prided herself on being. She could handle Heather, in her own way, in her own time.

"You have dog?"

"Yes."

"How sweet. I love animals. Now, about Alex—"

"Alex and I tossed around some great ideas tonight. I assure you we're both really excited about this, Heather. We can't wait to get started."

"Oh, I'm relieved to hear that. I can sleep now."

"Right. Get some sleep. I promise we'll be in touch soon. Good night." Before Heather could utter another word, Casey disconnected.

Brudy sat on his haunches and looked up at her with a *shame on you* look in his brown eyes.

"Stop it. I don't need your censure when lightning is probably going to strike me down at any moment anyway. Now let's go."

Casey slipped on her tennis shoes, grabbed her purse and headed for the front door. Brudy followed behind, his toenails clicking on the hardwood floor with each step.

"We're making a McDonald's run. I'm desperate for a chocolate salvation."

* * * *

Alex had no more dropped his suitcase onto the king-sized bed in his hotel room when his cell phone vibrated against his hip. Tired and worn out from a trying day, he wanted to let the call go to his voice mailbox and deal with it later. But since the Gridmore job hadn't turned out on a positive note, he was now without work and this call, even though it was late, could be a new opportunity.

Flipping open his phone, he saw it was his secretary, Dotty. In her mid-fifties and a widow, Dotty was as loyal an employee as Alex could ever hope for. She always put in more hours than her time card indicated and made sure Alex Roy Enterprises ran as efficiently as a trusty *Timex*.

"Hey, beautiful," he said, his customary greeting for the woman he owed his career to. "What's up?"

"Sorry to be calling you so late, Alex." Uh-oh. No teasing back, no smile in her sweet voice. Something was wrong.

"No problem, Dotty. I just got in when you called."

"Long business dinner?"

"Yeah." If you could really call it that. A total screw up with a talented and beautiful woman seemed more like an appropriate title for the night's events.

"That's good. I held off calling you earlier because I figured you'd be out to dinner, but I felt this really couldn't wait until morning, either."

The hair on the back of Alex's neck prickled. "What's going on? Are you all right?"

"Sweet Alex. Always thinking of me first. In spite of her faults, your mama managed to raise you right."

"So you've told me a million times," Alex chuckled softly, hoping to ease the tension he felt through the phone. "Now, tell me what's wrong."

"I'm afraid I have some tough news. We got word today that our bank, Mountain Financial, is being bought out by another, larger, financial institution called Western Bank. And unfortunately, they've thrown Alex Roy Enterprises into the high-risk category."

Alex suppressed a groan, not liking the sound of this. "Meaning?"

"Meaning your note with Mountain Financial was scheduled for renewal thirty days from now."

"*Was?*"

"Western Bank isn't willing to assume the old loan and write a new note."

"What? They can't be serious? I've banked with Mountain Financial for what, at least fifteen years? I've never defaulted. Hell, I've never even been late making a payment. Doesn't my track record mean anything?"

"I know. It's horse-hockey," Dotty cussed in her simple, old-fashioned way. "Alex. They're requiring that the full two-hundred and fifty thousand be paid-in-full by November tenth."

"Hell. Dotty, what am I going to do? Where am I going to find that kind of money?"

"Well, you do have a little in reserve, but that won't even cover a fourth of the note. I guess we'll have to go bank shopping."

Alex groaned, hating the thought of begging and pleading before some banker who saw him as nothing more than a series of numbers.

"Hey, look on the bright side. Since you're starting that new job in Omaha, I'm sure there's a bank who'll be willing to assume the loan," Dotty said with optimism. "It's not like you're totally destitute and unemployed."

Uh, yes—he was. Like an idiot, he'd turned down the job. Damn. Alex scrubbed a hand over his face. He hated the idea of eating crow, and telling Casey he'd changed his mind would be doing just that. But to save his business it looked like he had no choice.

"Listen, Dotty, I've got a few things to iron out here yet. Give me the weekend and then I'll be home to handle this banking…issue. In the meantime, see if you can line up some appointments with other banks for the first of the week."

"Will do, boss. And Alex, try not to worry. We'll work this out." Ah, bless Dotty, she was always the silver lining on his dark clouds.

"Hey, beautiful, with you watching my back, I can't lose. Get some rest. I'll talk to you Monday at the office. Night."

"Goodnight, Alex."

He flipped his phone shut and took a deep breath. Hell. "So much for Elvis leaving the building."

Chapter Five

"How did it go yesterday, Casey?" Sydnie Riley hollered as Casey tried to sneak past the open door. So much for escaping into her office undetected. That was the problem with having smart, savvy businesswomen for partners. She couldn't get away with nothin'.

Still, she kept her chin up and kept tiptoeing.

"Ca-sey," Syd said in a singsong rhythm.

Casey stopped short and sighed. There was no use in pretending she didn't hear her name. Sydnie wouldn't be put off. As President of Studs for Hire, Syd oversaw the entire operation and nothing, no matter how small the job, problem, or the success, she was on top of all company matters.

Casey closed her eyes, took a deep breath, and backed up three steps. Opening her eyes, she saw Sydnie sitting behind her desk with an anxious look on her face.

"Well?" Syd asked.

Casey groaned, hating like heck to be the deliverer of rotten, disappointing news.

"That bad, huh?" Syd asked when Casey didn't volunteer any information.

"That depends," she said at last, hoping to let her friend down easy. She plunked down on an overstuffed chair opposite the desk. Her jeans pinched her waist and now she wished she'd had the fortitude to say no to that late night chocolate shake run.

"Depends?" Syd asked. She arched one slim brow. "Depends on what?"

"Which part of yesterday you're asking about."

"Just how many *parts* did your day have?"

"Too many to talk about. So, let's leave it at that, shall we?" Casey sighed and let her head fall back against the softness of the chair. "You're here bright and early for a Saturday morning. Don't you ever take a day off?"

"Oh, no you don't, partner. I'm not letting you change the subject that easy. Fill me in on what happened at the Gridmore mansion yesterday. I've got a lot riding on this job, too."

Casey sighed. "I knew it. You aren't going to let this rest, are you?"

"Nope."

"Just once, why don't you surprise me? You're so predictable, Syd. And obsessive."

"When it comes to money and our reputation, I'm predictable and obsessive as hell. And so are you. If you weren't, you wouldn't be here now looking like you could use a pound of chocolate."

Oh, God. Even after her late night indulgence of a thick, chocolate shake, she still didn't look satisfied? If she ate much more, her waistline and hips would protest by refusing to let her even pry on a single pair of the jeans in her drawer.

"Do you think chocolate is the cure for everything? I mean eat chocolate and you'll forget your woes, forget you're sex-deprived, and your checkbook is dry," Casey said.

Restless and agitated, she got to her feet and grabbed a bottle of water from the stock of liquid sustenance they kept stashed in Syd's mini-fridge under the bar. Everything from caffeine to alcohol to healthy drinks cramped the compact space. Casey took a long swallow and leaned against the bar, proud she was at last consuming something with zero calories.

"Your checkbook being dry I knew. Now you're suffering from sex-deprivation, too?" Syd asked. "Tsk. Tsk. Tsk."

Casey shot her friend a tight smile. "Deprived isn't exactly the word I'd use. It's more like…limited. And that's just lately. When I said I'd partner with you on this business, I didn't expect to be run ragged working all the time. I don't have time to date anymore."

"Hmm. Is that it," Syd said, not sounding at all convinced.

"You, on the other hand, don't seem to be suffering these days," Casey stated. "How *are* things going between you and Trevor? Tell me. We never have much time to talk anymore, either."

"Things with Trevor are going great. And his new advertising agency is booming as much as Studs for Hire is. I'd love to girl talk more, Casey, but I'm afraid it'll have to wait. Heather has called twice this morning already."

Casey groaned. Man, the woman didn't give up. "What did she say?" she asked, but in truth she didn't want to know anything.

"To be honest, I'm not sure. She was rambling on so fast about deadlines, black leather and I don't know what all. What I did catch was that she wants you to call her ASAP. It's important, she said." Syd picked up two pink slips of paper and waved them in the air.

Casey pushed away from the bar and snatched the notes from Syd's hand. The messages said nothing more than what Syd had already told her, but the idea the moment of truth was at hand, and Alex was on his way back to Denver, made her stomach lurch.

"Ugh. What am I going to do?" She slapped the notes against her forehead, cradling the headache starting there.

"For starters, why don't you tell me what's going on. Didn't your hotshot architect fly in late yesterday?"

"Oh, he flew in all right. And flew the coop this morning." Casey stabbed her hand through the air.

"What? He's not taking the job?"

"Apparently he's not an Elvis fan."

"Who's not an Elvis fan?" Terri Alberry, Casey and Syd's third partner in Studs for Hire, asked as she breezed into the room with an armload of files to join her friends.

"The architect Casey hired for Heather's remodel."

"Oh. That's not good. Does Heather know? She might not be too happy to hear that there are actually people who don't like Elvis," Terri said.

"Truthfully, I don't think Heather cares," Casey said. "She's so hot for Alex she'd take him even if he thought Lisa Marie and Michael Jackson's marriage was a match made in heaven."

"Maybe she's thinking she can turn him into an Elvis convert. That can happen," Terri said.

"Well, he didn't actually say he wasn't an Elvis fan. He just thinks Heather's plan is a little...screwy."

"I for one, agree with him," Syd said. "But, it's not for us to judge. She's hiring us to do a job."

"Therein lies the problem. Alex maintains this type

of job isn't his area of expertise. His specialty is timber frame homes."

"We're all about giving the customer what they want," Syd said. "If Heather wants Elvis International, Las Vegas style, then that's what she gets. It's up to us to deliver."

"I know, Syd. I agree with you. His concern is if word gets out, it'll ruin his reputation, his credibility."

"All right. I can understand that considering what Heather wants. However, it's up to you, Casey, to convince him that won't happen. Besides, we're talking big money here. Didn't you tell him what Heather is willing to pay to make this quirky dream of hers come true?"

"Exact figures? No. We didn't make it that far. As he was doing dishes in my kitchen, I did try to convince him money wouldn't be an issue for Heather, though."

"Dishes? The guy does dishes?" Terri asked. Her eyes glazed over with longing and she sighed.

"Yes."

"Is he hot?" Syd asked.

"In a woodsy sort of way." Casey shrugged, not wanting to let on how he'd affected every nerve in her body. "He looks like a lumberjack. Normally I'm not one for red and navy checked flannel, but seeing it on him did give me a whole new appreciation for the fabric."

"In other words he's damn hot," Syd said, a huge smile covering her face.

"Hmm. I think Heather's not the only one who has her eye on the lumberjack," Terri giggled.

"Don't go getting carried away, you guys. Yes, he's good-looking. Very. But He's also stubborn, arrogant and—"

"Anyone I know?" a deep voice asked from behind them. Casey spun around to see one very handsome Alex Roy filling the doorway.

* * * *

"Alex? What the hell are you doing here?" Casey held out her hands, palms up, totally confused by his sudden appearance. Had he missed his flight and expected her to entertain him until he could catch another one? *Wrong*.

Or…had he changed his mind? A flicker of hope pecked at Casey, but she cautioned herself not to get excited just yet.

"That's a surefire way to make a guy feel welcome," he said with a hint of sarcasm.

"Well, gee. I didn't know I *was* welcoming you back," Casey said, hitting him with her own brand of retort. Two could play at this game.

"I suppose not," he said, his voice deep, smooth, and as intoxicating as it had been fourteen hours ago. He strolled into Sydnie's office and stopped a mere foot away from where Casey stood. A lazy smile tugged at one corner of his lips. "Sorry to intrude, ladies. I hope I'm not interrupting anything important."

Damn. He was even more handsome than she'd remembered. How could that be? And how the heck had she missed that amazing dimple in his left cheek when he smiled? Maybe it was because he hadn't done a lot of smiling yesterday. He'd been too busy trying to find a way to tell her, *forget it*.

"As a matter of fact we—"

"We're just finishing up," Syd jumped in. She threw Casey a stern look that warned her not to blow it. "You must be Alex Roy."

"That's me."

"I'm Sydnie Riley, one of Casey's partners." Syd came around from behind her desk and held out a hand to Alex. He accepted her gesture and the two shook hands like old friends.

"It's a pleasure, Sydnie."

"And this is Terri Alberry. She's the third partner in Studs for Hire." Sydnie turned to Terri, her arms still loaded with manila files.

"Hey, Terri. This is a triple pleasure." Alex winked and wasted no time in shaking Terri's hand.

"Great to meet you, Alex," she said, shifting the stack of files from both arms to one. "That was a nice profile I read on you in *Timber Home Living* a while back. I bet business has been booming for you ever since."

"Well." He shrugged. "It hasn't been too bad."

"I'm surprised you'd even be interested in Heather's crazy plans to—"

"So, what brings you down to the office on a Saturday morning, Alex?" Casey asked, interrupting Terri before she could run him off with any of her honesty.

"Actually, I was hoping I could talk to you. That is if I'm not too late."

"That depends on what it was you wanted to discuss," Casey said firmly. She'd done her best to convince him last night to take the job, and he'd still turned her down flat. No way was she getting on her hands and knees now and begging.

Casey lifted her chin and caught a glimpse of Syd giving her her, *don't blow it* look, again. "Let's go to my office." Casey took Alex by the arm and guided him from the room and out into the hallway.

As soon as they were through the door she let go,

not wanting to give him, or herself for that matter, the decadent pleasure of a prolonged touch. The buttery softness of his leather jacket had invited her fingertips to explore and sparked the desire to run her hands across his chest, down his arms, and around to his back. Far too much temptation for her own good.

The spicy, outdoors scent she'd noticed yesterday still clung to his jacket and didn't help her resolve, either. Right about now she'd be happy to bury her face in the crook of his neck and inhale until delirium swept her away.

Whoa. Time to put some serious distance between them.

Opening her office door, she flicked on the lights. To keep herself busy, and to get some of that much needed distance, she crossed the room and opened the vertical blinds. The sun peeked through the gray October clouds, offering a ray of hope that maybe this was going to work out all right.

Taking a stand behind her desk, Casey put her hard, no-nonsense business facade firmly in place. Crossing her arms beneath her breasts, she waited. He'd made her sweat last night, now she'd make him do the same— at least for a while. Then, if he didn't relent like she prayed he would, maybe she'd reconsider and get down on her knees and beg.

"Nice office," he said as he took his time inspecting her domain. "Sleek, yet sophisticated. Nice choice of colors. Butter cream, sage and rust with an Oriental flare. A fish tank to add tranquility. Even a green plant in a yellow pot. A lot of Feng Shui going on here."

"I'm thrilled you approve."

Alex chuckled. "Yeah. I can tell." He hooked his

thumbs in his jeans pockets and shifted his weight to one foot.

"So, what can I do for you this morning, Alex? Did you lose your way to the airport and need directions?" Casey knew that remark wasn't fair, and blamed the little devil on her shoulder for making her say it, but he'd walked out on her last night. He couldn't expect her to fall at his feet in gratitude since he'd come back. Well, that is, if, he'd come back. Knowing her luck, he probably *was* here for directions.

"You're not going to make this easy are you?" A heavy sigh escaped his lips.

"Easy? I'm not sure what you mean."

He groaned and rubbed his palm across his jaw. Casey's salivary glands kicked into overtime. What would the texture of his skin feel like next to hers? Rough? Smooth? Amazing?

"Okay. Let's do ourselves a favor," he said, slamming the brakes on her carnal thoughts, "and forget the games. I'm going to cut right to the chase."

"Cut to the chase?" Casey's heart stumbled in her chest. What was he cutting to the chase about? He'd already turned down the job. Had she missed something? Was he going to insist on being reimbursed for the trip out here?

"About what?" she asked with caution.

"First off, I'd like to apologize for last night."

Bam. She hadn't expected that one. "Apologize? What exactly are you apologizing for? Turning down the job? Walking out without so much as a goodbye? Male arrogance?" She shrugged and planted her hands on her hips.

As much as she hated him refusing the job, he'd had

every right—and he'd had a valid reason. As a business person she understood all too well that sometimes saying no, no matter how hard, was the right course to take.

He just wasn't supposed to say no to her. It had hurt her ego and her pride.

A short-clipped laugh escaped his throat, and he shook his head. "To all of the above. Things didn't end between us on the best note last night."

"Best note?" Casey narrowed her eyes and studied Alex. A man coming to her and apologizing, for whatever reason, was a rare commodity. How was she supposed to handle this one? Business school hadn't offered *Understanding the Male Psyche 101* in their curriculum. She was on her own.

"There was a misunderstanding between us," he said, raking his fingers through his hair. "I was expecting the Gridmore job to be…something it wasn't. And you expected me to be already on board when I got here. When we both realized differently, we got defensive."

"Defensive? I don't know what you're talking about. I never get defensive." *Joy.* The guy knew how to read her. Or else he was a pro at knowing what buttons to push to make a woman forget who was right and who was wrong.

Alex quirked a brow. "*Never?* Last night you did. And you're doing it now." He nodded at her, indicating her rigid body language.

Irked, Casey dropped her arms to her sides. He was right. As a partner in Studs for Hire she expected herself to be a professional and handle situations like this accordingly.

For cryin' out loud, she'd been in business long enough to know that sometimes you *had* to cut your losses and move on to the next deal, or you didn't survive. Yet, it wasn't every day she found herself drooling over a man who wore flannel and looked like he should be chopping down trees, not designing magnificent homes with them.

"Case?" There was a flicker of something in his eyes. Hope, maybe? Hmm. He did say there'd been a misunderstanding between them.

Her intuition kicked in, and if it was anywhere close to being right, he was going to give her another shot. This was no time to be stubborn. For the good of her friends, and their business, she'd swallow her pride—this time.

"Apology accepted." As Casey said the words, the tension in her body melted away.

"Then let's start out on a new note, shall we?"

"Okay." She took a deep breath. "I'm game. Let me begin by offering you something. Beer? Wine?" She moved across the room. "A job," she mumbled only loud enough for her own ears.

"Beer and wine? At the office? I take it you gals don't just work around here." He took off his coat and tossed it onto the couch. The two shirts he wore, a thermal under his usual flannel, made him look even more rugged.

"Work seems like *all* we do around here. That's why we pride ourselves on how well we stock our refrigerators." Casey opened the small fridge she kept hidden away in her office closet and showed off the full shelves.

"You weren't kidding about well-stocked."

"Life is short. A girl's got to sneak in some fun once in a while."

"Yeah." His eyes turned smoky, exuding a hunger for

some of that fun she'd been talking about. He cleared his throat and looked away. "Thanks for the offer. Maybe some other time."

Some other time? Could that be constituted as a rain check? She'd take it. Walking back around to the front of her desk, she leaned against its oak surface.

"Now, I'd like to offer a couple of apologies."

"Oh?" He splayed his hands on his lean hips.

"I shouldn't have allowed my emotions to get involved yesterday. This is business. I make it a rule not to let personal issues cloud my business judgment. Unfortunately I disregarded that. I'm sorry."

"It's understandable. You've got a lot at stake here."

Casey sighed. "Yes, well. That's an understatement."

"Business not going like you'd hoped?"

"Oh, no. That's not it at all. Business is good. But like I mentioned last night, we've invested a lot of time and money into this venture. None of us want to lose it. We're three single women with no one to support us if things go awry. It's a little scary to know that right now we're all one job away from destitution."

"Ah, the stresses of the ambitious entrepreneur. There's a lot of perks to owning your own business, but a lot of down sides, too. The pressure. The financial worries. Employee issues."

"Speaking from experience?"

"Well, I've had my share of trials and tribulations. Who hasn't?"

"True. I'm sorry about not being up front with you about what Heather wants. I did sort of lure you out here without much information."

"Sort of? I had no clue."

"Would you have come if I *had* told you Heather

wanted to turn her home into Elvisland?"

"No." Alex stepped forward, shortening the distance between them to mere inches. His gaze settled on hers, and he held her captive without even laying a hand on her. The tantalizing warmth of his body beckoned, making her tingle for the feel of his touch.

Damn. How was she supposed to focus on Elvis when her hormones were crying, begging for release with Alex? Maybe they should go ahead and sleep together? That way she could satisfy her Alex fetish and get on with the job Heather hired her to do.

"Even though it wasn't right," he drawled, "to be honest, I don't blame you."

"Blame me?" Casey asked, feeling a little breathless. The man had such a knack for throwing her brain off kilter.

Yes. Sleeping together, and soon, strictly for the pleasure—no attachments, sounded like a damn fine idea.

"What Heather wants…isn't exactly your run of the mill architectural project." Alex swept a lock of her hair off her shoulder and caressed the strands between his fingers.

Hell, why wait? She should lock her office door and refuse to let him out until he'd ravaged her on her ultra-suede couch.

"There isn't an architect in their right mind, myself included, who wouldn't run like hell from a job like this."

Casey swallowed hard. "And are you in your right mind? Or can I hope your appearance means you've lost all sense and are here for more than an apology?"

"Oh…I'm here for more." The sienna brown of his eyes darkened again, this time almost matching the black stripes running through the neutral tones of his shirt.

Casey's insides fluttered at his silent suggestion. Her
heart pounded in her chest. Pushing herself up from
her desk, the high heels of her black boots put her and
Alex almost nose to nose. At this close angle there was
no missing every detail, no matter how tiny, on his
handsome face. From the small crescent-shaped scar
below his left temple, to the whiskers peppering his chin,
the guy was all eye candy.

"And that more would be…?" she asked, teasing her
bottom lip between her teeth. Maybe she was being a
little too bold here, but then she'd never been very good
at restraint.

"To tell you…"

"Yes?" Casey watched, mesmerized as a muscle
worked at his jaw.

"I'll take the job."

Job? What job? Casey struggled to refocus her mind
from the image of Alex wearing nothing but a smile,
to one of blueprints and two by fours. *Crap.* The way
she was acting, putting a sexual spin on his every action,
his every word, you'd think she'd never had sex before
in her life.

"Heather is ready to start," he continued, his tone
sounding more businesslike. "I want to get the job done
and be back in Denver by the middle of December."

Reality kicked at Casey. *He wanted?* What the hell
was going on? She had the terrible feeling she'd missed
out on something—again. Probably because she was busy
lusting and not paying attention. *The Taboos of Office
Foreplay* was another non-existent college course she
could put to use right about now.

"Wait a minute. I'm confused," she said, shaking her
head. Feeling the need for some space, she circled around

behind her desk. "Last night you wanted nothing to do with this. You were worried about your reputation. Now?"

"To be honest, I still am."

"Then why? What changed your mind?"

"Does it matter? I've agreed to do the job. I thought you'd be happy."

Yippee-ki yay. Casey *was* ecstatic, but she knew how to read between the lines, too. There was a lot he wasn't saying. She'd better keep her fingers crossed that whatever had changed his mind was enough to keep him for the duration. Alex leaving her high-and-dry wasn't an option.

"I'm pleased, yes," she said, opting to play it cool. Not to mention relieved, thankful, and willing to bequeath her first born to him. Of course, she wouldn't mind Alex being the father of that first born. "And I have your word you'll see this project through to the end?"

"To the end." He gazed at her with rock-solid intention, making her think he wasn't just referring to the job.

"All right," she said a little breathless. Cripes, she needed to get focused—work focused that is. "Then we'd better get started."

"There's one condition we need to agree upon first," he said, holding up a hand.

Casey's back stiffened. Now what? And men thought women were difficult. Her eyes narrowed with suspicion and a tickle bit of dread.

"Condition? What condition?"

"I have to insist on no publicity."

"What? I can't do that!" Casey said, incredulous. She came out from behind her desk, ready to argue that he asked for too much. Fortunately she had the fortitude to keep about two feet, four inches between them. But damn. It wasn't enough. She backed up a couple steps.

"Why not?" he asked.

"I'll give you two big reasons."

"And those are?" He crossed his arms and waited.

"Well, for one, Heather is a publicity hound. She thrives on it, lives for it. Mark my words. She's already planning on letting the universe know she has her own private Elvis museum. People from all over the world fly in for her Elvis conventions. It'll be impossible to keep it quiet."

"What's reason number two? As if I really want, or need to know," he grumbled.

"Studs is counting on the publicity, Alex. We're like minnows competing against sharks for Omaha's business. We're the new kids on the block. A job like this can do more for us than thousands of dollars worth of advertising. You of all people should understand that." Casey held her breath. Somehow she had to convince him to give at least a little ground.

"Yeah. I do." He sighed and then looked up at her with dark, mesmerizing eyes. "And you understand my position?"

"You know I do." Of course, with eyes like his she'd be willing to eat worms if he asked her to. "So where does this leave us...besides in a gridlock?"

"Well, we're adults." He shrugged and a dangerous smile tugged at his lips. "I'm sure we can come to some sort of mutual agreement between us."

Casey's breath hitched. Adults? Mutual agreement? Once again his silent suggestions made it hard for her to focus on the business end of this arrangement.

Her feet exhibited a brain she didn't know they possessed and made her move forward. Inches of electrically charged air hung between them.

"How about..." her voice withered in her throat. *Focus, Case. Focus.* Boy, but that was hard when all she wanted to do was explore the taste and texture of his lips. Heather and Elvis could wait until Venus froze over, for all she cared. She had important things to worry about—such as one handsome, hunky architect. A young Harrison Ford had nothing on Alex Roy.

"How about what?" he drawled, his voice damned near hypnotic. He touched her, not with his hands, but with his gaze, wrapping her in a cocoon of silent seduction.

"We compromise." Casey tried to draw a breath, but her chest felt heavy, laden with the bedeviling weight of his attraction and her blatant desire. Her body leaned into him.

"How do we do that?" The warmth of his breath caressed her cheek. One of her knees wobbled.

"We..." The distant ringing of a phone echoed in the back of her brain, but she forced the intrusion aside. "Keep you...a secret."

"A secret?" This time Alex was the one to lean forward. He traced the line of her jaw with the pad of his thumb.

Her heart skipped a full minute's worth of beats. Knee number two quaked.

"No one but us," she struggled for air, "has to know you're working on this job."

"It might work." So close, so damn close, yet neither dared move. Instead sweet, agonizing torture kept them a hair's-breadth apart.

A firm knock sounded at Casey's door. She jerked and

Alex pulled his hand away. On knees as weak as an inebriated armadillo's, she scrambled backward.

"I'm sorry to interrupt," Terri said shyly. "But, Heather Gridmore is on line one for you. She's very insistent." Terri ducked back out of sight and Casey came up gasping for air.

"I probably better take it."

"Sure. I'll wait out in the lobby." Alex took a step back, picked up his coat and headed for the door. How come his knees weren't threatening to collapse like hers were?

Maybe she needed to do some serious strength training.

Chapter Six

Alex was getting in too deep, too fast with Casey by letting lust get in the way. She wasn't the reason he'd decided to stay and immortalize Elvis in Omaha, no matter how hot she was. This job was about avoiding financial disaster.

Period.

He stepped out of Casey's office and into the sleek, contemporary reception area. Taking a deep breath, he focused on regaining some semblance of sanity. What the hell was he thinking? And where the hell was his common sense?

Even though he'd tried to deny it, he'd come to the unsettling realization that Casey intrigued him.

Hell, in the thirty-five years of his life, not once had any woman gotten to him so fast, to such an extreme. Now, his curiosity to find out why she tripped his trigger, mentally and physically, stuck in his craw. This was dangerous ground he treaded, both professionally and personally. He'd been blind-sided by a woman once before, and had no desire to let it happen again. Ever.

In spite of the potential risks, however, he'd convinced himself that Omaha had a lot to offer, too. When he met with potential banks this next week, he could honestly say he was working and prove he wasn't a total risk.

Normally, Alex didn't mind the stresses of his own business. They were the elements that gave him an edge, kept him hungry and willing to push harder to produce the desired end result—happy clients and personal satisfaction. And, regardless of how screwball this Gridmore job might be, it provided a challenge, and a change. For months now, he'd needed both.

Without a doubt, Casey Burrows would deliver on those two counts. He'd fight the attraction all the way, but he couldn't ignore the fact she had captured his attention. Not only was she beautiful, she smelled good enough to devour. More than once he'd caught himself fantasizing about nipping her ears, her neck and those perky breasts.

When he'd touched her smooth skin only a few moments ago in her office... Damn. He should be running like hell, but a quarter -of-a-million dollar bank note was one big reason to stay. All he had to do was keep those dollar signs forefront in his mind, and keep Casey out of his bed.

He hoped—yet, he didn't.

The outer door opened and one of the *studs* Alex recognized from the photographs lining the reception room wall, walked in, white dust coating his clothes.

"Morning," the man said.

"Mornin,'" Alex said back.

"Have you been helped?"

"Yeah. I'm just waiting on Casey." Alex pointed a thumb over his shoulder toward her office. "She's on the phone. So, you work for Studs?" Alex asked, indicating the guy's drywall dust-coated jeans.

"You might say that. Name's Trevor Vanden Bosch." He held out his hand and the two men shook. "I own my own advertising firm, but I help Syd out with the smaller fix-it and remodeling jobs. And you? Just coming on board?"

"Sort of." Alex chuckled. "It's temporary. I'm Alex Roy. I'm an architect based in Denver. Casey called me in to draw up the plans for the Gridmore mansion."

"You came. Thank God. These women have been stressing over this deal for weeks. Heather's pestered the hell out of them the whole time. Maybe now that you're here, Syd will relax and we can get our love life back."

"You and Syd? Together?"

"Yeah." There was no mistaking the territorial tone in Trevor's voice. Sydnie was his woman—hands off.

"That's great. I met her this morning. She's a nice gal. Pretty as hell, too."

"We used to work together in the advertising game. But we didn't really hook up until after she started Studs. We're pretty tight. We're even thinking about making things permanent."

"Marriage, eh? That's a big step."

"Who's getting married?" Casey asked, excitement in her voice as she joined the two men in the outer office.

"Uh, the gal I'm doing the drywall work for, Case," Trevor said quickly. Obviously he didn't want Casey to know how serious things were between him and Sydnie.

"Oh. Well, everything is all set with Heather, Alex. I told her we'd be over in about an hour. What do you say we have some lunch and then get to work?"

"Sounds great."

"Do you have plans, Trevor?" she asked.

"I'm taking Syd out to a quick lunch and then I've got to get back to work. This drywall job has to be done before the happy couple gets home from their honeymoon in two weeks. Great to meet you, Alex. Good luck on the Gridmore job. You're going to need it." Trevor grinned and headed for Sydnie's office.

"Thanks. I think."

"Don't pay any attention to Trevor, Alex," Casey said as she slipped on her coat. "I'm confident Heather will love our ideas."

"Yeah. Well, I hope you have some because, I sure as hell don't."

* * * *

"No. No, no, no. That won't do at all," Heather said as she paced the length of the massive marble fireplace that filled one wall of Hector's former office, now the holding cell for every piece of Elvis memorabilia she owned.

She waved around the one page contract she'd insisted Alex and Casey sign—stating they wouldn't cease working on her home until the job was complete. She claimed she'd been burnt in the past by handymen who'd started a job and failed to finish on time, or if at all. And just to make sure they finished the job, they would be paid in four installments of five, fifteen, fifteen, and sixty-five percent.

Leave it to Heather to make things complicated.

Casey took a deep breath and prayed for patience. For the last three hours she and Alex had checked out every room in the mansion, scribbled pages of notes and measurements, took scads of pictures, and tossed ideas back and forth. Now, with every basic idea they suggested to Heather, she shook her head and gave them a thumbs down.

Alex pinched the bridge of his nose between his fingers and Casey knew she needed to get him out of here before he changed his mind, if he hadn't already, and high-tailed back to Denver, after all.

"Heather, these are ideas off the cuff. Alex and I haven't really had a chance to explore many possibilities. Now that we have a better idea of what you're wanting, we'll sit down and do some serious planning."

"I hope so. My confidence in you, Casey, is waning." She twisted a finger around the long beaded necklace she wore. "I'd hate to let you go since Hector was so fond of you. But, I suppose Alex and I could manage on our own if we have to."

Great. They hadn't even started and Heather was threatening to fire her. It was clear that since Hector's death, Heather had become even more independent and demanding.

Concern knotted Casey's insides. A quick glance at Alex told her that under the surface, he was struggling with some concerns of his own. He shot her a look that said, *do something*.

"Don't worry, we'll come up with a plan you'll love. I'm sure of it." Casey planed her moist palms down the front of her jeans, not liking how uptight Heather was making her feel. Even after all the wacky dealings she'd had with the woman over the years, not once had she gotten under Casey's skin. So, why now?

Because this was personal. Casey had more invested this time around. This wasn't just a job—this was her company.

"I hope so. This is a serious assemblage of genuine, certified Elvis artifacts. This isn't just a box of dusty, warped LPs and magazine clippings we're talking about here. These items need to be treated with respect and be preserved for generations. Elvis was the King of Rock 'n' Roll, for crying out loud. Need I say more?"

"No. I understand perfectly," Casey said, even though she really didn't. Assemblage? How the heck did Heather know a word like assemblage? Though currently a red head, Heather fit the dumb blonde persona to a T. Of course, this might simply be an act on Heather's part to to get what she wanted. The young widow had always been good at that trick. Hector had even said so on several occasions.

Casey sighed. They were heading down a long and difficult road.

"You're right, Heather," Alex said, ending the silence. "Elvis was a major influence in the music world. We'll do our best to preserve your collection and honor his memory at the same time."

"Oh, Alex. I knew I could count on you." Heather sidled up to him, wrapping her arm through his. Casey resisted the temptation to roll her eyes.

"I think we have everything we need, don't we, Casey?" Alex asked as politely as he could muster through clenched teeth. She needed to get him out of here or he was going to strangle her for this fiasco.

"I'm sure we have more than enough to get us started."

"Good." Alex carefully slipped his arm out of the tight hold Heather had on him. "We'll be in touch in about a week." He headed for the door, Heather trailing behind like a love-sick puppy.

"A week? That long?" she whined. "I want to get started right away. We're on a deadline. My next Elvis convention kicks off January eighth, Elvis' birthday."

"I promise we'll get started as soon as possible. I have to return to Denver tomorrow to finish up some other business first. And, it'll take some time to draw up plans for the addition. Casey will call when we're ready to meet again."

"What am I supposed to do in the meantime?" Heather asked.

Casey and Alex worked their way across the tiled foyer to the front door and Joey the butler appeared with their coats. The man was like a wisp of smoke, coming and going virtually undetected.

"*In the meantime*, I suggest you pack up your collection for safekeeping," Alex said and shrugged on his coat. "We'll be making a lot of dust. You wouldn't want anything to get ruined."

"Right. I'll do that. I need to finish cataloging the Elvis concert scarves anyway now that I've completed that part of the collection. I have exactly forty-two." Heather clapped her hands in excitement.

"Forty-two?" Casey asked.

"Yes. Elvis was forty-two when he passed away, so as a tribute I've collected forty-two scarves, complete with his sweat I might add, that he tossed out to concert goers."

"How do you know they're authentic?" Alex asked. "Any ol' scarf could be passed off as an Elvis scarf."

"DNA testing. I have every scarf tested for Elvis' DNA. Each seller has to agree to the test, or the deal is off."

"Interesting," Casey said, buttoning her coat. "It sounds expensive."

"Yes, but worth it. Each scarf is authenticated by a

letter from the lab stating that Elvis did, indeed, wipe his handsome brow with it."

"Did it take you a long time to find forty-two?" Casey asked, genuinely interested.

"I started with the one my mother got at Elvis' concert here in Omaha in June 1977. She was a huge Elvis fan, you know. So I only needed to find forty-one. Once I got the word out I was looking, people came out of the woodwork, hoping to make a quick buck. There's a lot of weirdoes out there, too, let me tell ya. Some real fanatics."

Alex and Casey exchanged looks, knowing that many would consider Heather herself a fanatic.

"Tell me, Alex," Heather said, "is there anything you're passionate about?" Heather slid one perfectly manicured hand up the front of his leather jacket. She pursed her lips in a seductive pout, her eyes heavy with desire.

"Building fine homes, Mrs. Gridmore. That's the *only* thing I'm passionate about." Heather's hand stiffened at the use of her married name. Her seductive smile gave way to a thin-lipped frown.

Casey figured she should intervene, but it was too much fun to watch Alex discreetly pull the plug on Heather's blatant attempts at seduction.

Heather stepped back, clearly insulted by Alex's put off. Oops. Pissing Heather off wasn't a good idea, either.

"But, I am a man who's open to finding additional passions," he said, his words laced with suggestion. He gave Heather a lazy smile that even Elvis would be proud of.

Heather's smile returned and she leaned forward just enough to give Alex a better view of her ample cleavage.

"Well, now. That's what I like to hear—a man who is open to passion."

Silently, Casey thanked Alex for making the save, but she didn't care for his methods. Standing here as if she didn't exist, like a third wheel, wasn't her idea of control. Time to get that control back. For good. Casey Burrows was in charge of this job, and she'd better act like it.

* * * *

"You aren't going to bug out on me now, are you?" Casey asked as she and Alex waited late Sunday morning for the flight attendant to announce boarding for the plane that would take him back to Denver. There was a teasing lilt to her voice, but Alex heard the underlying concern too. He had her worried.

"I agreed to take the job, Casey. No matter how bizarre this whole thing is, I won't leave you hanging. Trust me."

"Oh, I trust you, Alex. But if you do anything to make me regret my trust, it won't be pretty. I'll track you down myself." She grinned and gave him a playful slug on the shoulder.

"Don't worry. I don't relish the idea of pulling a three inch heel out of my backside," he laughed. He let his gaze take a slow, appreciative glance down the length of her shapely legs and to her feet decked out in a classy, yet sensible, closed-toe number. Mercy. What he wouldn't give—

"Good. I'd hate to ruin a perfectly good pair of shoes on a man," she said, curbing the lustful direction of his mind.

"Gee. I'm not worth a pair of shoes? I'm crushed."

Casey laughed, the lilt of her voice reminding him of the sound of low-toned wind chimes tapping softly in the breeze. His breath hitched.

She really was pretty. No, not pretty. Gorgeous was more like it. Dressed in a classy business suit, she looked nothing but professional. Yet, in spite of his resolve, he couldn't stop undressing her with his eyes and imagining what lay beneath the black fabric that fit her body to perfection.

Stop. Get over it. Continuing to think about her would only clutter his mind, and more pressing matters awaited him back in Denver. What he needed was a swift kick in the ass. Hopefully, a few days away from her, back in his own reality of financial troubles would be that kick he needed to scour his brain of any lingering lust.

Except for a year-long affair that had cost him dearly, he'd gotten along fine without a woman messing up his life. Women clouded a man's judgment and ripped away any common sense he possessed. He didn't need those kinds of distractions. Especially not now. His future depended upon it.

They announced his flight was clear to board and an unexpected pang of hesitation made him hold back. He glanced at his plane, then at Casey, and his gut tightened a fraction. He lifted a hand to touch her, but stopped himself.

Dammit. This was bullshit. He'd barely known her forty-eight hours, not enough time in his opinion, to develop any kind of attachment worth mooning about.

"That's me," he said, his voice purposefully hard for his own ears.

"I'll see you at the end of the week, then?"

"Yeah. Hopefully Friday. Remember, I'm driving, so it'll be later in the day. If something changes, I'll let you know."

"Okay. Give me a call when you reach the outskirts of Omaha. We can decide then if you feel up to dinner or not after a long day behind the wheel."

Dinner? With Casey? Alex gritted his teeth. Her suggestion sounded too much like a date, and he didn't want to give himself the pleasure of looking forward to taking her out for an evening.

"Sure," he said. The flight attendant gave the last call to board. "See you Friday." He held out his hand to seal their business deal with a shake, hoping to reaffirm the trust they'd placed in each other.

She accepted the gesture and his fingers curled around the slender length of her hand. Instantly, he knew he'd made a mistake. Searing bolts of awareness he didn't want to feel shot through his arm and straight to his chest—the exact reason why he'd avoided touching her earlier. Her smooth skin, hot to his touch, made him burn with the need to pull her close, feel her body pressed next to his.

In two days she'd consumed every ounce of his reasoning, and Alex knew from this moment forward, a sweet smile or a simple handshake would never be enough to satisfy his craving for her.

He wanted something more. He wanted something intimate.

He wanted something he couldn't have.

So, take this one moment and savor it, he told himself. *To hell with the consequences.*

He leaned in close. The subtle fragrance she wore surrounded him and beckoned him to take her into his arms. His eyes closed, the warmth of her skin his only guide.

Don't. Alex opened his eyes and forced himself at the

last second to shift to the right, placing a kiss on her cheek. Her skin was satin against his lips and still managed to ignite a fire down in the very depths of him.

She was something he couldn't have. She was something he wouldn't let himself have. Even though his body argued against his denial, he knew if he allowed himself anything beyond this one simple kiss, there would be no turning back.

And yet, he sensed it might already be too late. Breaking the contact, he turned and strode toward the airplane without looking back.

Casey Burrows had rocked his world.

Chapter Seven

"I had no idea there were so many web sites devoted to Elvis," Casey said as she perused through the long list of sites on her computer screen. "My hair would turn gray before I'd have a chance to look through all of these. That is if Heather doesn't turn it gray first. She pestered the hell out of me again today."

"Heather's rich. She figures she has the right to pester," Terri said as she lounged on Casey's office couch after a long and tiring Monday. She flipped her dark hair over the arm of the couch, took off her glasses and closed her eyes.

"Hey, *Elvis.com.* This is where I need to be," Casey said as she clicked on the official web site owned by Elvis Presley Enterprises. "It's amazing the man still has such mass appeal."

"Elvis is big business. Year after year he consistently stays on the top ten list of the highest money-making celebrities who have passed on."

"Yes, but you'd think after all these years he'd be a little less big business. Look at this. You can get an Elvis *VISA* card. And while you're at it, you can order a deluxe Elvis rose bouquet, complete with his picture imprinted on the blossoms, for the bargain basement price of one hundred dollars."

"Sweet."

"By the way, if you're in the market for *anything* Elvis, you have nearly eleven-thousand items to choose from right now on *E-bay*." She glanced over at her friend to see if she was still awake.

"Looking to buy something?" Terri mumbled.

"No. Looking for inspiration." She turned back to the computer. "Gee. It says here you can even get married at Graceland. They have a little chapel in the woods. Wow. An hour and a half ceremony will only set you back about six-hundred bucks."

"He was the King of Rock 'n' Roll," Terri stated simply as if there was no need to say more.

"So I've been told," Casey groaned, remembering Heather had said the exact same thing. "I just hope we can give Heather what she wants and still keep it tactful. I mean there's so much hokey Elvis stuff out there. I'd hate for this to turn out looking cheap, like a bad velvet Elvis painting you can buy on some street corner."

A new bout of concern settled in her stomach. No way, no how, did she want Alex coming back and saying, *I told you so. It can't be done.* They'd all be ruined.

"Quit stressing." Terri got up from the couch and walked over to Casey's desk. "Alex is good at what he does. You're good at what you do. You'll make it work."

"I hope you're right." Casey leaned back in her chair and combed her fingers through her hair. "I have this terrible feeling that before this is all over, I'm going to wish I'd forgotten interior design and stuck with accounting."

"Stop worrying." Terri waved a hand in dismissal, sat on the edge of the desk and slipped on her glasses.

"I'd stop *worrying* if I believed Alex really wanted a part in this. It's going to make for a long fall if he's just here for..."

What was he here for? Why had he changed his mind? Casey tapped a fingertip on the edge of her computer keyboard, her mind racing with speculation.

"Here for what?" Terri asked.

Casey shook her head. "I don't know. For being dead-set against it, he did come around pretty fast. I wonder if something happened after he left my place. Something or someone had to have convinced him to take on this job."

"Heather? Maybe she called him."

Casey shook her head again. "No, I don't think so. She doesn't have his cell number. At least not that I know of. I sure didn't give it to her."

"Oh, well. Maybe you changed his mind." Terri smiled.

"Me? I didn't talk to him again. Brudy and I went on a medicinal chocolate run."

"Then it had to be something you'd said to him earlier. Could be he needed some time for things to soak in a bit."

Casey laughed. Sure, she'd like to believe she'd convinced Alex to take the job, but she wasn't so sure. He'd been so adamant about the legitimacy of the job.

Second of all, Alex gave her the impression he wasn't quite sure what to do with her. One minute he acted like he wanted to kiss her, the next like he wanted to strangle her.

And that kiss in the airport. Even if it ended up being nothing more than a peck on the cheek, technically it was still a kiss. A mighty fine one at that, too. She rubbed the spot on her cheek where they'd come together, and her heart raced at the memory. Thanks to the warm, electrifying feel of his firm lips, she'd been off-kilter ever since.

"Terri, you're full of it," Casey said, more for the benefit of her own convictions than for the purpose of chiding her friend.

"I'm no dummy. I've seen the way he looks at you."

Looks at me? No. She didn't dare go there. Casey had a habit of reading more into a relationship than what was really there, and because of her assumptions, men always left, leaving her to fend for herself. The cycle had started with her dad, and in that area of her life, nothing, absolutely nothing, had changed.

"Besides, whatever his reason for staying, be thankful," Terri continued. "What matters is you landed the job with Heather. This will be a big boon for us."

"If we can pull it off. I hate to say it, but Alex is right. This is a risky endeavor. We could end up as major laughingstocks if we fail."

"Maybe what you need is some firsthand inspiration."

"What do you mean?" Casey looked up at Terri, her hazel eyes serious behind her glasses.

"Go to the source. Fly down to Memphis and tour Graceland."

"Go to Graceland? Why do that when I can check out the virtual tours? They also have the Graceland cam which is updated every sixty-seconds. It's almost like being there."

"*Almost,* is the key word here. Looking at postage stamp-sized images on a computer screen isn't the same as being there and experiencing it for yourself."

"That's true. And it would qualify as a bona fide

business expense." Casey tapped a finger on her chin, her brain starting to toss around possibilities.

"See? It would be a great opportunity to spend some time alone with Alex, too." Terri smiled and winked.

"Take Alex with me?" Was Terri nuts? The idea of spending time alone with Alex sent a quiver of anticipation racing through her veins. Normally, Casey didn't have any trouble devising clever ways to spend time with a man, or offering advice to her friends on how to attract a man's attention. For some reason though, when it came to Alex, she felt...lost and disoriented.

"Sure. Why not take Alex with you? He's so hot."

Hot was an understatement. And Casey was weak.

"I don't know. What about Brudy?"

"Your neighbor lady still looks after him during the week, doesn't she?"

"Yes. He practically lives with Mrs. Wiley while I'm at work. She loves him."

"Then I'm sure she won't mind watching him for a weekend."

"I don't know. This trip might be too expensive," Casey said, grasping for any excuse she could find to talk herself out this crazy, tempting idea and its *other* possibilities. Possibilities a girl should only fantasize about during the night in her cold, empty bed.

"Come on. Where's that adventurous spirit of yours? It can't cost that much for you two to fly down there for a weekend. Besides, you're working together on this. From what you've said, it sounds like he could use some inspiration, too."

Terri really was brilliant sometimes. A trip to Memphis could be the answer to their design dilemma.

There were only two minor problems. Sydnie. And Alex.

"What if Syd doesn't go for it?"

"What won't I go for?" Syd asked as she joined Casey and Terri, three wine coolers in her hands.

"Oh, marvelous," Terri said, reaching for a cooler. "After the day I've had, I need this."

"Me, too," Casey accepted the other cooler and moaned. "Heather has called five times today. The woman is tenacious."

"Quit changing the subject, you guys," Syd ordered. "What were you talking about when I came in?" Casey glanced at Terri and saw as much apprehension on her face as she was feeling in her gut. "Well? I'm waiting."

Casey took a long swallow of her berry cooler, building her resolve to push for this trip. "I'm struggling with this Gridmore project a little, and since I'm not an Elvis fan per se, Terri suggested that maybe what I need is some firsthand inspiration."

"So, you're going to go out and rent every Elvis movie ever made and have an Elvis marathon?" Syd asked, mischief in her voice.

"Very funny. I have something better in mind."

"And that better would be…I know," Syd snapped her fingers, "listening to *Elvis, Aloha from Hawaii* nonstop for a week." She grinned ear to ear.

"No," Casey said firmly, knowing Syd was being difficult for the fun of it.

"It's a great album." Syd took a drink.

"I don't doubt that. What I'm proposing is Alex and I take a trip to Graceland." Whew. That felt good to get that weight off her chest.

"Alone? Together? Graceland?" Syd set down her drink on the desk with a thud. Her face void of expression.

Uh-oh. Not a good sign. The weight returned, threatening to snap Casey's breast bone.

"It's not like we'd be totally alone. Hundreds of people visit everyday. You should see the list of celebrities who've toured Graceland. There have been so many they even list them alphabetically."

"And you think visiting Graceland will be the answer to all your problems?" Syd asked.

"Maybe not all, but it can't hurt. Terri, help me out here, will you? This was your idea." Casey gave her friend her best pleading look.

Terri shrugged. "I'm staying out of this. I did my part, now you do the rest."

Casey groaned. "Argh. Some friend you are. Syd, lighten up. I think this is a great idea. All we'd need is a couple of days. We go down, tour the place, and come home. Two airline tickets, two nights of hotel, a little food and we're set."

"You're making it sound like I'm against the idea," Sydnie chided.

"Well, you don't exactly sound like you're for it," Casey said defensively.

"Now who needs to lighten' up? You've been wound tighter than a guitar string for the last week because of this job."

"I'm under a lot of pressure here." Casey took a long drink of her wine cooler, the alcohol barely easing her tension.

"And that's why I think you should go."

"What?" Casey choked. "Really? You're serious?"

"Of course, I'm serious. Make arrangements and go— the sooner the better, too." Sydnie gave Casey a goofy look. Heading for the door, she stopped and turned to face her friend. "Oh. And don't forget to book *two* hotel rooms. You don't know Alex well enough yet to be making, *A Big Hunk o' Love.*" Syd shook her finger teasingly, then disappeared around the corner.

"Yes, mother," Casey mocked, catching Syd's reference to one of the King's songs. Now, all she needed to do was convince Alex and she was set. "Woo-hoo. Elvis, here I come. I hope."

* * * *

"It looks like all your paperwork is in order, Alex," the sleek, older bank president said from behind his oversized desk. "The other loan officers and I will confer in the morning. I assure you, we'll give your request for a loan due consideration."

Due consideration? That sounded like another snobbish way of saying, *sorry, can't help you.*

Alex leaned forward, resting his arms on the chair. This was his third bank stop today, and Colorado Financial was the first to at least let him fill out an application. The first two, after he told them how much money he wanted to borrow, simply said sorry and ushered him out the door.

"Look, I don't mean to be abrupt," Alex said, hoping he didn't sound desperate, even though he was. "I'm kind of short on time here. Can you at least tell me if the odds are in my favor of getting the loan?"

The silver-haired man, Jerry Shirley by his name placard, leaned back in his chair and laced his fingers over his trim waist. No doubt he stayed fit by playing golf and racquetball at the local country club, all paid for, of course, by the bank.

"We at Colorado Financial take all of our loan requests

very seriously and make every effort to grant those loans. However, sometimes we simply can't, no matter how much we'd like to. As I'm sure you're aware, credit history is crucial." He steepled his fingers and Alex sensed the man was looking down his nose at him.

He struggled to rein in his defenses. "And you're saying my credit history isn't up to your standards."

"Not at all. While it's true your credit score isn't as high as I'd like to see it, it is still within a range we can work with. However, since it falls on the lower end of the scale, it does throw you into a higher risk category."

The man sat forward and laced his fingers together on the top of his mahogany desk. His face was unreadable, but his thumb twitched.

Shit. This didn't look good.

"Alex, you are applying for a two-hundred and fifty-thousand dollar loan. A quarter of a million dollars is a lot of money. A request like this must be considered carefully. All bank officers must be in full agreement before the loan can be granted."

"And when you do your considering, do you take into account personal history? Or is it all up to a series of black and white numbers on a piece of paper to determine the outcome?"

"We, of course, rely very heavily on the numbers. As a smaller branch of locally owned banks, we do have the freedom to work closer with our customers—take into consideration their personal track records, if you will."

Alex took a deep breath and pushed forward. This was his best chance to get the loan he needed to survive. If he couldn't persuade the bank president to back him, he was out of luck here, too.

"Mr. Shirley, I hope you *will* consider my personal history. I didn't amass the debt for which is the purpose of the loan. My former business partner decided to go out and have a...good time at my expense. She did it so fast I didn't realize what had happened until the bills were landing in my mailbox. I was busy working to build the business and was taken completely off guard."

"I'm sorry to hear that. A tough setback for you."

"Tougher than you know," Alex groaned, remembering all of his partner's indiscretions. "It has taken time, but I've gotten a handle on things. I'm working diligently to reestablish my credit, and rebuild the reputation of Alex Roy Enterprises."

"Didn't I see you profiled in *Timber Home Living* a while back?"

Alex nodded his head. It was amazing how many people had seen that small article in a magazine with a very specific reading audience.

"It was a short piece," Alex said.

"Yes, but well done and interesting."

Alex relaxed a smidgen and eased back in his chair. His chances looked promising, now he needed to seal the deal.

"I've recently secured a major job in Omaha as a result of that article, too. I'm heading back there at the end of the week to get the project rolling."

The banker jotted down a few notes. "Do you mind my asking who you'll be working for?"

"I'll be working in conjunction with an Omaha contracting firm on the project," Alex said, purposefully leaving out the name of Casey's business. The Armani suited banker might frown upon a name like *Studs for Hire* and not take the job seriously. A risk Alex wasn't willing to take. "The homeowner is Mrs. Hector Gridmore," he added.

"Gridmore? As in Gangster's Pizza fame?"

"That's right."

"Great pizza. My wife and I order out at least one Friday night a month and gorge ourselves on pizza and beer. We've done it ever since the last kid left the nest." A twinkle shone in the banker's eyes as he grinned, making Alex think the guy wasn't only referring to gorging on food and alcohol. Maybe he wasn't such a stuffed shirt after all.

"We're not only remodeling the majority of the mansion for Mrs. Gridmore, but adding on an additional five-thousand feet to accommodate her collection of...antiquities." Alex figured categorizing Heather's Elvis memorabilia as antiquities might be pushing it, but it sounded more impressive, and right now he needed impressive.

"Sounds interesting," Jerry said. "Very interesting. I'll pass this information along to the other officers. Well, I hate to cut this short," he stood and extended his hand. "But I have another appointment waiting."

They shook hands and Alex left with a promise of a call from Mr. Shirley himself, in a day or two.

Now, all Alex could do was wait.

* * * *

Alex shut off the warm spray of water sluicing over his tired muscles just in time to hear his cell phone ringing. Stepping out of the shower, he grabbed a towel and reached for his phone where he'd left it on the vanity.

"Hello," he said as he juggled the palm-sized phone in one hand while attempting to wrap the towel around his waist with the other. Silence hung on the line and he wondered if anyone was there, or if the call had dropped. He pulled the phone away from his ear to check the number.

His heart hitched in his chest. Casey. He'd only left Omaha yesterday, but that didn't stop him from thinking about her most of the day.

"Casey? Is that you? Are you there?"

"Hi, Alex. I'm sorry. Must be a bad connection," she said. Was there hesitation in her voice?

Alex's gut tightened, sensing she had something important to tell him. Had the Gridmore job been called off? He hoped not. The last thing he needed was more stress.

"What's up?" he asked, not sure he wanted to know the real reason for her call.

"Ah, I have an idea I'd like to discuss with you. Is this a good time?"

Relief eased the tension from his shoulders. If Casey wanted to talk ideas that meant the job still had the green light.

"Sure. I just stepped out the shower."

"Oh…I can call back…at a better time," she said, sounding slightly breathless.

A grin tugged at his lips knowing that he, even over the phone, could affect her so easily. Glancing down at the towel tucked tight around his waist, he saw she'd aroused a response in him as well. Sudden desire for more intimacy than a phone call would allow made his pulse kick into gear.

Don't go there, Roy. He'd come home, hoping to get her out of his system, if only for a little while. So much for that bright idea.

"No, its okay," he cleared his throat, "what's this idea

of yours?"

"Promise me you won't laugh."

"Okay…I promise."

"And promise you'll hear me out before you say no."

"All right," he chuckled. "You've got me curious. Now, what's that amazing brain of yours thinking?"

"Well, since we've been struggling to come up with ideas for Heather's remodel, I thought maybe we could use some inspiration."

Inspiration? Alex could think of at least a dozen ways to get inspired with Casey, but not a single one had anything to do with Elvis Presley. Damn. Why couldn't he stop thinking like a hormone enraged teenager?

"You're not going to make me watch every Elvis movie ever made, are you?" he asked, forcing himself back to the real reason for her call. "There's more than thirty."

"Ohhh. You and Sydnie think alike, do you know that?" she asked, exasperation in her voice.

"We do? How so?"

"She asked me the exact same thing when I told her I had a great idea to help us on this project."

"Guess she's in outstanding company."

Casey's smooth, rich laughter drifted through the line and he found himself liking the sound far more than he should.

"Alex, you don't by chance own a copy of the album Elvis recorded live in Hawaii, do you?" she asked, forcing him back to business.

"Why? You need it?"

"No. Just curious."

"Hey, stop making me wait here," he said as he leaned a hip against the counter. "What's this idea of yours?"

"Okay. I think, strictly for business, of course…" she said as if wanting to make sure he didn't get the wrong idea about anything, "that you and I should fly down to Memphis for the weekend."

"Memphis? This weekend?" Alex froze, totally caught off guard by her suggestion. He expected her to talk about fabric, tile and paint, but this…? He raked his fingers through his wet hair. Now what?

"What better place to get the inspiration we need than Graceland?" she said with excitement. "We'd be able to see how Elvis lived, what his personal style was like."

Alex braced his free hand on the edge of the vanity. What the hell was he going to do? Agreeing to go away with her for a weekend to Memphis was an enticing idea—and a dangerous one. *Damn.* If he thought he was struggling to keep his libido in check now, what would it be like once they flew away together? Spent the weekend together? Slept in rooms right next to each other?

Alex suppressed a groan. He'd be crazy to say yes.

God, he wanted to say yes.

"Isn't there a web site or something we can look at?" he asked, hoping to thwart his temptation to tell her what she wanted to hear—and what he wanted to say.

"Yes. I've spent enough hours on it today that Graceland security is probably wondering if I'm a nutcase."

Alex laughed. "Did you find out anything?"

"Yes. A lot, actually. For instance, did you know Graceland is the second most famous house in America? The White House is number one. Speaks volumes about Elvis' popularity, doesn't it?"

"Oh, just a little," he joked.

"Alex," her tone turned serious. "Surfing a web site isn't the same as being there and experiencing the atmosphere for yourself. Just think. We can tour the grounds, walk the paths that Elvis walked, see his furniture, feel his spirit. We can even have dinner at a nice restaurant and maybe take in some live music. They say Memphis is where it all began—musically anyway."

"Why, Miss Burrows. If I didn't know better, I'd think you were asking me out on a date."

"Would a date...convince you to go?" she asked with a sultry tone.

Alex took a deep breath. She didn't have to *convince* him to do anything. He was ready, willing and able. Too damn willing. But he'd be certified crazy to agree to this.

Turning toward the mirror, he wiped away the moisture and studied his reflection. He didn't look crazy. Tired maybe, but not crazy. In fact, he looked like any other average American male. And therein lay his real problem. He was thinking like any other average American male lusting over a sexy woman.

How could he help it? Casey was beautiful, smart, and hot. Now, if he *hadn't* noticed her inviting lips, smooth curves and full breasts, then he'd definitely be crazy—and blind. Not to mention, demented. He'd simply noticed her like any normal, living, breathing guy would. No big deal.

But agreeing to go away with her for the weekend, even if it was supposed to be strictly a business trip, was a big deal.

Strictly business. Yeah, right. And Elvis was alive and well and living in Alex's garage.

Cripes. Didn't he have enough complications in his life right now without adding woman trouble into the fray? Hadn't he learned his lesson?

Yes. He had. The hard way.

"Casey, I...have something to tell you," he said softly, hating like hell to disappoint her and himself.

"What is it?" she asked, a mixture of caution and apprehension lacing her simple question.

His hand tightened into a fist. Ahhh. He couldn't do it. In spite of his resolve not to get involved on a personal level, he didn't have the strength to deny himself this chance to spend a weekend alone with her.

"*Elvis, Aloha from Hawaii* was broadcast in forty countries and seen in more American homes than man's first steps on the moon," he said, grappling for something, anything to say.

"And you're telling me this because...?"

"Well because...you asked about the album. Did you know that concert was the first of its kind to be broadcast via satellite? It was a worldwide ratings smash. The album not only hit number one on the Billboard album chart, but has gone Platinum five times." Son of a bitch. He was rambling like an idiot. He covered his eyes with a towel. *Somebody stop me.*

"Hmm. Very interesting, Alex. I didn't know all that. Sounds like you've been doing your homework since you left."

He laughed, feeling like an idiot and a fool. Just what the hell was he about to agree to here? "I didn't have to do my homework. I've known those facts for a long time."

"You did? But how?"

"Well." Alex scrubbed a hand over his jaw, not

believing he was about to make this confession. "I guess you might say I'm sort of an Elvis fan. When can we leave?"

Chapter Eight

Casey breathed a sigh of relief. At last they were here—Memphis, Tennessee, *home of the blues, the birthplace of rock n' roll*, according to the kind shuttle driver who'd dropped them at the front entrance of Elvis Presley's Heartbreak Hotel. Located down the street from Elvis' mansion, the hotel was one of the newer additions to the Graceland complex.

Casey couldn't remember a week dragging on like this past one since she was a kid anxiously waiting for Christmas morning. She was beginning to think Friday would never come. Now, here they were in Memphis, embarking on an adventure that she sensed would somehow change her life.

"You're really getting into this Elvis thing, aren't you?" Alex asked as they entered the retro style lobby decked out in blues, reds and purples. Low slung couches and chairs created comfortable seating for patrons who wanted to enjoy the vast array of Elvis photos adorning the walls. Elvis even crooned a ballad over the stereo speaker system, adding the ultimate final touch to the atmosphere.

"As a fan, you ought to love it," she said. "Besides, we came here to get inspired, remember? And I am already.

I plan to make the most of this experience." Casey whipped out her camera and snapped pictures of the furniture, wall decor, and the overall room design.

"I can see that." Alex shook his head.

"This is kind of a mini vacation for me, too," Casey said as she snuck a picture of Alex standing in the middle of the lobby, their luggage in his hands and a bemused look on his face. "It's been too long. I'm way past due for some time off."

"Whoa, wait a minute. I thought this was supposed to be a *strictly business* trip?" Alex arched a brow in question, and in Casey's opinion, Elvis had nothing on this architect in the good looks department.

"Well, sure. But you can't come to a place like this and not have fun. I mean, look at this." She spread her arms wide, indicating the hotel. "It's fantastic. I'm already starting to see why Heather wants to renovate her home in the Elvis style. This is so cool."

"It's neat." He nodded, looking around. "It seems a bit much though, at least for a person to live in twenty-four seven."

"Oh, Alex. Admit it. You like it, too."

"I'll think about it, but in the morning. It's after one and I've been up since five. You do realize that's four hours shy of twenty-four hours, don't you? Right now I'm not sure about anything except for the fact my body could use some serious shuteye."

That's not all your body needs—like a night of unbridled passion. No. That's what my body needs. Casey stifled a giggle and managed to keep her wild thoughts under wraps. The two drinks she'd enjoyed during the flight, mixed with her own lack of sleep, made her loosen her self-control a bit.

"Casey," he said. She switched her focus from a large black and white photo of Elvis to Alex and saw he stood only inches away. His gaze darkened and one corner of his lips hitched up seductively.

Lord, was he trying to seduce her with his rich, *let me have sex with you* eyes of his? If her sudden pounding heart rate was any indication, he was doing a fine job of succeeding.

Then again, it was 1:08 A.M. It could be she was hallucinating.

She jerked her gaze back to the photos on the wall and snuck a deep breath. His subtle mountain scent reached out and teased her nose, kicking up her desires. Oh boy.

Was this guy real? And were they really in Memphis together? Alone? For the weekend?

Casey stole a peek out of the corner of her eye and was rewarded with another awesome view of Alex. No. She wasn't imagining here. He wasn't a mirage conjured up by her overtired brain. He was a living, breathing man looking at her as though he might be undressing her with his eyes.

Casey swallowed hard and tried to act cool and in control, when in reality she wanted to forget the visuals, rip his clothes off, and get down to some serious business that had nothing to with blue prints, permits, or building codes.

"Casey," Alex said softly, angling even closer.

"Hmm." She leaned toward him. Her lips parted. Was he going to kiss her? Was he going to suggest they only needed one room?

"Sorry to spoil your fun, sweetheart...but I'm beat."

Her heart screeched to a halt *Beat?* What? He was

thinking about sleep while she was thinking about…
Her cheeks flamed with embarrassment. She widened
the space between them and turned her attention to
her camera.

How could she get the signals between them so
crossed?

What if she was the only one sending any signals?

"Oh, come on, Alex. You only went through one time
zone change between here and Denver. You can't be
that tired," she said in an attempt to cover her blunder.

"I spent close to eleven hours driving through insane
interstate traffic *before* our five-hour flight tonight.
Remember?"

"All right. I'll cut you some slack. No sleeping in
tomorrow, though. I've booked us for the Graceland
Elvis Entourage VIP Tour. It'll be a full day. Ticket office
opens at eight-thirty. Don't be late."

"Eight-thirty? Don't you think you're going to
extremes with all this Elvis stuff?"

Casey's defenses kicked in at his open challenge of
her decisions for this job. "No, I don't," she said with a
hardness to her voice. She lifted her chin. "With VIP
tickets we'll get to see everything. You know how
obsessive Heather is. This tour is going to give us the
edge we need. Desperately need, I might add."

She turned and strode toward the registration desk,
needing a moment to tamp down her frustration, and
the fatigue creeping over her body.

"Heather's not the only one bordering on obsessive,"
Alex mumbled.

Casey whirled around to face him, in no mood for a
man to challenge her control. Sure she was tired and
probably overacting to his words, but they were up

against the wall to make this job work.

"What's that supposed to mean? I'm just doing my job. A job I take pride in, for your information."

His expression eased, the guarded distance in his eyes dissolving a fraction.

"Okay. You're right. We do need all the help we can get. The VIP tour is a good idea. I promise I'll be ready by the time the ticket office opens."

"What about breakfast?" she asked, trying hard to stay the professional even though Alex insisted upon goading her. "Would you care to join me?"

"Sure." He leaned close. "I wouldn't miss finding out if you like your eggs sunny-side up...or over hard," he drawled.

His blatant suggestion combined with the warmth of his breath on her ear made Casey's heart skip a dozen beats. What was he trying to do, drive her crazy? She should be offended, she should walk away, but instead she longed for him to take her down.

"Stop...teasing me," she managed around a lump in her throat. She needed to be strong and put a stop to this.

"Who's teasing?" His lips brushed the sensitive flesh of her ear, sending shockwaves of awareness pulsing through her body.

Oh. My. God. She didn't have the strength to stop anything because she tingled—everywhere.

"You are...teasing," she said, breathless. In desperate need of air, smelling salts and a stiff drink, she managed to move her feet and turned to face him. She wasn't about to let him trifle with her heart and then drop her cold when this job was over. She stiffened her spine, ready to put him in his place. "You're a difficult man,

Mr. Roy."

He grinned. "Am I? I thought I was just the one *in control* for a change."

Casey's jaw dropped. Damn the man. He obviously got a kick out of riling her. Lifting her chin she attempted to exude a confidence she didn't feel. She headed for a safer territory—the registration desk.

"May I help you?" the young, pretty desk clerk asked in her easy southern drawl.

"Yes. We have reservations for two rooms under Casey Burrows."

"Burrows. Burrows." She tapped away on the computer. "Hmm. I'm sorry. I'm not finding any reservations listed under that name."

"There has to be. I placed them online last Monday night."

"I'm sorry. Do you have a confirmation number?"

"Yes." Casey placed her purse on the counter and rifled through the contents, confident she wouldn't find the reservation form she'd printed, but made a good show of looking anyway. She distinctly remembered placing the confirmation in a file marked Graceland—a file neatly organized with other pending files she kept in her desk. "But I don't have it with me. It's back at the office.

"Need some help?" Alex asked, joining Casey at the desk. The desk clerk shot him a pearly white smile and fluttered her eyelashes at him.

"No thanks. I've got it under *control.*" She gathered up the contents of her purse she'd placed on the counter and started stuffing it all back where it'd come from.

"Looks that way," he quipped.

"Would there be another name the reservation could be under?" the twenty-something woman asked.

"Susanna," Alex said, looking at the woman's name tag. "Did you look under Studs for Hire? Maybe our reservations got put under the company name."

"Studs…for Hire?" Susanna asked, a little breathless as she looked at Alex.

Casey gritted her teeth. God. Breathlessness was contagious. She could see the wheels turning behind Susanna's dreamy eyes—forming the wrong idea—as she drooled over Alex.

Alex stood there, a sexy smile on his face for Susanna, doing nothing to dispel her mistaken impression. By the look on Susanna's face, Alex was certainly making her night, heck, making her year.

"We're a *construction* company," Casey said, hoping to regain Susanna's attention. "You know houses? Two-by-fours? Plumbing? We're here to do some research for a remodeling project."

"Construction company?" Susanna asked as if in a daze.

"Yes," Casey said firmly, feeling tired and irritated.

And jealous. Yes. She was jealous. And she didn't want to feel jealous. Dammit.

"Well, if he works for Studs for Hire," Susanna said, nodding at Alex. "You're hired. Now I wished I owned a house," she giggled.

"I could design one for you. I'm an architect." Alex winked and Susanna blushed.

"Sorry, our territory doesn't branch out this far," Casey said, interrupting their flirting session. "Now, about our reservations. Did you find anything?"

"Reservation? Oh, yeah." She turned back to her computer and started punching in letters again. "Here it is. It is under Studs for Hire. Two rooms? Is that right?"

"That's right," Alex said. Susanna's smile widened and Casey saw a flicker of hope in the girl's blue eyes.

Casey pressed her lips together and groaned under her breath.

In spite of Susanna's flustered state, she managed to finish the appropriate paperwork and hand them two room key cards.

"Oh, and one last thing," she said as Alex and Casey started to step away from the desk. "One of the features of the Heartbreak Hotel is our free in-house channel that runs Elvis movies continuously. And I'm working tomorrow night, too, so if you need anything, don't hesitate to call. Enjoy your stay."

"Thank you. I'm sure we will," Alex said. They headed for the elevators and Casey threw Alex a perturbed smile as they walked.

At this late hour the elevator doors slid open within seconds of pushing the up button. Once inside, Alex hit the third floor button. Casey wasn't claustrophobic, but with Alex's imposing, hard-muscled body standing next to her, the space seemed minuscule, and suffocating, and hot. Damn *hot*.

"Looks like you're going to get your chance to watch those Elvis movies after all," she said, trying to refocus.

"Hmm. I don't know. I kind of had something else in mind for the weekend." He winked.

Something else? The elevator dinged, the doors slid open, and he stepped out into the hallway. Casey stood rooted to her spot, dreaming about something else.

* * * *

At eight o'clock sharp, Alex found himself outside Casey's door, not sure if he was ready for this day or not. For the umpteenth time he questioned his sanity for agreeing to this trip.

He should've known he wouldn't be able to look at her as just an associate, no matter how hard he tried. Her soft, tantalizing vanilla scent teased him mercilessly, and her green eyes bewitched him. How was he supposed to think about Elvis, blueprints and room design with Casey around?

Trouble. That's what this whole mess was. A big peck of trouble.

She'd accused him of being difficult last night, exactly what he'd wanted—or at least what his rational side wanted. He'd purposefully pushed at her control buttons and flirted with the desk clerk, trying to squelch the growing attraction he'd read in her eyes.

He'd gotten to her. Now, he'd see if her frustration with him had stuck.

He knocked and Casey answered the door with a bright smile.

"Good morning, Alex," she said with more excitement than a person should be allowed to have on a Saturday morning after too little sleep.

"Mornin' to you, too. Don't you look chipper," he said, irritated that apparently last night carried no long term effects for her. She'd pulled her hair back into a pony tail and was dressed in a pair of faded blue jeans, a Nebraska Cornhuskers hoodie sweatshirt and tennis shoes, giving her a youthful, spirited look. He liked.

"Thanks. I wanted to be comfortable, and since they don't let you carry in certain bags, I wanted plenty of pockets."

Alex let his gaze slip down the length of her jeans. The denim fit her figure perfectly, and oh, so nice. He doubted there was room to stuff much of anything into those pockets, but what he wouldn't give to find out—with his hands. Yeah, he liked too damn much.

So much for his resolve to stop fantasizing about her. How could he expect her to figure out he wasn't interested, when he couldn't stop acting like he was?

He cleared his throat and shifted his weight to his left foot. "Are you ready to go?" he asked, forcing his eyes to check out the pretty girls on the TV screen for a mere two seconds. The bad part of this whole deal was that nothing else captured his attention like Casey did.

"All set. I have my camera, a notepad, cash, credit card and a tube of apple-raisin lipstick. It's a great color for fall." She gave him a mischievous wink.

Your lips look sweeter than an apple pie fresh from the oven, sweetheart. Alex's pulse hitched. What he wouldn't give for a taste. When it came to apple pie, a man shouldn't have to stop with one piece if he didn't want to. He shouldn't have to stop with one kiss from a woman like Casey, either. Once he had a taste of her, he knew he'd want it all, à la mode.

All the more reason tasting was out of the question. So what if she was vibrant, exciting, and sexy to boot? She was off limits. There was no room for romance in his life. He had to make it through this weekend without throwing her down on the bed. And that was going to be harder than he'd anticipated.

"Taking advantage of the Elvis channel I see," Alex said as he nodded toward the TV, hoping to turn off his carnal thoughts. Elvis romanced a beautiful blonde in his arms as he sang. So much for blocking out the sexual suggestions bombarding his mind.

"You bet," she said. "I watched for a little while last night, then fell asleep. Elvis serenaded me in my sleep all night long. I think I'm in love," she said dreamily and sighed.

"You and how many other millions of women?"

"Oh, well. I guess I'll have to find my own Elvis." She gave him her own sultry smile and Alex's heart picked up its rhythm, rivaling the beat of the music on the TV.

Okay. What was she up to? Either she was oblivious to his efforts last night, or she was wise to his methods and playing a little game of her own.

"Are you hungry?" she asked.

Hungry was an understatement. "Famished," he managed to say around a lump in his throat.

"Then let's eat." She started to move past him on the way to the door, then stopped. Her soft, subtle scent wrapped around him, teasing and tormenting. "I'm starved, too," she whispered into his ear. The warmth of her breath pulsed against his skin, igniting a desire he hadn't allowed himself to feel for a long time.

She stepped away and strode down the hallway, leaving him behind. Alex narrowed his eyes as he watched her. The minx. She'd joined in the game all right and by the sudden tightness in his jeans, she was giving him one helluva run for his money.

* * * *

A quick breakfast later, Casey and Alex walked the short distance from the Heartbreak Hotel over to the Graceland complex. The sun shone bright and promised a beautiful fall Saturday in Memphis. Casey couldn't have asked for a more perfect way to experience a slice of Elvis' life, and get to know the man who was doing a good job of revving up her libido.

She knew she was playing with fire as far as Alex

was concerned, but she couldn't seem to help herself. He was handsome, witty, and under that tough-guy exterior he wore, she suspected he had a sensitive, caring side.

He was a good guy with enough bad-boy mixed in to make her want to flirt and have fun. During her teenage years she'd missed out on many of the thrills a boy's attention presented a girl. She'd been stuck at home looking after her younger brothers and sisters while their mother worked two jobs to assure their survival. Extra money and free time for teenage pursuits were luxuries she'd never had. And now, no matter how hard Alex tried, she wasn't going to miss out on this chance as a woman. So what if nothing came of their association. She wasn't in the mood for heartbreak anyway.

Their VIP tickets confirmed and their earphones in hand for the mansion tour, they boarded a shuttle with a group of other eager Elvis fans. The shuttle ferried them across Elvis Presley Boulevard and Casey held her breath as they drove through the famous, custom-made gates of Graceland.

Stepping off the shuttle, Casey and Alex walked up to the front of the house. Four columns towered tall at the entrance while two lion statues stood regally out front, still guarding Elvis' beloved home after all these years. The kaleidoscope of yellow ochre, sienna and orange on the trees framed the mansion, creating a spectacular scene.

"Wow. This is so cool. I can't believe we're actually here," she said with awe.

"Yeah. I can see why Elvis was so fond of this place," Alex said.

"I can't wait to see the inside."

"Well, you don't have to wait any longer," Alex said as a tour guide came out of the house and greeted them.

After a few brief instructions and a reminder flash photography wasn't allowed, the guide led them inside. Crossing the threshold, they filed into the house where Elvis had escaped the demands of his super-stardom. Behind these walls was where he'd felt the safest and most relaxed.

This is where Elvis, the man, had lived.

A tingle of anticipation raced along Casey's nerves. Anxious to see it all, she looked around the foyer and spied the staircase. A mixture of awe and sadness encompassed her body down to her toes. Off limits to the public, the second floor was where the man responsible for the entire phenomenon, the legend and myth, had met a tragic end at far too young an age.

A surprise hint of tears stung her eyes and she blinked, forcing them aside. Taking a deep breath, she soaked in the colors, the styles, and the very atmosphere of the house through her pores.

Elvis spoke to her through the headphones with his deep, sexy southern drawl, and she turned and noticed the portrait of a younger Elvis hanging along the stairs. Her breath hitched as he spoke of his life at Graceland, and Casey couldn't help feeling that the image inside the gilded frame reflected a man haunted by the high price of fame.

To her right, the front room beckoned with the specially designed stained glass peacocks adorning each side of the entrance into the music room. There a piano and a stack of well-used LPs waited to be played.

Soft white provided the main color for the rooms, including the carpeting, low-slung furniture and the walls. Accented by mirrors and royal blue and gold drapes, the area radiated elegant Hollywood chic.

"I wonder how many other famous people were entertained here," she said to Alex.

"Probably a few."

She saw another portrait of Elvis hanging above a black and white photograph of his parents. Three people gone from this world, but still very much alive. Casey took a deep sigh. Never in her wildest imagination had she anticipated the bevy of emotions assaulting her now.

Lifting her camera, she said a silent prayer her eight-hundred speed film would be enough to capture the interior without the benefit of a flash. The camera clicked away, capturing the home of a true American legend.

Alex touched her arm and together they walked through the house, taking notes and snapping pictures, all in an effort to capture at least a fraction of the real Elvis.

Seeing Elvis' personal effects, walking in the very places he'd once walked, evoked a sadness that tugged at her heart for all that had once been. Yet, his spirit was very much alive within these walls. So much so that she wouldn't be surprised to see him come walking around a corner, or sitting casually in one of his chairs smoking the cigarillos he enjoyed.

As they walked through the dining room, the audio talked about the dinner parties he hosted for his Memphis Mafia friends. And to Casey's surprise, the kitchen was very much like any other typical kitchen of the 1970's, complete with harvest gold appliances and an avocado-colored sink. The non-typical difference with Elvis' kitchen was the video surveillance TVs on the counter, and a set of red phones installed for his personal use.

Upon entering the jungle room, Casey smiled to herself, recognizing the green carpet as the same that had at one time covered her beloved grandmother's living room floor. An assortment of green plants and a large fountain dominated one wall. The odd assortment of furniture, some covered in striped fur, and a bamboo ceiling fan, added the final touches to the jungle feel.

They toured the basement next and the TV room where three TVs were lined up side by side, and learned Elvis liked to watch all three major networks of his era at one time.

Casey giggled. "Boy, times have changed."

"Yeah, he'd need hundreds of TVs now."

"That would be enough to make you cross-eyed, wouldn't it?"

"You bet."

They moved on, saw where Elvis played pool with friends, and all too soon found themselves exiting the house, ending the house tour in the backyard.

Alex gave her a warm smile. "So what do you think?" he asked after they removed their headphones.

An overwhelming sadness surrounded Casey and she took a deep breath trying to shake off the feeling. Geesh. She hadn't expected this.

"Are you okay?" Alex asked.

She nodded. "This might sound silly, but…I feel him. It's almost as if his spirit…that he still lives here."

"You mean Elvis?"

Casey nodded again, not trusting her voice to speak. Breaking down like a babbling idiot in front of Alex and dozens of other people wasn't her idea of starting the day out on the fun note she'd planned.

"I think you're more of an Elvis fan then you realize, Casey," he said with a light chuckle. Looking at her with his brown eyes full of understanding, he brushed a lock of hair that had escaped her pony tail from her cheek. "I know what you mean, though," he said softly. "I feel him, too."

Casey's breath hitched at the unexpected touch of Alex's fingers against her skin. Slowly, he rubbed the strands between his fingers, hypnotizing her. A tingle of awareness and anticipation raced down her spine. Desire for more than a simple touch from Alex hit her straight on.

She wanted more. Much, much more.

A group of older women exited the house, and their zealous chatter about how *Elvis the Pelvis* had once made their hearts flutter forced Casey back to reality. Her cheeks warmed and she took a quick step back, breaking the delicious contact with Alex. She focused her gaze on the other tourists, and forced her mind back on Elvis and away from Alex.

"When I was a kid I listened to Elvis' records all the time," she said. "It's been years since I've really paid much attention to him or his legacy. Now, it's as if all those memories I thought I'd forgotten are rushing back. God, I must be running a temperature or something." She laughed and took a deep breath, knowing in truth her sudden lack of oxygen had nothing to do with her memories of Elvis, but with sharing them with the man standing mere inches from her.

"It's nostalgia, maybe. Or a yearning for what might have been," he said with a hard edge, a muscle tightened in his jaw.

Casey pondered his words, wondering what Alex

yearned for. He said no more, and turned his attention to the house itself, no doubt studying every architectural line.

The house loomed before them and in spite of the bustle of activity around the grounds, the structure seemed sad and lonely. Casey's gaze was drawn to a second story window. She saw no one there, but she sensed a presence and goose bumps popped out on skin.

Good grief. What was the matter with her? She wasn't normally one for nostalgia, and she really didn't believe in ghosts, either. Had this whirlwind trip with the sexy architect thrown her into an emotional tailspin? Rubbing her hands up and down her arms, she tried to banish the goose bumps.

"Are you sure you're all right?" he asked.

"Don't you feel it? It's like he's watching us from behind those curtains up there."

"Stop. You're gettin' spooky," Alex chuckled, dismissing her apprehensions. "So, what do you think of the house itself? Do you think we can glean some ideas from it?"

Casey took a deep breath. Bless the man for whisking her back to business. Business was safe.

"It's much smaller than I expected. In the photographs it looks huge and sprawling."

"The power of photography. Speaking of which, do you think you got some good shots?"

"I hope so. We'll find out when I get the film developed. How did you do with taking notes?"

"Not the best. I got kind of caught up in checking out every detail." Alex gazed at her, his face full of silent suggestions. At least she thought his hooded eyes and the smile tugging at his lips constituted suggestions of a more sexual nature, or it could be just the bright sun blinding her from reality.

"I've got a good memory," he added. "I figure we can work on making more detailed notes later, while everything is still fresh in our minds."

"Fresh in our minds," she said absently. The only thing that was on Casey's mind at the moment was the idea of getting fresh with Alex.

"This place has a profound effect on a person," he said. "More than even I anticipated. I don't think there's much danger of forgetting the experience any time soon."

Graceland wasn't the only thing having a profound effect on Casey. And she realized right then and there that no matter where things went, or didn't, between her and Alex, he and Graceland would be forever linked.

She'd never listen to an Elvis song the same way again.

Chapter Nine

"Ready to move on?" Alex asked, nodding toward the back of the Graceland estate. "There's still a lot to see. I want to make sure we get your money's worth out of those VIP tickets."

"Even if we don't take another step, I feel like I've gotten a full bang for my buck," Casey said with a hint of sass in her voice.

Alex grinned and they headed for the business office where Elvis' father had helped run his illustrious son's career. Though dated in the seventies era, the office looked as if it was still very much in use, and concert bookings and movie deals continued to happen on a daily basis.

They walked past the small nook where Elvis and his friends used to target shoot, and then moved onto the racquetball building where Elvis had played in the wee hours of the morning the day he died. Knowing that he'd spent some of his final hours here made Casey's heart clinch.

Stopping by the kidney-shaped swimming pool, Casey knelt down and focused the lens of her camera. A tantalizing fantasy filled the frame as she shot picture after picture.

The image transformed to one of still water aglow with moonlight on a warm summer's night. Alex, his bare skin glistening with droplets of water, wore a sultry smile and nothing else.

In her fantasy Casey joined him in the pool and their arms quickly became entangled. His unique, spicy scent encompassed her senses. Their fingers probed. His smooth skin rippled with muscles and filled her hands. Their hungry lips craved, searched. Tongues danced, nipped, tasted. The two of them came together, body to body, under the watchful gaze of the Tennessee stars.

Oh, sweet Heaven. Oh, sweet, sweet, Heaven. *Take me now, Alex. Please, I beg of you.*

"Casey?"

The sound of her name flickered dimly in the back of her brain. She pushed it aside, not willing to let the fantasy end. Not yet. Not ever. Alex was about to—

There was a tug at her shoulder.

Yes.

"Casey." Alex's voice registered from above, startling her back to the present. "Are you sure you're all right?"

Daylight. Crap. There was daylight. *Oh, God.* She hoped she hadn't been moaning, and who knew what else, out here for the world to see.

"Uh, sure. I'm fine." She rose and her legs protested, threatening to drop her flat on her butt.

"Whoa." Alex grabbed her arm, steadying her. "You seemed...distracted. Did you see Elvis' ghost or something?" he teased.

Casey laughed, relieved, and a little disappointed, he hadn't guessed her true thoughts. "Would you think I was crazy if I said yes?"

Alex's forehead furrowed and he scratched his head.

"I refuse to answer that question on the grounds it might incriminate me."

"Chicken." Casey gave his shoulder a good-natured slug. "You know, Heather believes in ghosts," she said softly, walking toward the trophy building. This seemed like as good a time as any to break that piece of quirky news to Alex. "She thinks her house might be haunted."

"You can't be serious." He snatched her arm in a gentle grip, stopping her. His eyes were filled with a mixture of frustration and disbelief, and his mouth tensed into a thin line.

Okay, maybe she'd been wrong. Maybe this wasn't a good time.

"Well…" Casey held up her hands and shrugged.

"You *are* serious," he said, his voice hard.

"Let me put it this way. Heather has a fascination with the metaphysical. That's all."

"That's all? You're just full of surprises on this job, aren't you?" He planted his hands on his lean hips and shifted his weight to his left foot. Boy, she hated it when he did that. He always looked so rebellious, so damn sexy. And she always got this hot-n-bothered urge to rip his flannel shirt from his body and throw herself at him.

"It's no big deal, Alex." She crossed her arms in an attempt to keep her hands from grabbing him. She really needed more willpower, but every minute she spent in his company, her *strictly business* mantra crumbled a fraction more. At the rate she was going, she'd be in serious trouble by the time they flew home tomorrow.

"No big deal?" He threw her a sharp sideways glance.

"Why should it be? So what if she is open to…to possibilities outside of normal ways of thinking. As long as she signs the checks, it won't affect us and what we've been hired to do."

"Are you sure about that?"

"Well, why would it?"

A small group of Japanese tourists approached, eyeing Alex and Casey with curiosity. Casey stepped aside to allow them to pass. They smiled and chatted in their native tongue and since Casey didn't speak a lick of Japanese she didn't know if they thought she and Alex were having a lover's spat, or if they were simply commenting on the balmy October weather. The group mingled nearby, taking pictures and talking with animated excitement.

"Because she's a nutcase," Alex said with a low, exasperated tone that only she could hear.

"Alex, I wouldn't go that far. Sure, she's eccentric, but so what. She can afford to be. Don't stew. I've got everything under control."

"Un-huh," he said, doubt clear in his tone. He swiped a hand over his jaw.

"Besides, I owe her a note of thanks. Being here is making me see things...differently."

"Such as?"

You. But did she dare come clean and admit that Alex was *one* of those things? That he'd conjured up a desire for something sure, something concrete for her life? She'd fallen into other relationships, believing each subsequent Mr. Right was truly the one, only to find out she wasn't *the one* for him.

All her life she'd failed to keep men from leaving her. Why should this time be any different?

The crowd nearby increased in numbers and Casey worried if she and Alex *were* the big attraction, or if they'd missed out on some other excitement. People had to be bored with their lives if they thought the little scene playing out between her and Alex was more interesting than Elvis' backyard.

"Such as…this trip," Casey answered. She lifted her chin, dead set on regaining control of this bumbling conversation that was apparently amusing the Japanese tourists. "For one, it's given me a new appreciation and respect for one of the Twentieth Century's greatest icons." Now there was a safe and true answer that didn't reveal anything personal. But boy, did it sound corny.

"Yeah. And what else?"

Damn. "Does there have to be something else?" She threw up her hands and the Japanese group scattered like spooked geese.

"You did say *things*. Plural."

Crap. Why did Alex have to be so astute and catch every tiny detail? And why did he want to know? Was he fishing—hoping for more than a fleeting interest in him on her part?

"Well…coming here has also made me realize that maybe Heather isn't so far off the mark. I mean, look at this place. There are people everywhere and this isn't even the height of the tourist season."

"So what's your point?"

"My point is that maybe this remodel isn't as wacky as we first thought. There's no doubt it'll be a challenge to pull off, but there's not many people who don't like Elvis, at least a little bit. Six-hundred thousand visitors a year here has to mean something. We can do this, Alex."

"Excuse me," a small Japanese man said in broken English. "Would you…be so kind…take picture?" He nodded his dark head at Casey, his smile bright, his eyes sparkling with excitement.

"Of course," she said, returning the smile. He handed her the camera, pointed at some buttons and trotted back to his group as they bunched together, the house providing the backdrop for the photo.

Casey snapped the shot, took a second for good measure and handed the camera back to the little man. "Thank you," he said with sincerity and bowed. "Me? For you?" He smiled and pointed at the camera in Casey's hand.

"Oh. Sure. That would be fun, wouldn't it, Alex?"

"Yeah, sure."

The Japanese man took her camera while she and Alex moved to stand next to each other. He lifted the camera to take the picture and frowned.

"No. No," he said, shaking his head. He scurried over to them, his frown still firmly in place. "Closer. Like this." He clasped his hands over his arms as if he was giving himself a hug, clearly motioning for them to stand arm in arm.

Casey glanced at Alex apologetically. They scooted closer together. Draping an arm around her waist, he let his fingers brush across her backside just below the hem of her sweatshirt.

"Oh!" Casey bopped up onto her tiptoes and down again. He winked, and heat pricked at her cheeks. Who knew Alex could be so ornery?

She liked it.

"Good," the man said, nodding his head up and down. "Big smile." He pointed to the corners of his mouth and grinned.

Casey did as he prompted, and out of the corner of her eye she saw Alex's lips quirk up into the lazy grin that always made her heart palpitate.

"Aw. Good picture." The man held the camera out to Casey, but she couldn't move with Alex's arm still draped securely around her waist. And she didn't want to.

"Thanks so much," she said, forcing herself to lean forward enough to retrieve the camera. Alex didn't loosen his hold.

"My pleasure. My pleasure." He bowed again and hurried back to his waiting group. They disappeared in a flurry of excited chatter.

Alex's fingers pressing on her hip scorched right through the denim of her jeans and down to her skin. Casey closed her eyes and leaned into Alex, refusing to relinquish the comfort of his strong arms.

Oh, yeah. His muscles were warm, rock-hard and lean. Images of their bodies entwined, exhausted and slick with sweat after a round of raucous lovemaking consumed her mind.

Alex cleared his throat, snapping Casey out of her second fantasy of the day. She took a quick step to her right, afraid Alex was either thinking she was horny as heck, or completely off her rocker. So much for keeping this trip under control. And so much for her brain ruling over her weakening heart, and over her traitorous body.

"You suppose that's really what all the fuss was about earlier—them trying to figure out how to ask you to take their picture?" Alex asked, acting as if she hadn't fazed him one bit and that nothing had even happened between them.

Casey shrugged, more than a little perturbed by his nonchalance. So what if he wasn't hot-and-bothered like she was. That realization was exactly what she needed to keep her focus, her control.

"Time to get back to work," she ordered. "We've got

a lot more to see."

Leaving behind the bright sunlight of the October sky, they stepped into the darker interior of the Trophy building. Casey blinked and waited for her eyes to adjust. When they did, her jaw dropped. Here in this building, every element of Elvis' professional career was impressively displayed. While the house reflected Elvis as a person, this building showcased the King of Rock 'n' Roll in all his glory.

Gold and Platinum records and other awards lined the walls. Stage costumes, including many of his famous white jumpsuits, studded with their vast array of gems, glittered under the lights while they stood protected behind glass.

"They're magnificent," Casey said barely above a whisper as she and Alex admired a suit adorned with a large eagle. Made entirely of multi-colored gemstones spanning the torso, the suit took Casey's breath away. She wanted to break through the glass and touch it, hold it, and pack it in her suitcase.

Wouldn't that be a nifty souvenir? "I can see now why Heather is so excited about acquiring one of these."

"Impressive," Alex said, sidling up next to her. In no time flat the warmth of his body once more seeped through her sweatshirt and into her skin, making her sweat. Okay, perspire. According to one of Casey's grade school teachers, girls didn't sweat, they perspired. Yeah, right. She was sweating. And panting. And drooling.

Great, she still wasn't fully recovered from the photo session in the yard, and now she was dealing with the second four alarm fire of the day.

"It's been years, but I remember seeing some of

these," Alex continued, his voice as intoxicating as aged whisky. He stood so close his breath riffled the hairs on the top of her head.

That did it. She was damned near lost. Her toes danced in her tennis shoes. Her fingers itched to touch. Grabbing Alex by his flannel collar and pinning him up against a gold record-covered wall was pretty darn tempting.

Get it under control, Case. Sydnie wouldn't be happy to get a call from an incarcerated Casey because she'd busted Elvis' gold records while jumping Alex.

She swallowed hard, so hard she thought she'd popped a muscle in her neck while trying to curb her increasing desires.

"I wonder how many suits he owned?" she managed to croak around her protesting vocal cords.

"Elvis owned about one hundred different stage costumes," a velvety voice said from beside them. Startled, Casey turned to see a petite brunette tour guide smiling at them. "We have more than seventy of those costumes here in the Graceland collection," she continued.

"Ah…incredible. I had no idea," Casey said with a wobble in her voice. Her cheeks flushed with heat. God, could anyone else tell what she'd been thinking? Probably not. That didn't stop the guilt, however, from crashing over her like a tidal wave for having such racy thoughts in a place bordering on the sacred.

"What happened to the other thirty or so costumes?" she asked, attempting to act the part of the interested tourist. She had to admit though, she was curious to know how Heather planned on getting her hands on one of these flamboyant, magnificent pieces.

"Elvis was very generous," the guide said. "He often gave away items to individuals and charities. The charities would then auction the items to raise funds for their respective organizations."

"So it is possible for private collectors to obtain some of his stage costumes, even now, after all these years?" Alex asked.

"Absolutely. In the world of Elvis collecting, some items have changed hands several times. It might surprise you to know that pieces of his personal clothing are in the hands of private collectors as well."

"These jumpsuits certainly are fabulous," Casey said, eyeing the collection with awe. "So colorful. Breathtaking."

"They looked fabulous under the stage lights, too," the guide said with enthusiasm. "The fans loved them, but the jeweled ones are very heavy."

"They look like they'd be really hot, too," Casey said, the subject of heat forefront in her brain.

"Actually, they weren't too bad. The jumpsuit was a popular fashion style of the 1970's and Elvis' costume designer, Bill Belew, had these made of wool gabardine imported from Italy because the wool breathes."

Clothes that breathe? Sounded exactly like what Casey needed right about now. Either that or stripping off every stitch of material on her body. *Yeah, like that's an option.*

Feeling restless and in need of air, Casey thanked the guide and she and Alex left the building. The last stop on the tour was the Meditation Garden and together they stood, gazing upon the graves of Elvis and his family. Reverence and a profound sadness surrounded them as they read the markers and marveled at the number of flowers left by adoring fans.

And Casey got it—Elvis' impact on the world, and the world's fascination with him.

She stole a glance at Alex and wished she understood her own growing fascination for this man she'd hired.

* * * *

Alex's cell phone buzzed against his hip as he and Casey made their way back to their hotel rooms after a long day of experiencing everything Elvis. From clothing to furniture, to automobiles and airplanes, they'd lived and breathed Elvis for the last nine hours.

His phone buzzed again and he checked the number. Dotty.

His gut tightened. Dotty calling late on a Saturday afternoon signaled a problem—and not just a plumbing or deranged client problem. Those minor issues she could handle. The woman was the goddess of efficiency. No. Her calling him now, with less than an hour before the members of her weekly poker club were scheduled to descend upon her condo, meant something else was awry.

Dotty worked hard for Alex all week long, but when it came to the weekends she was as possessive about her time off as an alley cat with a fresh chicken bone. She never called him on the weekends.

Unless there was an emergency.

Casey turned and looked at him, concern in her eyes. "Is something wrong?"

Only the feeling that all hell was about to break loose, but he decided to keep his thoughts to himself.

"No. It's my secretary. I'd better give her a call back."

"Sure." Casey shifted the sacks overflowing with Elvis goodies she'd purchased in the gift shop, and pulled her key card out of her back pocket. Damn nice back pocket, too, Alex thought. "I'd like to freshen up, anyway," she said.

"Okay. Let's meet in say…thirty minutes? I'd like to get a serious start on this tonight. I've got a few ideas and I'd like to get them down on paper while they're still fresh."

"Sounds great."

"Good. I'll bring a sketch pad and come to your room. We can order room service if you're hungry."

"You don't want to go out?"

"I don't like a lot of background noise when I'm trying to work. Makes it hard for me to focus."

"Oh. Well, we can discuss ideas on the plane tomorrow, too. And there is always Monday." Alex cringed at the disappointment he heard in her voice. And for two seconds he almost reconsidered. It was damn tempting to take her out for a night on the town, but he knew that wasn't a wise move. Already today the impulse to make this into more than a *working* relationship between them had hit way too many times.

"I'd rather start now," he said. "I can't be away from Denver forever. The sooner we get things in motion, the sooner I can get back."

"Right. I understand." The light shining in her eyes all day had since dimmed and Alex felt like the biggest kind of heel. But it was better to keep things in check now, rather than suffer the consequences later.

"Well, times a wasting. I'll see you in a half-hour." Casey disappeared behind the door. The slide of the deadbolt ramming home sounded like thunder.

Shit. He'd blown that one. *Real subtle, Roy.* He'd much rather follow and find out how Casey planned on spending those thirty minutes than calling Dotty to find out what was wrong now.

He had his own ideas how he'd like to spend his half-hour—like with Casey. Relaxing. Under the sheets. Well, relaxing wasn't exactly the right word. In fact, with Casey by his side, relaxing would be the farthest thing from his mind.

There was his biggest problem. He couldn't trust himself. All day her soft, alluring scent had teased him unmercifully, driving him crazy with need for more than a platonic, business relationship. On more than one occasion he'd come close to acting on his urges only to thankfully be interrupted by a tour guide or a horde of crazy Elvis fans shoving by to see the next amazing artifact Elvis had either worn, touched, played, donated or drove.

If he was alone with her he couldn't count on an unwanted interruption to save his ass.

Alex's phone buzzed again, temporarily stilling the carnal desires boiling in his system. While flipping his phone open, he unlocked his door and entered the dark quiet of his room. The air conditioner hummed methodically, spewing out its frigid air.

"Hey, Dotty. I was just about to call you back. What's up?" He turned on a light and dropped his key card on the dresser.

"Alex, I'm glad I caught you," Dotty said in a breathless rush. "I was afraid that you might have your phone off or were out of range or something."

"Whoa. Calm down. Dotty, are you okay? There hasn't been an accident or—"

"No. No, nothing like that." She took another deep breath, and so did Alex.

"Well, it must be something to get you all riled. You're

breathing heavy into the phone. If I didn't know better, I'd say you were coming on to me."

"Stop goofing," she chided in her usual good-natured tone. "This is serious, could mean big things for you. What am I talking about? It *will* mean big things for—"

"Slow down. Tell me what's got you so excited? You recruit some rich, new player for your Saturday night poker game or something?"

Dotty moaned. "No. It's the same 'ol crew. But this isn't about me. This is about *you*. Aren't you listening?"

"Me? Where are you?" Alex asked, trying again to get to the bottom of what had her so excited she'd taken time out of her sacred poker game preparations to call him.

"I'm at the office."

"Why? Was there a fire—?"

"No. I'm telling you, nothing bad happened," she blurted out, interrupting him.

Alex let out a deep breath and every tight muscle in his body relaxed. "Okay. So, why are you at the office on a Saturday then? You never go in on a Saturday."

"I had some work to finish up since I left early yesterday for a dentist appointment. And it's a good thing I was here, too, or I would have missed it."

"Missed what?" Alex smiled to himself. Good ol' honest Dotty. He'd never find a truer employee or anyone better to watch his back, and his business. She reminded him of a poodle on steroids.

"Alex," she said, her voice rising an octave. "You'll never guess who called."

Alex scrubbed a hand over his face and groaned. "Dotty, enough with the guessing games here. Just tell me. Who called?"

"Okay. Okay. Be that way, spoil the fun. But you aren't going to believe this."

"Try me," he said with a huge dose of sarcasm.

"Hunter Dierks called about ten minutes and fifteen seconds ago. He, himself called. Can you imagine? I thought I was going to pass out. Well, at first I thought it was some kind of prank so I quizzed him on some of his movies and—"

"Whoa. Hold on. Hunter Dierks? The actor?"

"Yes. The actor. He wants to build a get-away-from-Hollywood home in the rural Aspen area. And he wants you to do it."

Holy shit. This was it. This was the break he'd been hoping and praying for. If he landed this job and satisfied the world-famous actor, Alex would never hurt for work again.

"Alex? Are you still there?" Dotty asked. "The call didn't drop, did it?"

"No. I'm still here."

"Isn't this exciting? It's just what you need."

"Dotty, did he give any details? When he wanted to get started? Completion date?" He plopped down on the bed and scrubbed his hand over his face to make sure he wasn't dreaming the whole thing.

"He didn't get too specific, but he mentioned something about after the first of the year."

First of the year. Okay. Alex could handle that. He'd be done with immortalizing Elvis in Omaha long before that and would be ready for a new job.

"But he wants to talk to you as soon as possible," she continued. "He's on a short three day break from filming and he wants to get things in motion while he's home.

I'll text you the number where you can reach him. And he gave me some specific times he'll be able to take your call. I'll text those as well."

"Sounds great. I'll get in touch with him as soon as possible."

"In the meantime, go out and celebrate, Alex. You deserve to. As for me, I'm late for my poker game. I hope I can catch my breath and focus on the game. Hunter Dierks. Who would have thought." They said goodbye and Alex flipped his phone shut.

Hunter Dierks. Yeah. Who would have thought. Here Alex was, a quarter of a million dollars in debt, struggling to rebuild his business, and living in a tiny apartment. Provided everything fell together right, his luck could be turning around. After fifteen months of hell, he was ready.

Alex's rational business side, however, kept him from getting too excited. He hadn't even spoken to Dierks yet, they were a long way away from a deal. A lot could happen between now and then.

"Yeah, like I wake up." He laughed.

But Dotty was right. Alex deserved to celebrate, and what better place to do that than Memphis. And he was with a smart, sassy and beautiful woman who made his chest ache and his jeans tighten. Nothing was going to take away his chance for a night out on the town with Casey.

Flipping his phone back open, he pushed the end button and watched the screen go black as it shut down. He set it on top of the dresser and headed for the shower.

Tonight he wasn't going to be disturbed. He had other business on his mind.

* * * *

Casey double-checked her lipstick in the mirror while Elvis and Nancy Sinatra crooned out a tune in the movie *Speedway*. A thunderous pounding beat at her door.

"Uh-oh. That can't be good." Checking through the peep hole she saw Alex. He'd changed his clothes and even through the distorted view, he looked hot. She took a deep breath, planed her hands down her jeans and unlocked the door.

"Where's the fire," she teased. He stood there, hands on hips as usual, his ever present cell phone absent. A nice chambray shirt tucked into the low waist of his jeans highlighted his broad shoulders. His dark hair, slightly damp, proved he'd showered. A day's growth of beard dusted his chin.

Yes. Hot. Hot. Hot.

What she wouldn't give to bury her face in his neck and inhale his fresh, musky scent, feel the roughness of his whiskers against her cheek.

"We're going out," he said, the huskiness in his voice making her quiver all over.

"Going out?" she asked, a little breathless.

"Yeah." Slowly, he walked into the room, forcing Casey to take two steps back for every one of his. "You ready?" He shut the door, blocking out the world. His gaze darkened like a building thunder cloud as he watched her.

"Oh. Sure. But I thought…"

"I changed my mind."

The hard edge of a chair pressed into the backside of her legs. Holy cow, she'd backed across almost the entire room and didn't even know it. Who was coming on to who, here?

"Is that so?"

"Looks like you figured I would," he said eyeing her clothes.

"It never hurts to be prepared."

"Hmm." He hooked a finger under the thin strap of her white cami top peeking out from beneath her blouse. "Nice." The intoxicating combination of his approval, and the brush of his touch against her collar bone, revved her pulse into high gear. She could feel the heat of him down to her painted toenails.

Casey scrambled to gather her wits. "What about all that talk of staying in? Room service? Working the night away?"

"Work can wait. This is our last night in Memphis. Let's enjoy it."

"What did you have in mind?" she asked, throwing in a hint of her own seduction for good measure.

"How about we check out Beale Street?" He let the strap fall back into place and lifted a length of hair off her shoulder. He caressed the strands between his fingers. "Let's find a great restaurant to please our taste buds. Share a few drinks. Enjoy some blues." Brushing her hair back, he let his thumb trace the line of her jaw.

The tingling sensation of his touch nearly made Casey whimper out loud with want. And her taste buds craved a lot more than Memphis cuisine.

"Sounds like you've…got the whole night planned…"

"Could be." His eyes darkened even more, looking dangerous with intent. Intent to throw her down on the bed and take full advantage? Oh, she hoped so.

"What changed your mind?" she asked, the rational side of her wanting to know. Sometimes her rational side could be a real pain in the ass. This really wasn't the time to be asking questions—this was a time to be *going for it.*

One corner of his mouth lifted. "My secretary talked me into it."

Casey's speeding gears came to a screeching halt.

His secretary? *Not* the answer she'd expected. Or hoped for. She had to ask. Yeah, her rational side could be a major, royal, pain in the ass.

Chapter Ten

Casey and Alex left the dark, noisy interior of the Platinum Record restaurant and stepped out into the balmy autumn evening. Beale Street hummed with the Saturday night life of buzzing neon signs and couples strolling arm in arm.

Casey stole a peek at Alex and a longing to share such an intimacy with him, like what those couples shared, tugged at her insides.

Right. Like our fire and ice association is going to allow that. But, I can dream.

"Doing okay?" Alex asked, breaking the silence hovering between them as they walked.

"Uh-huh," she said, shoving aside her yearnings. "I think I ate too much, though." Casey placed a hand on her tummy and smiled. "That was some of the best barbequed pulled pork I've ever had. The potato salad had a different taste to it, but it was still good. I'm afraid I overindulged."

"A person has a right to overindulge every once in a while. Don't you think?" One corner of his lip curved up into a smile.

"I suppose so." She laughed. "Unfortunately I have a tendency to overindulge…a lot."

"How so?" He tugged at the collar of his bomber jacket and shoved his hands in his front jeans pockets. A light breeze tousled his hair, making him look every inch a rebel. Wild, erotic fantasies sauntered through her mind. *Don't go there.*

Casey averted her gaze to safer territory, like the vast array of flashing neon signs up ahead. A rainbow of blues, greens, yellows and reds flashed with precise rhythms, beckoning passersby to stop and enter the doors beneath. Everything from music clubs to quaint, unique shops lined the street. That's what she needed to cure her Alex woes—shopping. Nothing like a good, hearty round of power shopping to distract a girl from pining over a man. Casey knew that from first-hand experience.

"I sort of like to shop." She shrugged—as if her sometimes financially crippling habit was no big deal.

"Sort of? How do you sort of like to shop?" He quirked a brow in question.

"Okay. I admit it. I love to shop." They stopped at a street corner and waited for the light to go through its cycle.

"So do I, sugar," an extremely tall, ice blonde said to her left. Dressed in scarlet sequins and wearing bright red lipstick, she smiled, revealing the most perfect set of teeth Casey had ever seen.

Casey gave a smile in return and with one quick assessment, realized the woman was no woman. Although, she had to admit, the guy did look pretty hot. In comparison to his dazzling clothes, he made her feel like a drab, frumpy wallflower.

And he smelled terrific, too. The scent was light, refreshing, yet mysterious. "Nice fragrance," Casey said.

"Thanks, sweetcakes. It's the latest from *Estée Lauder.*

Cost me a small fortune, but it's worth every penny," he said in his breathy and sultry voice.

Casey saw a grin tug at Alex's lips. The stoplight switched to green and like a herd of cattle, they and the ten or so other people, including the blonde, hustled across the street.

"You might say shopping is my own form of therapy," Casey said. Drawn like a mosquito to a dangerously glowing bug light, she pressed her hands against the plate glass of a shop window. Gaping at a vast collection of handbags on display, Casey's mouth began to salivate. A quick inspection of her reflection showed that at least she wasn't drooling. Yet. *Saliva dripping down my chin, now that would be attractive.*

"Therapy?" Alex asked, surprise in his question. "What could a bright, beautiful accountant like you need therapy for?"

Bright? Beautiful? He thought she was beautiful? A flash of heat warmed her cheeks. Feeling unsure and restless, she moved away from the window and started walking.

"Oh, nothing much, I guess. Just my parents' divorce. Maybe a broken heart. Or two." She laughed to hide her discomfort. Peeking at him from behind her lashes, she hoped to see she'd been successful, but instead saw a flicker of raw emotion cut across his face.

"Sounds like plenty to me," he said softly. "My parents are divorced, too. I know what it's like."

"I'm sorry."

Alex shrugged. "Ah, it was for the best. I guess. They loved their work more than they did each other. Even as a kid I saw they were really married to their respective careers. They spent so much time apart I often wondered how I was even born."

"That must have been tough to understand."

"That's just the way their relationship worked. The sooner I accepted it, the easier it was for me to cope and get on with my own life. That morsel of acceptance came in damn handy when they split for good."

They passed by a blues club and the deep, soulful music coming from inside the brick and mortar building vibrated the sidewalk beneath their feet as they walked.

"How about you? Why did your folks opt for the big D?" he asked.

Even though Casey wasn't cold, she pulled her jacket tighter and tucked her arms around her middle. "My dad was a…free spirit. A restless soul. Or so he claimed." She took a deep breath, reminding herself to stay calm— that according to a thousand dollars worth of therapy sessions, talking about her dad didn't always have to raise her hackles. "Deep down, I think he really did love my mom, though. It was the restrictions and responsibilities a wife and five kids presented that he couldn't handle. No matter what we did—no matter how hard we tried, he wasn't happy. Blamed us for holding him back, keeping him from what he really wanted in life."

"So your mom got stuck holding the bag."

"Exactly. And since I was the oldest, so did I," she said with a bitterness she hadn't intended to reveal. Even after years of psychobabble and shopping therapies, Casey still struggled to control the resentment she harbored toward her father.

Deliberate, self-centered abandonment was a hard act to forget. And forgive.

"So, what about the broken hearts?" Alex asked. "Engaged? Married?"

Casey's pulse quickened at his question. Was he interested? Or simply curious? She hoped *interested* because Alex sure had a way of making her want to rattle a few skeletons from her closet, bequeath her dog to him, and pledge her undying devotion. Of course, she could be experiencing a moment of insanity brought on by indigestion after eating too much barbeque.

Whatever it was, she'd learned a long time ago that admitting she stunk in the relationship department wasn't the best way to garner a man's interest, especially when hoping for something long term. It was better to leave him guessing as to the true reason she shopped until her credit cards groaned under the strain. Of course, admitting her credit cards groaned on a frequent basis wasn't the smartest way to catch a man, either.

"No marriage. Not even an engagement," she said with an air of conviction. She stopped walking and leveled her gaze on Alex. Time to test the waters of attraction. "Finding a good man is hard these days. And I won't settle. I'm holding out for Mr. Right."

The neon lights reflected in the depths of his smoky eyes as he returned her stare. He stepped closer and she could smell the subtle combination of leather and Alex. Yummy.

He stood only three inches taller than she, but at the moment he seemed as tall and encompassing as a rugged mountain top. Boy, she'd loved to go mountain climbing right about now.

"And if Mr. Right doesn't exist?" he asked, his voice whisky smooth.

Casey swallowed hard and tried to calm her racing heart, gasping lungs, and sparking nerves. She hoped like hell Memphis had an excellent ER. If Alex didn't back off, the EMT's would be scraping her melting body off the sidewalk like the smoldering Wicked Witch of the West.

Shouting erupted down the street, breaking the connection between them. They turned in unison and saw two men pushing and shoving one another. The crowd on the street backed away as the scuffle turned into an all out fight. Police rushed up to pull the men apart. As they scrambled to subdue the offenders a fist flew through the air and dealt one officer a hard blow to the jaw. He hit the ground with a hard thud.

"Looks like the night is heating up," Alex said. "Maybe we should head back to the hotel. It's getting late, anyway."

The intensity she'd seen in his eyes only moments before had disappeared like an elusive wisp of smoke. Casey groaned under her breath. She wouldn't mind throwing a few punches at those two idiots herself for their piss-poor timing.

"Sure," she managed to say around a lump of aggravation lodged in her throat.

Alex stepped to the curb and hailed a cab. Within seconds a taxi zipped up beside them. Alex placed a strong hand on the small of Casey's back and helped her into the backseat. The simple touch, even through her jean jacket, made certain parts of her anatomy tingle with heat and desire.

The cab took off with a jolt and careened around a corner. Casey slid across the seat from the force of the turn and found her body pressed up against Alex's.

She reached out to brace herself and realized her hand was gripping Alex's firm upper thigh. Shoulders, knees, elbows and hips weren't the only body parts making electrifying contact. All she had to do was move her pinky finger a quarter, no an eighth, no, make that a sixteenth of an inch, and she'd be making full blown contact with a very prominent piece of Alex's anatomy.

Oh, God. Heat that had never really died in the first place exploded like gas thrown on a simmering flame. She fought the urge to crawl on top of him and give him her own version of lap dancing in the back of the careening cab. Daring a glance into his eyes, she saw the intent she'd seen there earlier had returned. Her heart pounded in her heaving chest. She clamped her mouth shut, afraid if she didn't, Alex would notice she was panting like a dog. Not a good idea to appear too eager. A girl should always play at least a little hard to get.

The cab sped around an opposite corner and Alex slipped his arm around her to keep her from catapulting back the other way. His hand squeezed her waist. Holy crap. His fingers were touching her bare skin where her shirt had ridden up against the seat.

Okay, if she wasn't panting shamelessly before, she was now. But really, who gave a damn? Panting was a natural, reaction to being tossed around in the backseat of a city cab with the hottest man to ever walk the earth.

The cab screeched to halt in front of the hotel. Someone really needed to give the cabbie some serious driving lessons, but since Casey was entangled in Alex's arms, she wasn't going to complain. In fact, she was feeling a little disappointed the torrid ride was over.

"That was a ride to remember. Are you all right?" Alex asked after paying the cab driver. The cabbie tore out of the hotel parking lot, barely missing a parked car.

"Not really," she said, breathless from the crazy, exhilarating experience. The night air did little to cool her still burning cheeks.

"You're hurt?" Alex lightly squeezed her shoulders, a mixture of concern and desire in his eyes.

Casey's already quivering insides jolted from his touch. She was hurting all right. Hurting for wild, passionate sex. She wanted to reach out and touch him in return, but if she dared, there would be no holding back. Concrete never looked so good.

"No. I'm fine," she lied through her teeth. "Just a little…shook up from the ride."

His brows furrowed and he stepped back, letting his arms fall to his sides. Casey groaned. Alex looked as disappointed by her admission as she felt by the loss of his touch. Since when had she become such a tongue-tied idiot around men?

Since she met Alex.

Suddenly, Alex grabbed her hand and pulled her into the Heartbreak Hotel. Ignoring the bustling activity going on in the lobby, he pulled her down the hallway toward the stairwell. He shoved the door wide and without letting go of her hand or breaking his stride, he led the way up three flights of stairs, his grip tightening with each step. By the time they reached their floor, Casey's chest heaved from the exertion and her hand hurt, but Alex didn't slow is pace. Halfway running to keep up, Casey started to ask him what the heck was going on, but she let the words die on her tongue. The last thing she wanted to do was say something stupid again and change his mind. He was clearly a man on a mission.

They reached their rooms and Alex immediately dropped her aching hand. He stepped back, as if he couldn't bear to be near her, putting several long, agonizing feet between them. Geesh, had her deodorant quit working?

"This is your room," he said, one hand firmly planted on his hip, the other pointing at her door. "That's my room." He pointed to the door to his right. "You belong here. And I belong there," he said, moving his hand back and forth in a chopping motion. "Get it?"

"Oh, I get it all right." She grinned, her heart jumping for joy. "You're as sexually attracted to me as I am to you. And we're both trying so damn hard not to be that it's getting in the way of hot, wild sex." There, she'd said it. And it felt wonderful to speak up and be her old self again—throwing caution to the wind, going for what she really wanted.

And she wanted Alex.

His eyes turned as dark and turbulent as a stormy spring sky, and for a few seconds she couldn't tell if it was a good turbulence, or a bad turbulence. Had she goofed and misread his signals? He leaned forward as if to kiss her, then in a split second, stopped himself. Intense, animalistic desire smoldered in those eyes of his.

She was right on target. She'd bet the one Armani suit she owned on it.

"Look, I've tried all along to be a good girl and play the professional game with you," she said, determined to make this trip to Memphis one she'd never forget, "but after today, I'm through. I can't take this agony of denial between us anymore. Life is too short. Why waste it?" So what if she ended up with another broken heart and a maxed out credit card after he'd had his fill of her and walked? The hot, electrifying sex they were bound to have would make all the pain worth it.

"Damn," he said huskily, and grabbed her, pulling her tight up against him. Capturing her mouth with his, he kissed her deep, kissed her hard, as if he couldn't get enough.

Instantly, Casey's body responded like a match held to a firecracker fuse. Explosive currents raced through her veins to her fingers, her toes, hell, even her eyelashes.

Oh, yeah. Could she call it? Or could she call it?

The familiar earthy scent of leather and spices teased her nose, tempting her beyond belief. Her purse fell to the floor as she slipped her arms around his neck. The force sent them plummeting backward. They hit against the solid door with a thud, shifting their hunger into overdrive. She held on tight, desperate to climb on top of him right here, right now.

Alex's tongue sought and found hers. He tasted of beer and mint and she plunged her tongue deeper, hungry for more, silently begging for more. He answered her call and their tongues twined together, dancing and mating in perfect unison.

His day's growth of beard rubbed against her chin, giving her a rough caress, and a new series of sparks exploded inside her, spiraling down to her core. Her body throbbed with longing, making her wet with desire.

A moan echoed in the back of her throat. Her needy hands pushed at his coat and managed to find their way beneath to his shirt. She tugged and yanked at the material, desperate to remove any barriers keeping their flesh apart. The shirt pulled free and she ran her hands up the hard six-pack of his stomach. Casey groaned with pleasure.

Alex buried his hands in her hair and cupped the back of her head. Pulling her up on her tiptoes, he kissed her harder, with fervor and urgency.

The solid, unforgiving door pressed into her back and Alex's erection pressed into her front. *Holy, shit.* The only thing standing between his pulsing manhood and her screaming O zone were two layers of blasted clothing. And well, they *were* gettin' it on in the public hallway of the hotel. But who gave a damn about that? All Casey cared about was getting rid of those sexy, inconvenient jeans of his.

Without warning he broke the kiss and Casey heard herself whimper from the sudden loss.

"Your…key?" he asked, his words coming in a short raspy breath, tingling the lobe of her ear. His chest rose and fell against her breasts, tormenting and teasing her nipples.

He peppered her cheeks and lips with more kisses. Smooth strong hands and cool air brushed against her back as Alex pushed up her shirt. Without hesitation his hand slipped down into her jeans, massaging and caressing the small of her back before diving lower down to her backside. He squeezed. She gasped.

Her head fell back against the door. Feeling possessed, she moaned from the desire consuming every ounce of her body. So, this is what Elvis meant when he sang *Burning Love.*

She pulled at Alex's coat. Her fingers dug into the soft leather as she struggled to remove the damn thing. His lips worked magic against her feverish skin, and with each touch, each caress, her knees threatened to fold.

"Where's your key?"

"Key?" she asked, panting. What was he talking about?

"We need your goddamn key," Alex rasped against the hollow of her throat. "*Now.*"

Casey blinked once, twice. "Key? Uh…"

"Casey," he groaned. "I'm a desperate man, here." He nipped at her ear.

"Back…pocket."

"I should have guessed." His fingers slid down into her jeans pocket, tickling and teasing as he grabbed the plastic in one slick move. Without breaking his hold on her, he managed to slide the card into the slot and pull down on the door handle.

Talented.

The door gave way and they stumbled into the room in a frenzy of tangled arms and legs.

"My purse," Casey breathed against his lips.

Alex groaned and let go just long enough to snatch her bag from the hallway floor. Within seconds the door slammed shut and he was yanking off her jean jacket and pushing her down onto the queen-sized bed.

"Dammit. This is wrong and you know it," he growled as his hand slipped under her shirt and pushed the fabric up to below her breasts.

"Wrong? Why?" Her questions came in short, breathless gasps as she tugged off his coat.

"I make it a rule to never mix business and pleasure." He kissed the sensitive flesh between her breasts. "It's too dammed expensive."

"Oh, yeah? I make it a rule," she grabbed the front of his shirt and pulled at the buttons, "to never date a guy who wears flannel." One button let go and the rest followed with blessed ease. *Thank, God.*

"What's wrong with flannel?" he asked seconds before recapturing her mouth with his own.

She dug her hands into the material of his shirt and moaned, feeling the rock-hard solidness beneath. The tips of her fingers burned with fire and hunger for the feel of his skin against her own. Shoving aside his shirt, she worked it down over his arms and back, freeing him of the soft, sexy material.

They broke the kiss, coming up for air. "It's always in the way."

"Not now, it isn't."

"True. And I have a new…appreciation for it," she gasped.

"Appreciation?" His hand pushed up higher beneath her top and snuck under her bra. He cupped her breast.

Her breath hitched.

He smiled.

"Oh, yeah." She pushed up from beneath him, knocked him off balance and rolled him over onto his back. She climbed aboard. "I've discovered flannel is…*hot.*" Running her hands over abs and pecs as hard and solid as bricks, she leaned forward and pressed her breasts against his chest.

He pushed her back long enough to strip away her top, exposing the latest addition to her bra collection.

"Sweet heaven," he said, his gaze soaking up the sight of her breasts showcased in scarlet satin and lace.

"You like?"

"Like is an understatement." He sat up and laved her breasts with his tongue—teasing and tormenting her into oblivion. Her head fell back. A moan escaped her throat.

"It's a Venus," she panted.

"Mmm. Nice. It's got to go," he said against a deep swell of breast the bra helped accentuate to perfection. Alex's hands encircled her waist and skimmed up her back to the clasp.

Her stomach rumbled. Casey froze. Her stomach rumbled again, only this time it lurched, too.

Alex pulled back. "After all you ate, you can't be hungry."

Casey's stomach did a second major pitch. She scooted off of Alex, clutching her stomach. Dots of sweat broke out on her forehead. Damn. She was going to be sick.

"It's not hunger," she moaned.

"You look pale. You okay?"

"No." Clutching her stomach, she fled for the bathroom, stopping only long enough to kick the door shut and fling up the toilet seat.

What a lousy way to end the date that wasn't.

* * * *

Casey walked through the Studs office door at a snail's pace, the only speed her aching, tortured body would allow this early on a rotten Monday morning. She'd never spent a more miserable thirty-six hours than these past ones. Contracting food poisoning, flying home while sicker than a dog, and trying hard not to throw up in the lap of her handsome architect, had been exhausting. Not to mention humiliating.

Through the dark sunglasses shielding her eyes, she tried to focus on her steps and prayed her leaden feet would carry her down the hall to her office without an embarrassing incident.

The last thing she wanted was to put up with a round of ribbing from her partners because she'd passed out in the lobby of their office with drool on her cheek.

Terri worked diligently at her desk, and Sydnie was nowhere in sight. Thank God.

Casey held her breath and tip-toed her way along the paisley carpet. Terri didn't look up from her computer screen. Yea. She was going to make it.

"So, you are alive," Terri said softly as Casey reached the magazine rack overflowing with the latest home decorator issues. Casey stopped and wobbled on her feet. Thunder crashed in her head from the sound of Terri's voice.

Damn. So much for sneaking by and saving her aching body from the pain and exhaustion of communication. Slowly, she turned around. Her ankles threatened to collapse and let her crash to the floor. What the hell had she been thinking to wear heels today? The dumb shoes added a good three inches to her height, giving her head exactly seventy-one inches to fall to a concussion—if she was lucky. A concussion was the only way to avoid any more major embarrassment and pain. She'd experienced her fair share over the last day-and-a-half and didn't care to add to the tally.

"Why wouldn't I be alive?" Casey asked after getting her bearings straight.

"Your wild weekend in Memphis…?" Terri shrugged, a grin twitched at her lips, implying far too much.

"It wasn't a wild weekend. It was a business trip," Casey said defensively. Her stomach muscles screamed in objection to talking above a whisper. "And I got food poisoning."

"Uh-huh. If you say so." Terri giggled, but she didn't stop typing on her computer. The light clicks of the keys sounded like gunshots to Casey's ears.

"It's true. Now quit. Quit typing. You're killing me."

Terri stopped her work and Casey sighed in relief. She closed her eyes and squeezed the bridge of her nose, hoping that minor discomfort would take away the pain in her stomach.

"Maybe I ought to check out Memphis," Terri continued, for whatever reason not taking Casey seriously. "I need some excitement in my life. Things have been boring for me lately."

Casey wanted to protest that getting food poisoning far from the comforts of one's own bathroom, and then having to endure a five-hour flight, didn't constitute a wild weekend in Memphis. But even the idea of uttering a word required more energy than she could muster.

"Oh, hey. Alex is here," Terri said.

"What? Already? It's so early," Casey groaned. Her cheeks warmed in embarrassment, knowing he'd witnessed her at her very worst with her head stuck in a toilet bowl. Thankfully he'd endured her misery on the plane with good humor, and had been as attentive to her needs as a mother hen—tucking her in the best he could with a blanket and pillow in a tight airplane seat. During the moments she'd really felt tough, he'd offered words of comfort and tried to keep her mind occupied with silly words games and trivia.

He'd been sweet, caring, and wonderful. The man deserved five gold stars.

She just wasn't in any condition, mentally or physically, to let Alex see her looking so bad again. She'd hoped he wouldn't come in until late afternoon, giving her a few hours to collapse under her desk and make a feeble effort at recouping.

"It's ten o'clock," Terri said.

"It can't be that late."

"Sorry to disappoint you, but it is."

"How long has he been here?"

"About an hour."

An hour? Casey closed her eyes again and prayed for strength.

"I wasn't sure what you two had planned for today," Terri continued. "So I told him he could wait in your office."

Great. Now Casey couldn't even commiserate in her private domain while gulping doses of Alka-Seltzer.

A new round of stomach pains pierced her insides, and the floor swayed beneath her feet. Okay. Either the floor was rising up to meet her, or was she well on her way toward meeting it. Maybe curling up into a fetal position right here in the middle of the waiting area wouldn't be such a bad idea.

"Boy, you are sick. Do you need some help?" Terri asked.

"I'll be fine as soon as the fire-breathing monkeys quit jumping around in my stomach."

"That says it all." Terri sprang from her chair and put an arm around Casey. "I'll help you to your office."

"No, it's okay. Really. I can...do it." Casey grabbed her stomach and moaned.

"I don't think so. You should have stayed home, Case. You're in no condition to be here, let alone get any work done," Terri scolded.

"I thought I would be fine by now."

"Thought? Obviously your stomach is impeding the rational thinking side of your cranium. You have food poisoning."

Cranium? What a big word for a crappy day.

"Now, it's as simple as putting one foot in front of

the other," Terri instructed. "Sing it with me. You…put one foot in front of the other—"

"Very funny. You're a real comedian."

"I try."

"Do me a favor and let's keep this between us, okay? It's bad enough Alex heard me puke my guts out, I don't want the whole world to know about it."

"It's food poisoning, Case. It's not like you went out and got smashed and thrown in jail. This isn't your fault."

"I know. It's just embarrassing. Especially…Alex…we were on the bed…"

"On the bed?" Terri stopped short in front of Casey's office door. "You mean you two were *gettin' it on* when you got sick?" she whispered so Alex wouldn't hear through the door.

Casey closed her eyes and grimaced at Terri's words. "Don't remind me. Every time I think about what I gave up because of some stupid potato salad, I could scream."

"Was it good?" Terri asked. "Did you have time to do much before you hurled?"

Casey groaned. "Thanks for making it sound even worse."

"Sorry. But come on. Tell me what happened."

Casey thought back to every touch of Alex's hands on her skin, every brush of his whiskers against her breasts, every kiss. A sigh escaped her lips. "It was magnificent, amazing, incredible. It was shaping up to be the best sex I've ever had. Oh, life is so unfair."

"What rotten luck."

"Par for the course for me. Look, Terri." She grabbed her friend's arms not only for support, but to plead her case. "You've got to help me get out of here, now. I can't face Alex, not yet. And especially not looking like this. I have major circles under my eyes that I didn't have yesterday."

"That explains the glasses."

"Yes." Casey whipped off her sunglasses to prove just how bad she looked.

Terri grimaced. "Ah, yeah. You do sort of look like a raccoon."

"Gee. Thanks for the charming analogy. What the hell was I thinking? I should have stayed home."

"You weren't thinking, remember?"

"Okay. Okay." She cupped her forehead trying to stop the massive pounding against her skull.

"Hey, it's not too late. Alex doesn't know you're here. Go home and get some rest."

Casey put her sunglasses back on and sighed in relief. "Right. Now help me get out of here before—" Her office door swung wide, cutting her off in mid-sentence.

Casey froze. There Alex stood, tall and imposing. And as intoxicating as ever.

Chapter Eleven

Casey's heart lodged in her throat. So much for a quick escape.

"Good morning, sweetheart," Alex said with a smile way too cheery for decency's sake. He braced a hand on the door jamb and leaned forward. "I was wondering when you'd make it in today."

"When? You knew I'd come?"

"You're too stubborn not to."

"Stubborn, am I? Well, I think you're...overconfident."

"Is that right," he stated dryly. His eyes blazed with challenge.

"Uh," Terri caught her bottom lip between her teeth, "I think the phone is about to ring. I better get back to my desk so I can answer it. She's all yours, Alex." Terri placed Casey's hand in his and scurried back down the hall.

Casey inhaled sharply at the touch and tried to pull away, but Alex held fast.

"Thanks," he said. "I'll take good care of her."

In spite of feeling lousy, little tingles of desire zipped through every aching inch of Casey's body. And he'd made it happen with only the simple touch of his hand,

and six little words. *I'll take good care of her.* Casey's heart stilled. How long had she waited to hear such words? More years than she cared to count. Did she dare let herself believe them? Believe Alex?

"Do you always wear your sunglasses inside?" he asked, forcing her to refocus her thoughts. "Or do you have something to hide?"

"Why would I have anything to hide?" Casey pulled her hand away, lifted her chin, and breezed past him into her office. The move hurt to high heaven, but she'd never let Alex know how much. Making a beeline for the vertical blinds, she grabbed the chain and yanked them shut.

"You tell me."

She turned and pretended to look through some papers on her desk, hoping to appear too busy to answer his question, but even that small effort took more energy than she had at the moment. Groping behind her for the arms of her plush office chair, she slowly eased down into the leather softness without bothering to remove her coat. She let out the breath she'd been holding and closed her eyes.

"Do you have any toothpicks on you?" she asked.

"I seem to be fresh out. Why?"

Taking off her sunglasses, she tossed them onto the desk, too tired and spent to hide her affliction from him any longer. Besides, if he didn't run at the mere sight of her, he'd prove once more he was a man with a heart. "I want to use them to prop my eyes open so I can get something done." She heard Alex chuckle, and with Herculean effort she forced open her left eye. "It's not funny."

"No, it's not. But you are."

"Me? Should I take that as a compliment, or as an insult?"

"A compliment, sweetheart. You make me laugh. And I haven't laughed in a long time."

She made him laugh? Casey had the feeling she'd just been paid one of the highest compliments Alex Roy could bestow. Her heart warmed.

Yet, the urge to ask him why he hadn't laughed for so long, nagged at her insides. She shifted her gaze and saw a dark intensity brewing in the depths of his eyes, warning her away from the subject.

"Look," he said, breaking the sudden, awkward silence. "Let me run you home so you can rest. I'll come back and work. Then if you feel up to it, we can meet later and weed through the ideas we haven't come up with yet."

"I appreciate the offer." Gingerly, Casey shook her head. "But I can't leave. We need ideas fast. We're working on such a tight schedule the way it is."

"Case, as you found out, food poisoning is no picnic—no pun intended. You need to rest. A few hours here or there isn't going to make that much difference. Besides, with the condition you're in, you won't accomplish much anyway. And we don't have time for screw-ups, either."

"Thanks for your vote of confidence. You make me feel so much better," she quipped.

"My pleasure."

Her stomach rumbled, and a new wave of exhaustion slithered through her body. At the moment she felt like she could sleep for a century and still be tired.

"All right. For once I'm in no mood to argue. I'll take you up on your offer for a ride home. I'd hate to fall asleep at the wheel and wreck my new car." She rose, grabbing her purse and sunglasses.

"I'd hate that, too. Before we go anywhere though, I need your okay on a place to work. Can I set up a drafting table somewhere?"

Casey pointed to a vacant area by the aquarium. "That works for me, if it works for you?"

"Are you sure? I'd hate to crowd you, invade your privacy."

"No worry." Casey flipped a hand in dismissal. "I come from a large family. I'm used to a small herd of siblings taking over my space." *Besides, I like the idea of being able to salivate over you all day long.*

"Must've been nice," he said with a hint of regret.

"Most of the time, no, but we did have a few moments I wouldn't trade for the world."

"Brothers? Sisters?"

"Two of each. All younger, and each one was so full of fire they could have burned down the city in their own right. In spite of their wicked ways though, they all turned out pretty good. How about you? Any siblings?"

"I was an only child."

"Wow. Bet that had its perks—like no sharing the bathroom, no fighting over what to watch on TV, or who got the window seat in the car, all that good stuff."

"Not when you get lost in the shadow of your parents' careers."

Casey's heart pinched at the flat, cold tone of his words. She remembered how lonely she'd felt when her father left—how lonely she still was at times. Sure, she had good friends and her family, but there was still a void in her life created by the absence of her father. And Alex had a void, too—made by his parents' lack of interest in their son.

She searched for something profound to say, but she could barely add two plus two at the moment. Pulling words of wisdom from the depths of her struggling brain was impossible.

And like Alex said, there was no time for screw-ups. Professional or personal.

"Hey. Look on the bright side," she said. "At least you didn't have to baby sit all the time. Count yourself lucky on that score."

"Yeah. Lucky." His words gave the impression he didn't care, but his eyes still said differently.

Casey's stomach gurgled again and she knew she was pressing her luck. She needed to get home. Rummaging through her purse, she dug out four rolls of film and tossed them to Alex.

"Graceland?" he asked, holding up the film.

"Yes. Do me a favor and see that they get developed, will you? There are plenty of one-hour places around. Terri can help you. And if you should need anything, just let her know. She'll take care of it. She's as efficient and as organized as a worker ant."

"There is one thing I need."

Was he suggesting what she hoped he was? No. She couldn't let her mind go there. Not today when she felt like death warmed over and she couldn't do a damn thing about being sick or wanting to jump his bones.

"What's that?"

"I need the original blueprints for Heather's house."

Disappointment rolled over Casey and compounded her body aches, but what the hell did she expect? She was a mess, and with her chalky complexion she looked like she was the Bride of Frankenstein's sister. She wouldn't want to be intimate with herself, either.

"Blueprints I can handle," she said. "I'll make a call and see that they're delivered to you by this afternoon."

"You know. You're pretty efficient yourself."

"It comes from years of working in a male-dominated corporate world where women really are the backbones."

"You'll get no argument from me on that score," he quipped. "I'll get these pictures developed. They should give us a lot to work with."

"I hope so. Keep your fingers crossed those inside the house turned out all right. A photographer I am not."

"I'm sure they'll be great. In the meantime, I'm going to start working on some drawings for the addition."

"Super. We'll need concrete plans as soon as possible. Sydnie's dad and brothers, Riley and Sons, is scheduled to do the heavy construction and they only have a three-week window to do it. Then our guys will step in and take care of the electrical, drywall and finish work. Hopefully by the time the addition is ready for us, we'll have the majority of the remodel done. And of course, all of this hinges on if the weather holds."

"For an accountant, you know quite a bit about construction."

"I'm a woman of many talents."

He shortened the distance between them, his steps slow but full of intent. Intent upon throwing her down on the desk and finishing what they'd started in Memphis? Damn. Why did she insist upon torturing herself?

"That you are," he drawled. He brushed the back of his fingers along her cheek. His touch was comforting, mesmerizing, and Casey wouldn't be at all surprised if she was dreaming the whole thing. But her popping nerves and buckling knees told her she wasn't dreaming—she was dying of need.

Her stomach lurched again, reminding her she was also dying of food poisoning. And the food poisoning was winning the game. She clamped a hand over her stomach.

"Alex—"

"Come on, sweetheart. I'm taking you home."

* * * *

"Sorry to interrupt, Alex," Sydnie said as she came into Casey's office late that afternoon. "Here are the pictures. Four rolls, right?"

"Right." Alex turned his attention away from the preliminary blueprints he'd been working on for the last five hours and watched Sydnie place the packets of photos on the desk. "And you're not intruding. I could use a break." He stood and stretched his stiff muscles. Autumn dusk encroached on the windows, proving he'd lost track of time.

"How are the plans coming?" she asked.

"Good. I've come up with a couple different possibilities. Hopefully Heather will be satisfied with at least one of them."

"I hope so, too. But don't be surprised if she isn't. She can be...picky." Syd arched a brow and smiled.

"I take it that's your polite way of saying she's difficult."

"You got it."

"That was my impression when I first met her. I'm glad to know it wasn't just me."

"She's also impatient in case you missed that one. She's called five times today alone."

Alex laughed. "Drawing up blueprints takes time.

There are codes, city ordinances and structural considerations."

"We know that but Heather, well she's used to getting what she wants, and when she wants it." Syd crossed the room to Casey's refrigerator. "Can I get you something, Alex?"

"Sure. Something nonalcoholic, but loaded with caffeine."

"Feeling the need for a boost?"

"You know it. I haven't caught up from the weekend yet."

"Speaking of the weekend—sounds like you and Casey had an *interesting* one," Syd said as she handed him a can of cola. Her pretty green eyes sparkled with mischief.

Interesting was one way of putting it. He popped the can and downed a long swallow. He turned back to his drafting table. "Memphis is a neat place," he said, not wanting to reveal what did and didn't happen between him and Casey. She'd been so ill the last two days he doubted she'd had much of a chance to confide in her friends about their trip.

"Alex." Syd let out a deep sigh and walked over to him. "I don't want you to think I'm sticking my nose into your business, but Casey is a dear friend. I'm not sure what your intentions are toward her, but I don't want to see her hurt again."

Alex stiffened. Intentions? Sydnie obviously knew something he didn't. Did he have intentions toward Casey? And if so, what were they? Friendship? Lover? Something permanent? All of the above?

Hell. He was on the verge of bankruptcy, and in no position to offer her anything more than his architectural know-how. He picked up a pencil and twirled it between his fingers, relishing in the familiarity of the one constant, sure element in his life.

"Again?" he asked, diverting the direction of the conversation, curious to know more about the woman who intrigued him more than he liked to admit.

"It's not really my place to say much," Syd said. "But she's been in some relationships that didn't work out. Those weren't easy times for her."

He'd suspected as much, she was a beautiful woman—there had to have been some men in her life. The idea of Casey loving another man, and receiving a broken heart in return, made his insides pulse with a mixture of jealousy and anger.

He couldn't go there. Allowing himself to feel, to care, was a move in the wrong direction—for both of them. He'd already made a major mistake this past weekend by letting his guard down. He didn't wish food poisoning on anyone, but he had to admit, Casey's bout had been a mixed blessing and saved him from getting in too deep.

"Some men are fools," he said coldly. "And some women never learn."

"I see," Syd said dryly. Her eyes told him she'd gotten his message loud and clear. "I'll let you get back to work." She headed for the door. "Oh, I almost forgot." Reaching into her jeans pocket, she pulled out a key. "Here. This is for the back door of the office building. Lock up tight when you leave, will you?"

He accepted the key and Alex wished it was Casey's warmth he felt through the brass. "Sure."

"I'll see you tomorrow. Good night."

"Night."

Sydnie left him to his work, but Alex knew it was going to take more than solitude and caffeine to get his mind back on the unfinished blueprints in front of him.

A sudden urge to call Casey, hear her voice, feel her vibes through the line made him reach for his cell. Flipping it open, he scrolled through the long list of numbers. He selected hers, but paused before pushing the send button.

What excuse would he give for calling her? *Hey, just checking in to see how you're feeling? Going to make it to work tomorrow? I miss you. I can't stand not seeing you. The memory of the scent of your hair drives me crazy.*

Alex groaned. Why did he keep drifting into dangerous territory? Since Valerie's deception, he'd steered clear of temptation and intimacy traps. And he needed it to stay that way.

Letting out a heavy breath, he closed his phone. It was past time to get back to work, and past time to put Casey out of his mind.

Restless and edgy, he crossed the room and saw the packs of pictures Syd had left. He reached for the envelopes, but his hand stilled. For the first time he noticed the top of Casey's desk revealed nothing of her personality. The oak surface was void of any typical office knickknacks except for a two by four wooden block stamped with the words *Studs for Hire* and their logo of a heart and a hammer. The only personal item set out for the world to see was what he assumed to be a family portrait. An older woman sat in the middle with five grown children, three women, and two men, surrounding her.

An easy smile played at Casey's lips, as if she and her siblings shared some secret. Alex couldn't help wishing he knew the feeling of being a part of something so great, to know such a connection.

Some things, he guessed, weren't meant to be.

He took the Graceland photos and laid them out in order on the extra table Terri had brought in earlier that day. Casey claimed she was no photographer, but the photos proved otherwise. They clearly showed she not only had an eye for detail, but had a way of capturing the emotion behind the subject as well.

He picked a photo up off the pile, but it was the one beneath that caught his attention. His breath hitched in his chest.

Slowly, he picked up the photo taken by the Japanese tourist. Casey and he stood arm and arm, autumn leaves framing Graceland behind them. Flashes of their weekend together flooded his mind. His body responded to the memory of how the small of her back felt pressed against his arm, the way his hand cupped the top of her hip. Soft, curvy, and oh, so right. The vanilla scent of her hair that day still tantalized his senses.

She really was beautiful. And smart. Witty. And sexy.

And he was a fool to think he had anything to offer her.

"I have to see him!" a demanding female voice said from down the hallway. Alex stiffened. A bad feeling filled his gut.

"He doesn't want to be interrupted," Sydnie insisted.

"I won't take no for an answer," the irate voice said again.

Alex dropped the photo, intent on seeing what all the ruckus was about, but the office door flew wide before he took two steps. Heather marched in, her eyes ablaze with emerald fire.

"Alex. Finally. I've been trying to get to you all day," Heather exclaimed. She sauntered into the room in a flurry of mink and scarves, reminding him of an eccentric 1940's movie actress.

Sydnie followed on the heels of their star client, threw up her hands in frustration, and mouthed the word *sorry* to Alex.

"I have to talk to you," Heather said dramatically as she rushed into his arms.

"Whoa. What's the trouble?" He tried to dislodge her hold on him by taking a couple steps back, but she wasn't so easily put off and held on tight.

"I know you don't like being interrupted, but I figured by now you'd be done for the day and it wouldn't be a problem."

"Actually, I planned on working pretty late."

"Oh, no?" she cooed. Brushing her hand slowly up and down his arm, she laid on the seduction thicker than dry wall mud. "I was looking forward to us having dinner. My treat."

"Thanks for the invite, Heather, but I'm afraid I'll have to pass. I need to get these plans done. We're on a deadline, remember?" He twisted in her arms and this time managed to break free.

The painted-on smile on Heather's face faded from seductive to one of blatant disappointment. "Surely you can take an hour or so to relax. You have to eat."

"Sydnie has already ordered me something." Glancing at Syd, he hoped she'd play along with his ruse and help him find a way out of this.

"That's right. I was about to run and pick it up when you came, Heather."

"Oh. Well, maybe some other time, then?" Heather

arched a brow higher than Alex thought physically possible, and shot an irritated glare in Syd's direction.

Syd got the hint. "I'll run now and get your supper, Alex. But I'll be back in *just* a few minutes." She hurried from the room, an aggravated frown on her face. Alex didn't blame her for being pissed. In fact, Alex was feeling a little pissed himself.

"Alone at last." Heather wasted no time in shortening the distance between them again. "I've been hoping for some private time for us to get to know each other better. I feel like you've been avoiding me." She stuck her bottom lip out in a pout.

"I'm sorry you got that impression. That wasn't my intention," he fibbed, and hoped he wouldn't be struck dead by lightning for it. "Casey and I have been busy working on your remodel."

"Don't you think getting to know me better is important, Alex? After all I'm the one who is going to be living in the house after it's done. I'd think you'd want to fully understand my tastes and personality so it reflects in the design of the house."

Not really. "There's no fear of me missing your dynamic personality, Heather," he said reassuringly. "You've made my job easy. I understand exactly what it's going to take to make you happy."

"Oh, yes," she drawled. "I think you do." One corner of her red lips curved up in a seductive sneer that would have made even Elvis proud.

Damn. He wanted to tell her to back off, but Alex held himself in check. He needed the income from this job too much to run the risk of losing it. Pissing Heather off wasn't an option.

"So, what was so important that it couldn't wait until

tomorrow?"

Heather's eyes darkened, obviously not happy he'd turned the conversation back to business. She circled the room inspecting the artwork, the furnishings, reminding him of a lioness sizing up the strength of her intended prey.

Casey better watch her back. And he'd better watch his front.

"I've recently acquired another, quite large, private collection of Elvis memorabilia," she said casually. "And I'm always interested in acquiring more. I wanted to make sure you fully understood how much room I'm going to need before you got too far along with the plans."

"Don't worry." Alex turned toward the blueprints, lifting one off the table. "As you can see, this addition will not only be large enough to accommodate your current collection, but will allow you plenty of room to expand."

Heather didn't bother glancing in his direction. She was too busy eyeing the groups of photos spread out on the table. "I'm sure it will. I have great confidence in you, Alex. That's why I insisted Casey secure you for the job."

Alex held his breath, hoping she didn't notice the picture of him and Casey. Not that he really cared, but he didn't want to give this lioness anything more to sharpen her claws on.

"You went to Graceland." She turned around to face him. "I'm impressed. I appreciate a man who takes his client's desires so seriously."

"I take my *job* seriously."

"And what else?" she asked, walking his way, her hips

swaying with purpose in every high-heeled step. Slowly she pulled the red silk scarf from around her neck, letting the fabric caress the expanse of bare skin at her throat.

Alex gritted his teeth. Heather was purposefully backing him into a corner where he could see no escape.

Shit. This was a lose-lose situation if he ever saw one. If he returned her interest just to pacify her, he'd only be digging himself into a deep hole with another conniving woman. If he turned her away, he'd blow the job for both him and Casey. And neither one could afford the loss.

He was screwed—hopefully just metaphorically.

She flicked the scarf and it landed on his shoulder. An overly sweet flowery scent, so unlike Casey's soft and subtle vanilla, filled his nose. His gut reaction was to toss aside the damn thing, but he restrained himself. This situation called for tact and professionalism if he hoped to survive unscathed.

She slipped her hands under the thick fur lapels of her coat and lifted the garment off her shoulders and down her arms. A lump formed in his throat at the sight of the skin tight, white satin jumpsuit she wore encrusted with sparkling colored stones. The front v'd open down to her belly button, showing off more than cleavage. She slipped on a pair of silver-rimmed dark glasses, completing her Elvis look."Do you like it?" she asked with a dare in her voice.

Man, was he in trouble. "What's the occasion?"

"It's my Halloween costume, silly."

"Halloween isn't for a couple of weeks."

"I know, but I wanted to try it out—see if you like it." She struck a pose and winked.

"It's…" She licked her full, red lips, interrupting his

train of thought. *Son of a bitch.*

"A man of few words, aren't you, Alex," she drawled. She sauntered toward him, her intent clear. *Double son of a bitch.*

"Yeah. Few words."

Chapter Twelve

"I still need Alex to draw the final rendering sketches for these, mine are just temporary, but what do you think?" Casey asked Syd as she laid out the design boards she'd slaved over for the last two days. In spite of being at home sick, she'd managed to work with the photos of the rooms in Heather's mansion and pull together paint, fabric, and furniture ideas.

"I think you need to watch your back," Syd said sternly. "After Heather's little show here at the office last night, I'm even more convinced the woman will stop at nothing to get what she wants."

Casey's spine stiffened. She set down the layout for the Hawaiian suite and fisted her hands on her hips. "What happened last night?"

"Heather showed up after hours in a flurry of fur and scarves."

"And?"

"And Alex had his hands full."

"His hands? Literally? Or figuratively?"

Sydnie took a seat on the corner of Casey's desk and folded her arms. "You have to ask?"

"Against his will, I'm sure. Alex tolerates Heather. He's not interested in her personally." She turned her attention back to the room designs and hoped Syd didn't see through her nonchalance. In reality she was sweating bullets.

"Maybe, but she's sure still interested in him. She was practically pawing him when I left. And I heard her ask him what he thought of her Halloween costume."

"You left?" Casey spun around and stared at her friend. "Why?"

Syd explained about Heather's surprise invitation for Alex to join her at dinner, and how he'd fibbed that Syd had already ordered out for him. "So, you see, I had no choice but to go and bring him something. By the time I got back, Heather was gone."

"And what happened while you were gone?"

"Your guess is as good as mine. Alex was working on the blueprints when I came in, and Heather was nowhere to be found."

"Did he say anything?"

"Thanks. For bringing him supper."

"Did he offer any kind of explanation? Any clues?"

"Nope."

"How did he appear? I mean, did he have a guilty look on his face, like they'd been up to something?"

Syd shook her head.

"Did you see lipstick on his collar, or on his cheek?" Casey pressed. "Was his hair messed up?"

"No to all of the above," Syd said, still shaking her head. "He looked just like when I'd left him. Cool, confident, and sexy. So I handed him his cheeseburger extra value meal, he said thanks and that he'd see us in the morning. That was it. I got the impression he was in no mood to talk. So I went home."

"Why didn't you call me? I need to know what's going

on around here," Casey said, aggravated—no, make that ticked off, at Heather and her conniving, man-stealing ways.

"It was late. I figured you'd be sleeping after being so sick. Excuse me for being wrong."

"I'm sorry. It's just, what am I supposed to do about this…fiasco?" Casey threw up her hands in frustration and started pacing. "I can't demand she leave Alex alone. She'll fire us all."

"True. But you can play along with her game, too. If she sees you and Alex getting *friendly*, she's bound to get the hint and bug off."

"I don't know, Syd. She's not easily deterred. Plus, she might see me as a threat, and still fire us. I don't want to take that chance. It's too risky."

"Do you want to risk losing Alex?"

Casey stopped in her tracks and turned to face Syd. "You're forgetting one thing. Alex isn't mine to lose."

"And he never will be if you don't step up to the plate."

"I know," Casey sighed. "I'd just rather finish this job first and collect our paycheck. It's safer that way."

"You might not have that much time."

"That's a chance I'll have to take."

The phone rang out in the reception area, but stopped after only two rings. Within seconds Terri raced through Casey's office door, panic covering her face. "I think we've got trouble," Terri said.

"What is it? Has something happened?" Syd asked.

"Heather called. She insisted we bring Alex's drafting table and tools over to the house right away."

"What? Why?"

"She said she and Alex are working at her place from now on and that he needs his table ASAP."

"Did she say anything else?"

"Only that Alex had been there for hours already and they were making great progress," Terri said with a dramatic flare.

"Progress? What kind of progress?" Casey's eyes narrowed to slits. The woman was going too far.

"I don't know. She hung up before I could ask."

Syd was right. Casey needed to step up to the plate and *get friendly.*

"Girls," she said with determination. "Help me get this drafting table loaded into my car."

* * * *

"So, you've moved out on me," a smooth, sassy voice said from behind Alex.

Casey. His breath hitched.

He turned away from the large windows lining the south wall of Hector's former home office to see she stood just inside the large double doors, her arms folded below her breasts, questions on her face. Dressed in a black turtleneck sweater and black slacks, she looked sleek and hot.

The glow had returned to her skin and her green eyes were bright with mischief. It had been two days since he'd taken her home to recoup from her illness, and he hadn't realized how much he'd missed her until this very moment.

"Feeling better?" he asked, sticking to a safe topic.

"I was. Then I found out you'd decided to pack your drafting tools."

"It was kind of a spur of the moment decision."

"Ahh. Well, thanks for including me in the decision making process."

"Sorry. I didn't want to bother you if you still weren't

feeling well."

"But I thought we were partners." Slowly, she walked across the now empty room. Every piece of furniture and Elvis memorabilia had been removed, leaving the room a huge, hallow cavern, but Casey lit up the space like a thousand shining stars. "Aren't partners supposed to tell each other everything?" she asked, stopping only a few feet away from where he stood.

"That depends," he said with a hint of challenge in his voice. He'd missed sparring with her for the last two days, too.

"On what?"

"On what kind of partnership we share." For the first time in almost two years the word partnership didn't make him cringe.

"Hmm. *Strictly business.* Wasn't it?" She bit the tip of her finger in question while a hint of a grin tugged at her red lips. Alex suppressed a groan in frustration. What he wouldn't give to nip and tease those lips into submission once more. Their tryst in Memphis had only been four days ago, but it felt like an eternity. Especially since they didn't get to finish what they'd started.

He was a tortured man.

"I still can't believe you left me for this," Casey said, spreading her arms wide to indicate the room. "I thought you liked the Feng Shui I had going in my office."

"I do." *And a whole lot more.*

"So, what are you doing here? And more importantly, what were you doing here without me?"

"Following the boss's orders."

"Boss? As in Heather?"

"You got it."

"It sounds like she's taken Elvis' *Teddy Bear* song

literally and put a chain around your neck."

"Not quite. I'm still my own man." He winked.

"Are you now?"

"Yes," he said firmly. "Besides, it was going to have to happen sooner than later anyway. I'll need a base point here during construction."

"Well, Mr. Your-Own-Man, I have something for you." She gave his collar a light tug, then smoothed the fabric with the steady, sensual pressure of her fingers.

"And that would be?" he asked, his breath sounding ragged to his own ears. A light, spicy scent clung to her hair, reminding him of the crisp autumn day outside.

Yeah. Casey was feeling better all right. She was in full-blown tease mode. And if she kept it up, he'd be in full-blown mode himself.

"Why don't you follow me and find out? Boss's orders." As she turned, she let one long fingertip blaze a trail along his jaw, ratcheting up the fire already building inside him. Without looking back she headed for the door and left him standing there like a dumbfounded idiot.

"Aren't you coming?" she asked without missing a step. "I'll need your help."

Alex mentally kicked himself into gear and joined her out in front of the house by a hot red Chevy Avalanche.

"What's this? A new ride?"

"New, yes. Mine, no. This is Terri's. We decided trying to stuff your drafting table into the trunk of my Mazda wasn't going to work."

"Smart conclusion." Alex laughed and dropped the tailgate. He removed the folded drafting table while Casey gathered items from the front seat. Fifty pound bags of dog and cat food were stacked at the front of the truck bed. "What's up with all the pet food?"

"Terri volunteers at an animal shelter. She's always donating to the needy."

Alex felt a major leap in his own needs as he watched her lean into the vehicle. The black slacks she wore fit her shapely backside to perfection, outlining her firm, just-right-for-his-hands cheeks. *Oh, yeah. He was needy all right.*

They returned to the house and immediately Alex put his mind and hands to the task of setting up a work area next to the windows to take advantage of the best light. Casey handed him his bag of drafting tools and he made a point not to let their fingers touch. If they did, he wouldn't be responsible for his actions—like pinning her down on the top of his drafting board.

"What do you have there?" he asked, nodding toward the poster boards she held, and trying like hell to keep his mind on work.

"The room layouts." Was that apprehension he heard in her voice? "I finished them last night. That is except for the final room renderings. I just temporarily put my sketches on the boards to give you an idea of what I have in mind."

"But you've been sick. How did you—"

"I was bored. And I knew we needed to get rolling, so I worked while watching hours of HGTV."

"Speaking of getting rolling. Terri handled acquiring all the permits we need, and Riley and Sons will be here later today to start digging the footings for the addition. And the blueprints are done and have been approved. We're on our way."

"Wow. Sounds like I wasn't missed at all."

Alex wanted to tell her he'd missed her as much as he missed the sun on a cloudy day, as much as the snow capping the Rockies, but the last woman he'd felt similar feelings for had betrayed him.

But Casey was no Valerie. He was certain of it.

"So how much did you have to change to get Heather's approval?" she asked, bringing his brain back around to the job.

"Not a thing."

"What? You can't be serious? She didn't have you change one single thing? No moving a door, window or a wall? Nothing?"

"Not one single thing. She was, surprisingly easy to please." Alex saw Casey's brow furrow, and her lips formed a tight, thin line. Her wheels were spinning— no doubt wondering what had transpired between him and Heather. Alex hid a smile. A little jealousy could be good. Right now Casey didn't need to know there was nothing to be jealous about. He only had eyes for one woman, and she was standing right in front of him.

"So, let's see those room layouts," he said, tugging the boards from her white-knuckled fingers. "We have a house to remodel."

"Okay," Casey said, a little breathless from Alex's sudden demand. Would he be just as demanding in bed? Oh, boy. She couldn't go there. Not now. Her heart hadn't stopped pounding the way it was since she'd walked into the room—she didn't need to add to its rhythmic pace by thinking lusty thoughts.

Focus. Focus on work. But work only added more pressure to her nerves. Showing her layouts to Sydnie and Terri was one thing, but putting them out for a professional like Alex to see and judge, was something else.

Casey wrung her hands and took a calming breath she hoped he didn't see. Heck, she hadn't been this nervous when they were tearing at each other's clothes in her hotel room. Funny how a few drinks and a burning desire had a way of taking away one's inhibitions. Too bad she couldn't call upon those two elements to rescue her now. Well, she could the burning desire part.

"Promise me you won't be too hard on me," she said, trying to get a grip. "Remember, I'm still learning."

"I promise I'll go easy." Alex chuckled and the deep, easy sound offered a bit of comfort. He placed the boards on the drafting table and eased back to sit on the window ledge, giving her some space.

"First, we'll discuss the grand foyer." Holding up the design board she said, "I personally don't see anything wrong with the foyer other than it's currently too dark. Agree?"

She looked at him and knew instantly she'd made a huge mistake. His shirt sleeves were rolled up, exposing his muscular forearms and strong wrists that lead to big, rugged hands. Hands that had cupped and fondled her breasts not so long ago.

"Agree," he said, reminding her she wasn't in the room alone, that this wasn't just some fantasy she was enjoying all by herself.

"Since…this is the main entrance," she said, a little short on breath, "and where the Gridmore family portraits hang, I thought we'd simply lighten the paneling with a nice, soothing neutral shade of Indian Summer." She pointed to a paint chip and the rendering she'd done to bring the room to life and hoped to God he didn't notice the tremble in her hand.

"The color will lighten the area considerably," she continued, "and there's just enough neutral fleck in the black marble tile to pull it off while still being classy and sophisticated. I also suggest we leave the other woodwork untouched."

"Sounds good." Alex crossed those muscular arms of his in front of his broad, powerful chest. She'd felt the power of that chest, felt the heat of his skin, the rhythm of his heart beneath. Taking a deep breath, she forced her gaze up and discovered he watched her intently. His eyes darkened and she was afraid he'd read every single thought dancing through her head.

Casey took a step back, hoping increased distance would keep her in check. "I didn't do anything...for this room yet," she held out her hands to indicate their surroundings, "since this room will lead into the addition, I figured we'd tie the two together with an all-out Elvis theme. But I need to see your design for the addition before I can do too much."

"Do you have any ideas?" he asked, his voice low and seductive as hell.

Oh, yeah. She had ideas.

"A few."

"Let's hear 'em."

Oh, God. This was torture. Sweet, agonizing torture. How much longer could she stand here and babble about room design when all she could think about was Alex?

"Well. Heather hosts a monthly Elvis meeting as well as an annual convention, and with this room being so big, I thought it would be the perfect area for her guests to gather, mingle and party. I see the walls in this room lightened as well, a bar added at the west end, and low slung, retro style furniture in eclectic colors placed in groupings, and photos of Elvis in groupings on the walls as well."

Crap. Was she rambling? To her ears she sounded like she was rambling.

"What about the other rooms?" he asked. He pushed away from the window and stepped over to the drafting board. "Show me what you have in mind."

Casey felt a whimper rumble at the back of her throat. Was it her imagination, or was Alex really that tall? That big? That deliciously bad?

With a quick catch of her breath she was once more surrounded by the mesmerizing scent of him.

"I thought…what we could do is…" *Forget about the damn house and ravage each other. It's only a job, right? Who cares about money and a reputation anyway?*

"What? What could we do, Casey?" He brushed a tendril of hair away from her cheek. The backs of his fingers breezed lightly against her skin, sending a wave of heat pulsing through every square inch of her body.

"Uh." She took a deep breath. "I think…it would be fun to…theme the rooms to not only some of his songs, but his movies, too." She scrambled to find the right design board in her pile. This impromptu presentation wasn't going anything like she'd planned.

"How so, sweetheart?" His warm breath tickled the shell of her ear as he spoke, the husky sound seeping down, fanning her desire.

Sweetheart? Yeah. Nothing like she'd planned. Holy crap.

"Elvis made…several movies in Hawaii," she said, her focus wavering to point she could barely think. "I designed a 60's Hawaiian room…for *Girls, Girls, Girls,*

Blue Hawaii and—"

"*Can't Help Falling in Love*," he whispered.

Casey's body froze. But her heart still pounded in her chest. "*Can't Help...Falling in Love?*" she asked, her breath, her sanity gone. "What—"

"Elvis'—song, from *Blue*—"

"Shouldn't I be sitting in on this little discussion?" Heather asked from the open doorway, jerking Casey from Alex's seductive spell.

Chapter Thirteen

"Get in and let's go, Terri," Casey said as she put her friend's Avalanche in gear and tore out of the Studs parking lot later that afternoon.

"Will you take it easy, Case," Terri hollered over the classic rock blaring on the radio. For nine blocks she twisted back and forth in the passenger seat, scouting for unsuspecting cars, making her pony tail bob around her face.

"Relax." Casey punched down the accelerator and merged into the rush-hour traffic clogging six-eighty. "I'm an excellent driver. I promise we'll make it to the animal shelter before they lock up for the night."

"I'm not concerned about making it before they close. I'm concerned about making it in one piece." Terri braced one hand on the dashboard and gripped the arm rest with the other as Casey zoomed in between and around cars.

Casey giggled, feeling free and reckless after being under Heather's watchful eye all day. She loved the thrill, the exhilaration of a fast drive, preferably on the open road, but she'd take what she could get. Putting a pedal to the metal was one way to release frustration, especially sexual frustrations.

Damn. Why couldn't she get a break? Between a rotten relationship record, food poisoning and Heather Gridmore, Casey's sex life was forever in a holding pattern of near misses and mishaps. Honestly, how many more hot-and-bothered starts and stops could a girl take and still survive?

Casey asked the Avalanche for more speed and glimpsed Terri's cheeks paling to the color of chalk. Casey smiled. She loved to rile her sensible, predictable friend.

"Woo-hoo. Your ride really gets out and moves for a truck. Sweet," Casey said as she zipped around another car.

"Slow down, Case," Terri ordered. She reached over and turned off the radio. "You're going to get pulled over in *my* truck. Or worse, wreck it."

"Argh. You're such a fuddy-duddy." Casey eased up on the gas and the truck's speed began to drop.

"What's gotten into you?" Terri asked.

"Nothing. I'm just having some fun." After the day Casey had had, she needed some fun. Working beside Alex, the heat of his hard body next to hers as they discussed room plans, yet being unable to touch like she was dying to, had Casey wound tight. She was ready to explode. She needed release.

Taking a deep breath, she noticed the musky scent of Alex still lingered on her clothes, driving her even crazier.

Make that sexual release.

With Alex.

Yeah. Like that's going to happen.

"Tell me again why *you're* driving me to the animal shelter in my ride?" Terri asked.

"Because I need sex," Casey said between clenched

"Oh, God. Stay away from me." Terri plastered herself up against the passenger door.

"Stop. I'm not that desperate."

"Gee, thanks."

"No, I mean I'm a man only kind of woman. I need sex with a man."

"Oh, so that's it. I should have guessed." Terri rolled her eyes and let go of her hold on the dash long enough to throw up her hand. "Do you think driving eighty in a sixty zone at rush-hour is a really good substitute for—"

"I need sex. I can't have sex. And since I can't have it, getting out and driving is...the next best thing. Dammit. What else am I supposed to do?" Casey tightened her grip on the steering wheel until her hands hurt, but she didn't loosen her hold. Pain could be a good distraction. She hoped. Or she'd go nuts.

"This wouldn't have anything to do with Alex, would it?"

"Right on, girlfriend. But I'll get over it. I have to. Hey, after we drop off the pet food, do you want to make an ice cream run? I've got a massive craving for chocolate and peanut butter smothered in vanilla soft serve."

"Oh, Case. Quit being such a girl scout," Terri grumbled.

"What's that supposed to mean?" she asked with a huff as she turned left onto another street.

"It means, quit putting everyone else first. Don't you deserve to be happy? Deserve to do what you want for a change?"

"Well, I..."

"And I'm not talking about shopping or food, either. I'm talking serious stuff here, like sex with a man *you love*—not think you love, but really, truly love, a solid relationship, and anniversaries to mark the years, not just months."

Casey heard a tinge of longing in Terri's voice and sidled a glance at her as they drove down the quiet street. Her friend was wiser and smarter than most people gave her credit for, oftentimes providing the right answers for some really tough questions, only in a roundabout way.

And in Terri's simple way, Casey was certain her friend was telling her to go for it—to take a chance with Alex. But Casey needed to hear the words spoken out loud—just to be sure—then she'd etch them in the concrete of her mind.

"Are you suggesting what I think you are?"

"Of course I am. You want sex. You want Alex. You want sex with Alex. So have it. What's stopping you?" Terri shrugged.

What was stopping her?

Ethics and responsibility to name a few.

But Terri was right. All Casey's life she'd taken a back seat to everyone else—their wants and needs, and she wasn't even a wife and a mother. Where the hell had she gone so wrong?

No. She hadn't gone wrong. Had she? She didn't have a ton of regrets dragging her down, she had a good family. And she didn't get to where she was—co-owner in a growing company, owning a nice home and a new car, by not paying attention and working hard.

She'd wanted all those things, hadn't she?

Yes, she had.

And, she still wanted the one thing that had always eluded her. Terri was right. Casey wanted the anniversaries that marked the years, not the months, or in her case, sometimes weeks.

For some reason the men in her life always had a habit of bailing. What made her think Alex would be any different? Right now the only clue she had was an inkling of a gut feeling that Alex was different.

Was an inkling enough to take a chance on? She wanted so much to take the chance with Alex, but she couldn't forget what was at stake.

"Look. My personal wants and needs aren't important at the moment," Casey said as turned the truck into the shelter's parking lot, the beam of the headlights arcing over the building's white exterior. "Taking care of the job is."

She put the truck in park and cut the engine.

"And what about when the job is done, Case?" Terri asked. "Then what?"

"I…" whatever words she intended to say didn't come.

"Don't wait, Casey. Because once this job is done, Alex is going to go back to Denver. Then you're back to square one."

"And what if I go for it? What if Alex still goes back to Denver? I'm not sure I can take another heartbreak, Terri."

"Then make sure he doesn't go back, at least not without you." Terri got out of the truck and stood by the open door, the sun dipping low on the horizon behind her.

"My life is here."

"Don't regret the chance you didn't take, Casey. Call him." Terri shut the door and hurried into the shelter, leaving Casey to make her decision on her own.

"Don't regret the chance you didn't take," she repeated slowly. "Okay. Here goes nothing." She snatched her phone from the seat and dialed Alex's number before she could change her mind.

✳ ✳ ✳ ✳

"Damn," Alex grumbled as he ended the call from Dotty. He raked his fingers through his hair, wondering why things had to be so complicated all the time. Hunter Dierks, action star, had broken his leg while getting out of the shower and was now on a six-week leave instead of a three day break. Not one to lay around and do nothing for a month and a half, Dierks wanted to go ahead and start the building process of his new Aspen home. And he was willing to pay handsomely to make up for the inconvenience to Alex.

"How am I supposed to be in two places at once?"

"I'm sure I wouldn't know," Heather drawled. Alex stiffened at the sound of Heather's voice and dropped the papers he held onto the drafting table. Slowly he turned to see her saunter into the room with two glasses of wine in her hands.

"You've worked hard all day. Obviously it's time for a break." She winked, her eyes overflowing with silent suggestions.

Alex groaned under his breath. Complicated was an understatement. He'd discovered over the last few days that Heather was cunning, manipulative and fearless when it came to getting what she wanted. And he had no patience to sit and sip wine knowing she had an ulterior motive. But she was the boss, and refusing her offer of a simple drink might come across as rude. Keeping the boss happy was a necessary part of any job. This one, in particular, was no exception.

"Thanks, I was just finishing up," he said, pushing his chair back from the table. A fire, compliments of Joey the butler, blazed in the fireplace across the room.

Alex stood. He accepted the glass and Heather's fingers touched his, a deliberate move on her part. He stifled a curse.

Too bad he couldn't drink wine like he did beer—in a couple of chugs.

Taking a drink, he found the wine smooth and not too sweet, proving Heather had excellent taste and deep pockets when it came to stocking her wine cellar.

"How are things coming?" she asked over the rim of her crystal wine glass.

"Good. We got the footings for the addition dug today. Providing the weather holds, we'll start pouring the foundation tomorrow."

"Wonderful," she said with excitement. "I can't wait to see the walls go up."

"Things will move relatively fast once we reach that stage. We'll try to get the addition framed in as soon as possible. At this time of year though, each day is a race against the clock. Keep your fingers crossed for a mild fall."

Her body swayed as she moved closer to where he stood, giving him a front row view of the cleavage her low-cut knit top revealed. At least she wasn't dressed like Elvis tonight.

"Hmm. I'm curious, Alex. What have you come up with for my bedroom? Have you thought of any more ideas for my *Burning Love* theme?" She took another sip of wine and licked her bottom lip.

Alex silently cursed and studied the condensation

beading on the side of her wine goblet. "As we discussed earlier, Casey is handling the majority of the work for the remodeling."

"I know, but I hired you to do that." A frown covered Heather's otherwise perfect face. Just how many dollars did it take for a woman to look like a red-headed Barbie doll?

"I'm the architect. I mainly handle the structural end of things." He set down his barely touched glass of wine. "If Casey has an idea that includes adding or eliminating a wall, door, or window, she confers with me to see if it's structurally possible to do it. If we are able to make that physical change, we go from there. If we can't, she'll come up with a new idea."

"But I want you to be in charge of the whole project." She leaned forward, giving him an extra close up view of her professionally enhanced breasts. No matter how much Heather's cost, they didn't come close to the perfection of Casey's perky, yet soft breasts. Casey's had a gentle swell that rounded into a globe of creamy sweetness that fit nicely in the cup of his hand. He should know, he'd touched and held them in Memphis and hadn't stopped fantasizing since.

"And I thought that's what I was paying for," Heather continued, intruding on his thoughts.

Aggravated, Alex took a step back. Somehow he needed to let Heather know he wasn't interested in *her* project, but he was walking one helluva fine line.

"Don't worry. Casey and I are working closely on all facets of the job. She won't proceed on any plans without first consulting me."

"Well, it's nice to know I'm at least getting some of my money's worth." She picked up her glass and walked around a series of long tables they'd set up to lay out all of the room plans. Her hips swayed gently in skintight blue jeans, and three inch pink heels completed her outfit. Alex marveled how women managed to walk in the damn things.

Heather glanced at the fabric, tile, and paint samples Casey had chosen for each room.

"As you know, Casey is very good at what she does. I'm sure you'll be very happy when we're done."

"She's an accountant. What can she really know about design?" There was no mistaking the disdain in Heather's voice.

She picked up a sample of scarlet-colored fabric and worked the material between her fingers for a few seconds before letting it flutter back to the table.

"A hell of a lot. And you know it, or you wouldn't have chosen her for this job." Alex's jaw tightened. Paycheck or no paycheck, he wasn't going to let Heather cut Casey down.

"Well, I do have to admit these room layouts are rather impressive. I do like what I see. Did you draw these?" she asked, pointing to the colored room renderings centered in the middle of each work board.

"No. Casey drew them."

She frowned. "As the architect, isn't this a part of your job?"

"No need. Casey did an excellent job. She's very talented."

"As I'm sure you are, Alex. With your eye for detail, have you ever considered painting?"

"I've dabbled some."

"Some?" She arched a perfectly sculpted brow. "Don't you want to do more than some?"

Alex's jaw tightened. Every word she uttered hinted at underlying meanings."Maybe someday. Right now I prefer to focus on architecture."

"That's right." She circled back around the tables, shortening the distance between them once again. "Your passion is for timber frame homes."

He nodded and narrowed his eyes in suspicion. What was she up to now?

"Yes, it is."

"I think passion is important. Don't you?" She placed her index finger on a button in the middle of his shirt. "Life would be boring without passion." Ever so slowly, she worked her fingers from one button down to the next.

Alex's hands clenched into fists as he moved to the table where the room designs laid, pretending to straighten them. "I suppose it would be," he said dryly.

"Tell me, Alex. Besides two-by-fours and blueprints, what else are you passionate about? Fine wine? Sports cars? Beautiful women?" She gazed at him, her eyes heavy with sexual intent.

Walking over to him, she slowly traced a line on his sleeve with her finger tip. There was no denying the feel of her touch through the material, but rather than turning him on, she annoyed and bored him. Her touch was nothing like Casey's.

Casey made his blood pump and his body harden just by bestowing him with a saucy smile. And her touch— well, it was explosive.

Heather set down her wine and sidled up even closer. With both hands she drew lazy circles across his chest.

Looking up at him from behind long lashes, she teased her bottom lip between her teeth. She was attractive all right, and rich. Any man thinking with his *other* brain, would jump at the chance to give her exactly what she wanted.

She twined her arms around his neck and he could feel her fingers messing with his hair. Her warm breath brushed lightly across his chin.

Damn. She was backing him into a corner again with her little play of cat and mouse, and he wasn't certain how to put an end to it this round. Last time he'd saved his skin by doing some fast talking and a promise to move his makeshift office to her house.

But now? He was out of options. Being honest and telling her flat out he wasn't interested in her sexually was one way to douse her fire, but it was also a sure way to get him, and Casey, fired.

He glanced at his phone and saw the stupid thing sitting there silently on the table, mocking him. Normally his phone rang off the hook with calls regarding the job he was working, but not tonight. No saving his ass by the bell this time. That's what he got for working late. Everyone else had called it a day hours ago.

"You know, I'm more of a beer, football, and heavy-duty truck kind of guy," he said, finally answering her question, hoping for a way to cool her interest. "It's pretty hard to haul lumber in a sports car."

"I suppose it would be." She traced the length of his jaw with a slender finger, studying his face as if he were a priceless piece in her collection.

Okay. Time for drastic measures.

Out of the corner of his eye he caught a glimpse of a wine glass on the table to his right, and he got an idea. Was it close enough for him to reach? Stretching his fingers, he felt around the table top without moving his hand too far, not wanting to appear obvious.

At last, the cool feel of crystal met his fingertips. Carefully he inched the glass closer to the edge, gave it a quick flick and raised his arm as if he intended to return her caress.

"Oh! Oh, no!" Heather jumped back. The dull ping of crystal hitting the carpet echoed in room.

They looked down and saw red wine dripping down her left leg to her foot and into her pointy-toed shoe.

"Heather. I'm sorry." He reached down and picked up the glass. "At least it didn't break, or you'd be taking it out of my paycheck," he said as he set it back on the table with care.

She gave him a tight smile as she shook her foot. "Yes, well accidents happen."

"I'll run and get something to clean up this mess."

"Don't bother. This carpet is going anyway," she said, waving her hands.

Damn. So much for a quick escape. At least she wasn't fawning all over him anymore. In fact, she looked like she was trying hard not to be miffed. That was all right by Alex. Maybe if he succeeded in irritating her a little each day, her infatuation would wane.

"Yew, this is feeling kind of sticky. I think I better go and change," she said, shaking her foot again.

"Right. I should get going, anyway. I have some phone calls to make." He grabbed his coat and slipped it on before she could suggest something crazy like he stay and help bathe her foot.

He snatched up his phone and notebook and headed for the door. With a quick wave and a goodnight, he left Heather fuming and dripping in wine.

* * * *

"I'm telling you, Rory, you have to help me out again," Heather said with more desperation in her voice than she normally allowed, even in desperate situations. She drummed her polished fingernails on the top of a stack of plastic totes containing her precious Elvis collection. The small, third-floor bedroom overflowed with the containers she'd packed with meticulous care.

"How? How else am I supposed to help you, Sugar?" his smooth, comforting voice asked from the other end of the line.

"You're a theater person. Use your imagination. Where have you been anyway? I've been trying to call you for two days."

A huge sigh reverberated through the phone line. "Busy. I work for a living, you know. Now, tell me exactly what it was you need my help for."

"I caught Alex and Casey getting friendly."

"Friendly? What do you mean by friendly?"

"He was nuzzling her ear, whispering, all the things he should be doing with me. Even across the room I could see the desire in his eyes. Dammit. The only time he even comes close to me is if he needs my approval for something. Otherwise, it's like I don't exist."

"Heather. You hired the man to do a major remodel and add on to your house, not romp with you under the sheets. I'd say if he's not paying any attention to you, it's a good sign."

"How can ignoring me be a good sign? I write the checks," she said in a huff. Whose side was Rory on, anyway? "He should be focused on making me happy. Giving me what I want."

"He is focused on making you happy, and on doing a

good job. Be thankful. He could be a schmuck and not give a damn and leave you in a nightmarish mess."

"All right." Heather plopped down on one small corner of the bed that wasn't covered with large portraits of the Gridmore family, and noticed her husband staring up at her. She groaned and wished the portraits were back on the walls of the entrance foyer, but Casey and her crew were now in the process of painting the dark paneling. "So he's a good kind of focused. But I want him to focus on me, too. I could have gotten any architect from Omaha to do this job, but there was a reason I wanted Alex Roy."

"And that reason is? You never did tell me." A long pause stretched between them. "Heather?"

"He's...cute."

"Cute? You commissioned an expensive architect from Denver, who specializes in magnificent, one-of-a-kind timber frame homes, just because he's cute?"

"Yes. And he's sexy, hot, and young."

"Well, stupid me. I should have known. Must be nice to have money to burn. You should try struggling from paycheck to paycheck like the rest of us poor saps."

"This isn't about money, Rory, and you know it. I've been lonely since Hecky died. And I'm tired of being alone in this big ghostly house. I want a companion."

"I told you a long time ago that you should get a pet. Dogs are great. I have a friend of a friend who knows the guy who runs Missouri River Kennels. We could drive out. I'm sure we'd find—"

"I'm not looking for that kind of companionship, Rory. I want— No. Make that need. I need a man."

"How can you be lonely for a man when you're always entertaining? There are always men around doing something or other at your house."

"The staff—the chef, the gardener, security, caterers, florists. Staff doesn't count."

"What about the clubs you belong to?"

"You know our Elvis antiquities club only meets once a month, and we don't get many new male members who are young, handsome, and eligible."

"Well, you've got a lifetime membership to the country club. Go golfing. That's a great way to meet men."

"I don't like to golf," she whined. "Hector loved it and during the summer he lived on the course. I have no desire to take a backseat to a set of golf clubs again. Besides, so many of the men there are old. I'm ready for a man who can satisfy me for hours, not minutes."

"Oh, the perils of our sweet, deprived Heather," he said with enough dramatics to rival the screeching of fingernails on a chalkboard.

"Stop. This is serious. What am I supposed to do? With the house under construction, it'll be weeks before I can host any kind of party again. How am I supposed to meet anyone else?"

"Take a trip? Go to Mexico, the Bahamas, take a singles cruise. It'd be good for you to get away for a while. You can avoid stumbling around in the remodeling mess, too."

"And leave my priceless collection here alone, unprotected with so many strangers working on the house coming and going? I can't do that."

"Well—"

"Besides, the Elvis jumpsuit I acquired should be here next week. I have to be here when it arrives."

"That's right. You'll call me immediately when it

comes, won't you? I'm anxious to see it."

"If you help me, I'll let you be the first. I'll even let you touch it, with gloves on, of course. If you help me."

"That's blackmail."

"Personally, I think that word is a bit extreme in this case, but call it what you will, as long as you agree to come to my aid."

"It's blackmail in my book," he said, blowing off her lame threat.

"Rory, please. It's been two years since Hecky passed away. I need to move on."

"Heather, you're a beautiful…amazing woman. I've never known you to have trouble finding a good-looking man."

"Good-looking, no. Eligible? That's the challenging part. You date. You know how hard it is to find someone who doesn't either have kids, survives life on anti-depressants, has a criminal record, or is about to kick-the-bucket."

"All right," he said, resignation in his voice. "I know it's tough."

"So, you *will* help me?"

"If I don't, you'll probably also petition to have me kicked out of the Elvis club."

"Now there's an idea."

"Some friend you are," he quipped. "What did you have in mind to drive lover boy into your arms?"

"I want you to haunt my house."

"What? You can't be serious?"

"Very serious. You know I've always suspected there's a ghost in the house. Unfortunately, the spirit is too unpredictable and rarely makes it's presence known."

"And this involves me how?"

"Since we can't depend on the real ghost, I want you to create one."

"And just exactly how do you propose I do that?"

"You're the one with the imagination. Remember?"

"No way. I'm not brainstorming this alone. You're the one with the interest in the metaphysical. You will help."

"Oh, all right."

"Good. And have your checkbook handy."

"My checkbook? What do you need that for?"

"Sugar, nothing in life is free."

Chapter Fourteen

Casey changed her mind.

Calling Alex was a rotten idea.

Showing up at his hotel room was ever so much better.

She double checked her trench coat, making sure the collar adequately covered what wasn't underneath. Her mouth hitched up into a saucy smile. Alex was going to be surprised.

And if he wasn't? She couldn't go there. If she did, she'd chicken out and leave without so much as a hello. But the solidness of his hotel room door, staring her down and daring her to knock, made a cache of butterflies flutter in her stomach.

Who was she to think she could waltz into the Embassy Suites, up to Alex's room on the eighth floor, and seduce him into a night of wild, passionate, mind-altering sex?

Don't regret the chance you didn't take.

No. No way was Casey going to regret anything as far as Alex was concerned.

She, Casey Burrows, was going for it. She'd talked herself into this, driven herself halfway across Omaha dressed in the hottest lingerie, heels, and her long black trench coat to cover her secret plans. Turning back now wasn't allowed. Especially, after she'd endured the pain of waxing in places that rarely saw the rays of the sun. Walking across the hotel lobby, knowing she wore only a few pieces of strategically placed satin under her coat had been nerve wracking, and yet one of the most exciting things she'd ever done.

Casey took a deep breath and knocked. Seconds ticked by and Alex failed to answer.

Great. Just what she needed—to be left standing out in the hall feeling more and more like an idiot with every passing moment.

"Maybe he's in the shower," she said under her breath. A delicious vision of Alex standing buck-naked, his body glistening with droplets of water, filled her mind. Hmm. Wasn't this the second time she'd had the fantasy of Alex wearing only water?

Time to stop fantasizing and start living in the real world. Squaring her shoulders, she knocked, harder this time. The click of the lock sent her nerves into a frenzy, but it was too late to bolt and run.

The door opened and Casey was greeted by a fully-clothed Alex, his cell phone at his ear. So much for the water fantasy. But the evening was young, and Alex looked as rugged and as handsome as ever with his shirt sleeves rolled up and his faded blue jeans slung low on his hips.

A hint of surprise touched his eyes, but then he smiled and waved her into the room. Closing the door, he held up a finger to indicate he'd only be a few minutes, then disappeared into the adjoining bedroom.

Damn. Talk about rotten timing. "Stop it. No negative thoughts. Stay positive," she mumbled.

Seconds ticked by into minutes. Restless, Casey started to remove her coat, but caught herself. Shedding her coat now would ruin the whole surprise. Of course, she could strip and lounge in a chair, her feet up, wearing nothing but a tie like Julia Roberts in *Pretty Woman*. An act like that took guts, though, and Casey was shaking in her black stilettos. Besides, she didn't have a tie.

"Sorry about that," Alex said, startling her. Casey spun around. "No problem."

"You should have taken your coat off, made yourself comfortable."

Casey's breath caught. "Oh. I didn't even think about it." She shrugged and smiled as innocently as she could manage.

"Can I get you something? I don't have anything fancy, just a few beers in the frig."

"A beer sounds great." Liquid courage. She could use a twelve pack right about now.

Alex headed for the bar and pulled out two long-necks. Removing the tops, he handed her one.

"Thanks." She accepted the cold bottle and took a drink. The icy liquid slipped down her throat and soothed like she'd hoped it would. Alex downed a long swallow and Casey watched, mesmerized by the flexing of his neck muscles as he drank. The man had one delicious neck—strong, lean and tan. If she were a vampire, she'd love to sink her teeth into him and show no mercy. Heck, who needed a vampire?

"So, can I take your coat?" He raised a brow in question.

Oh, yeah. Please do, handsome.

"You look uncomfortable," he prodded, interrupting her secret wish.

"Actually I'm a little chilly," she fibbed. "My system hasn't adjusted to the cooler fall weather yet. I guess I'm still on Memphis temps," she said with a hint of suggestion.

A flicker of desire danced in his eyes and she knew he'd caught her double meaning. He took another swallow and leaned against the bar, one booted foot over the other, his arms folded across his wide chest.

"So, what's up?" he asked. He leveled his gaze on her and Casey's hormones sizzled from head to toe.

The man had to ask what was up?

Let the games begin.

"I need…to talk to you," she said, a little breathless. Damn. She didn't want to come across as a desperate, panting virgin. She was supposed to be the sexy siren who had it all under control.

"About the job?"

"No. I mean yes. Sort of." *Shit.*

"Lose my cell number?"

"No." Great. Now she was starting to sound like a CD with a major hiccup problem. "What I need to say can't be said over the phone."

"Sounds serious."

Casey took a deep breath, stepped forward, shortening the distance between them, all the while trying really hard to be brave, smart and sexy. "It is."

Alex shot her a half-assed grin. "Did I get fired?" He downed another deep, long swallow of beer and Casey couldn't help wanting to be the bottle.

"No. Nothing like that." She inched closer. "But my reason for being here does have to do with fire." She was dying to touch him, explore every sweet inch of his amazing male perfection, but held herself in check, not wanting to rush the night she'd savor forever.

"How so?" he asked huskily. He unfolded his arms and braced them on the bar behind him, causing his collar to widen. Snippets of hair peeked out for her pleasure. Yum.

"I've been hoping we could start a fire…between us." She took a quivering breath and held it, bracing herself for his answer.

"Don't you mean *stoke* the fire between us?" He traced the line of her jaw with the pad of his thumb, sending shock waves of desire racing through her body. "I've been smoldering since the day I stepped off the plane."

"Smoldering?" She reached out to touch him, but he stopped her by sliding his hands down over her arms, forcing them to stay by her sides. Then he cupped her face in his hand and she leaned forward, dying to be closer. Their gazes locked and held. Intense sexual hunger vibrated between them.

"Burning," he drawled. He brushed her cheek with the back of his hand, letting his fingers brand a blazing trail down the slope of her neck and to the hollow of her throat. Casey's knees weakened.

Pushing aside her collar, he let his hand slide beneath the heavy fabric. His fingers caressed and explored the skin above the swell of her breast. Casey's heart rate bucked into action.

His fingers moved to the right in a stealthy exploration. His eyes hooded with intense desire when he discovered very little in the way of clothing stood between them. A mischievous smile played at his lips, and Casey restrained herself from jumping him right then and there.

Hooking a finger under the strap of her bra, he gave

a slight tug. A low moan escaped his throat as he slowly slid the satin between his thumb and forefinger.

Casey's chest rose and fell, matching the rapid rhythm of her heart. Pushing the strap down over her shoulder, he gently kneaded her flesh, his touch electric and dominating as hell.

Oh, yeah, she was definitely in control here. Quite the sexy siren she was. *Not.* More like a woman possessed.

A tug at her waist told her he'd undone her belt, letting her coat part and a whisper of cool air sweep over her skin. But Alex pulled her tight up against him, replacing the cool with his flaming heat. The solidness of one very aroused body part pressed into her thigh.

Sweet, Jesus.

Before Casey could recover from the realization he was happy to see her, he stepped back and brushed the coat off her shoulders. The garment slipped down her arms and fell to the floor in a pool at her feet. His hungry gaze turned all out ravenous and trailed down, then back up, leaving blazing fires at every strategic location on her body.

"Nice," he rasped, cupping a black satin and lace-covered breast in his hand. Even through the fabric his thumb worked magical, intoxicating circles over her nipple.

Casey groaned and let her head fall back. This wasn't the way she'd envisioned her grand seduction scene. She was the one who was supposed to be in control, stripping off her coat, driving him crazy.

But so what. Alex taking control was better than she'd ever imagined. Maybe she'd overrated her personal control.

He pressed his lips against the hollow of her throat

and nibbled and sampled his way down to her collar bone.

Yeah, way overrated.

"Come here intent upon seducing me, Burrows?" he asked between kisses, the warmth of his breath pulsing against her already feverish skin.

"Maybe." The minute she said it, Casey mentally kicked herself. Alex pulled away and she groaned at the loss of his lips against her skin, his hands on her body. His brow furrowed. His eyes deepened to the shade of dark chocolate—decadent, yet dangerous.

"Maybe? Should I be insulted? Or embarrassed?" He backed up, widening the distance between them, but his questioning eyes never left her.

Casey swallowed hard, feeling half-naked and vulnerable. Hell, she was half-naked.

"Did I say maybe? It was a slip of the tongue." A whimper lodged in her throat. One little, teeny, tiny word and she'd blown the most amazing prelude to sex she'd ever known.

"A slip of the tongue," he drawled. Was he suggesting, or condemning? He placed his hands on his hips, his body language screaming, *don't mess with me.* "So, which is it? And your answer better be the right one because if I find out you're on your way to seduce someone else, I'm not going to be happy."

She sucked in a deep breath. Okay, he was backing up the body language with the *right* verbal language. Alex Roy had a tinge of jealousy brewing in his blood.

Lifting her chin, she turned to hide the smile threatening to cover her face. "What makes you think I was planning to seduce anyone else?"

"So, you make a habit of running around the city dressed in just lingerie and a trench coat?"

"Of course not. But it is kind of an exhilarating exper—"

"Then you are here to seduce me." In two strides he reached her, pulling her hard up against him. His mouth captured hers in a searing kiss that demanded and gave at the same time. Casey tunneled her fingers into his hair, and returned his kisses with equal fervor.

His tongue sought and found hers and they joined in a wild, out-of-control dance of pent-up passion.

The palms of his hands were calloused from his work, but they felt like the finest velvet as they skated down the length of her back. He reached her derriere and wasted no time in slipping his hands beneath what little material was there. Cupping her buttocks, he squeezed, kicking Casey's libido into turbo mode. He rocked her hard against him.

"I," she managed between kisses, "can't take it anymore." She grabbed the buttons on his shirt and sent them popping, revealing the broad chest that she'd dreamed about since that Saturday night in Memphis. A peppering of hair covered his torso, funneling down below the waistline of his jeans, inviting her to follow the path.

Alex shrugged out of the shirt and sent it flying across the room. Casey explored his broad chest and firm belly with her hands, not stopping until she reached the front of his jeans. The denim did nothing to hide the solidness of his desire. He groaned from her bold touch, urging her to do far more.

She kicked off her shoes and answered his request by freeing the button of his jeans. By the time she'd managed to handle the zipper, she was panting shamelessly, ready to cross the bridge of no return.

Reaching into his jeans, she took him into her hand. Her thumb glided over his tip.

"Casey," he gasped. "Oh, sweetheart."

In one swift move, he lifted her off her feet and pressed her up against the wall with his rock-solid body. He braced one hand on the wall behind her, with the other he shoved aside the small strip of satin standing between them and ecstasy. His fingers wasted no time in finding their intended target.

Casey's breath died in her throat at his touch. Her eyes fluttered closed. Alex explored and teased, driving her insane with a harried rush of unrelenting need. Her fingernails dug into his shoulders, desperate for more, desperate for it all.

"Alex," she pleaded. She pulsed against his hand, seeking, demanding release. Then it came, spasms of desire, joy, and relief hitting her all at once. She cried out and Alex covered her mouth with his, capturing her explosive desire deep in his throat.

When she regained a small semblance of control, he pulled his hand away and left a trail of her feminine release along her inner thigh.

"Alex?"

"Dying for more?"

"Yes. Oh, yes." Her head fell back.

He braced his hands on either side of her head and pressed his shaft against her core. Casey inhaled sharply at the shear size of him.

"I want you," he growled. "And I want you now. Fast and hard."

Their lips met once more, dipping and plunging, fast and furious. They devoured each other up against the unforgiving wall. He forced her panties down over her slim hips, and they slipped down to the floor in a soft whoosh. She kicked the satin garment aside, freeing her legs. Reaching behind her back, she unclasped her bra, wanting to give Alex every bare inch of her.

"Casey," his rasped against her lips. "Back pocket." She pulled his leather billfold from his jeans. "Inside. Protection." She opened it, found the gold package, then let his billfold fall to the floor.

Ripping open the foil, she removed the condom. He took it from her and sheathed himself. Within seconds he was lifting her back against the wall, burying himself deep inside her. Casey wrapped her legs around him and together, their bodies slick with sweat, they rode the wave of unexplainable pleasure.

Casey shuddered, on the verge of a second climax.

"Hold on, sweetheart. I'm comin'."

"Alex— I—" He thrust deeper, harder. Spasms rocked her out of the universe. Together they raced neck-and-neck to the finish line, and ended in a dead heat.

Alex's body jerked from an aftershock, then his tense muscles relaxed and they slid to their knees, spent and satisfied.

Satisfied. Oh, yeah. For the first time in her life, Casey was totally, completely satisfied in the sex department. And the night was still young.

* * * *

Alex snapped the band of his watch closed around his wrist as he walked back into the bedroom. Casey lay in a tangle of sheets, her hair tumbling about her face on the rumpled pillow.

One long, smooth leg peeked out from beneath the covers, tempting him to climb back into the queen-sized bed with her for another round of lovemaking.

They'd played, teased, and climaxed so many times he'd lost count before collapsing in exhaustion during the wee hours of the morning. And now she slept peacefully on her side, exhausted from their wild night. Reluctantly, Alex had left their bed, forcing himself to shower alone. With his celebrity client waiting to meet with him in Denver later today, he didn't have time to get distracted with a much fantasized about rendezvous in the shower.

But he was distracted. Big time. Hell. He raked his fingers through his damp hair. Casey Burrows was distraction personified.

Be tough, Roy. Be strong. If he had anything to say about it, there would be more nights, more mornings after—allowing for many future showers.

A soft sigh escaped Casey's lips as she stirred. The sheet slipped lower, giving a peek at the plump roundness of a gorgeous breast. Alex's jeans tightened and he knew he had to get out of here before he said to hell with his celebrity client, stripped off his clothes, and jumped in beside her.

Leaving just yet, though, was out of the question. Gently, he sat on the edge of the bed and she stirred again from the shift of weight on the mattress. Exhausted by the intense pleasure they'd shared, Casey needed her rest, but he needed one more kiss before saying goodbye.

A low moan escaped her throat as she stretched. The sheet slipped further, exposing one deliciously pert breast. Her nipple hardened from the room's cool air that kissed her skin. Alex groaned, an intense desire to take the sweet orb into his mouth, to taste the tangy saltiness of her skin on his tongue, was about more than he could stand.

All night long she'd responded like wildfire to his every touch, so sensitive, so responsive. And she in turn had made sure he was pleasured to the hilt. Never in his life had he experienced such a night of intense passion. A man could get used to Casey's fire in his bed every night.

Alex could get used to Casey in his life.

It had been way more than a year since Valerie had trounced on his heart, and his dreams. Was he finally getting over her betrayal? His head wanted to argue, demand it was too soon to think about any kind of a relationship with a woman again, but his heart was either weaker, or more open minded than his head. His heart wanted to feel, to live again. His heart wanted to move on. With Casey.

Deep down Alex knew he should listen to his head. He wasn't ready for anything more than a casual association. It was too soon to let his heart fall. His heart and his head both needed more time.

And as much as he hated to admit it, he needed absolute proof Casey wasn't another Valerie.

"Casey, sweetheart." He lifted a lock of blond hair that had fallen in her face and tucked it behind her ear. "Casey. Wake up."

"Hmm?" she said dreamily. "Are you ready for more?" She looked up at him, her lips swollen from a night full of passionate kisses. Her eyes heavy with sleep, still smoldered with the fire he'd seen a few short hours ago.

Oh, was he ever. More than ready.

"Good morning," he said, forcing himself to tamp down his surging desire.

"What time is it?"

"Six."

"Six? Why are you up so early? We just went to bed, well, I mean, sleep." She gave him a saucy smile.

"Yeah. We did."

She placed a hand on his chest and the heat of her touch seared through the fabric of his shirt. He didn't want to leave now, not when she was there before him, ready, willing and simply so irresistible. But his future waited back in Denver. It wasn't every day a celebrity came calling, asking Alex to design his multimillion dollar house. For Alex to throw away this opportunity would be ludicrous.

She fiddled with the row of buttons and silently he begged her to work her magic once more, but then her hand froze. "You're dressed already. Is something wrong?" she asked.

"No. Nothing's wrong. Sorry to wake you. I just didn't want to leave without saying goodbye."

"Goodbye? Why say goodbye when we'll see each other all day. And besides, we don't need to be to Heather's for at least a couple more hours."

"I won't be at Heather's today. I have to take off for Denver."

"Denver? What? Why?" Her green eyes widened in surprise.

"I have some other business to take care of."

"Now? Alex, you can't leave. We're knee-deep in this job. Can't whatever it is wait?"

"Unfortunately, no." She pulled her hand away and tugged the sheet up over her breasts. "Look, I'll only be gone for a few days. And you'll do fine. You've got everything under control."

"What about the addition? They've started

framing—"

"Don't worry. I've discussed everything with Riley and Sons. They know what to do. They're handling all the major parts of the construction anyway. If they have any questions, they know where to reach me."

"They'll know where to reach you? What about me? Will I know where to reach you? And by the way, thanks for giving me so much *advance* warning." He saw her shoulders stiffen. She pulled the sheet tighter against her breasts, tucking the folds under her arms.

"I'm sorry. This all happened kind of sudden. My new client had a change in his schedule and wanted to get things rolling on his house plans immediately."

"New client? You have a new client?" She bolted upright, giving the sheet a chance to slip a fraction. His gaze dropped and she grabbed a chunk of fabric before it could fall far enough to reveal what she apparently no longer wanted him to see.

"I was going to call you about it last night, but you showed up here instead and we got…sidetracked." She lifted her chin. Damn. She was getting all defensive. "This is business, Casey. Working with more than one client at a time is what you hope for. It helps keep you in the black."

"You know that. And I know that. But Heather isn't going to like another client encroaching in on you. As far as she's concerned, you belong to her while this job is in progress."

She climbed out of bed on the opposite side of where he sat, wrapping the sheet around her as she went. Either she was feeling a little shy in the light of day, or no longer wanted him anywhere close to what he'd touched, pleasured and loved for hours. The possibility that her desires could turn stone-cold so soon was like a double whammy, hurting more than he cared to admit, and made him feel the part of the biggest kind of fool once more.

So much for learning his lesson with Valerie.

"Heather doesn't own me." He stood, frustration tensing his muscles.

"In her mind she does. Can't you tell your other client he'll have to wait? That you're too busy right now."

"It's not that simple." He faced her, the bed seeming more like a wall between them now, not the special haven where they'd shared so much only hours ago. Her eyes darkened and she took another step back.

Yeah, once a fool, always a fool.

"He's sort of…high-profile. His job takes him away for months at a time. He's got a break right now," he said, for some odd reason feeling compelled to explain.

"High-profile or not, it's not going to be that *simple* on this end, either. Heather will have a fit when she finds out you've left. What am I supposed to tell her?"

"Just explain that I have business to take care of. She doesn't need to know anything more than that."

"Un-huh. Like Heather is going to be satisfied with that lame answer. And I'm the one who has to suffer her wrath when she finds out you've left." A myriad of emotions crossed her face. Alex didn't blame her for being disappointed, even a little bit angry. Heather could be a handful when she wanted to be—which was ninety-nine percent of the time.

Casey glanced around the room as though searching for something, then her gaze landed on the chair where he'd placed her coat, shoes, and lingerie. Snatching up her things, she headed for the bathroom.

"Case...wait." She stopped, and glared at him with impatience.

God, with her hair tumbling about her face, the rumpled sheet draped around her curvaceous body, and her temper blazing in her green eyes, she was as beautiful and sexy as ever.

Dammit. He wouldn't go there. This wasn't about sex. Personal involvement. This was business. *Strictly* business.

"Casey. Come on, understand. Designing this house for Hunter Dierks will help reestablish my reputation as an architect of timber frame homes. I need this—"

"Hunter Dierks?" she asked with surprise. "You don't mean Hunter Dierks the actor?"

"Yeah. I do."

"Next to the President or the Queen of England, that's about as high-profile as you can get. No wonder you're so anxious to get out of here." She frowned, looking angrier than ever. *Son of a bitch.*

"Dammit, Case. You of all people should understand why this is such a fantastic opportunity. It'll shoot my business off into directions I can't even begin to imagine."

She shook her head. "What I understand is you're bailing on me for a bigger, better fish. Hell." She stomped into the bathroom. "In your pond, I'm just a lousy guppy."

"That's not true and you know it," he said, his own temper flaring. He followed, unwilling to let them part on short-sided stubbornness. She grabbed the door in an attempt to slam it shut, but his hand and the wood met with a loud slap, stopping it half-way. "Casey, this has nothing to do with you. It's simply the name of the game—"

"Oh? I think it does. From the start you didn't want this job. It wasn't good enough. You didn't want anyone to know you were involved with Studs for Hire and their client with the Elvis fetish because you were afraid it would hurt your precious reputation. Well, let me tell you something, buddy." She shook a finger in his face. "You insult my company. You insult me."

"Casey, you're blowing this all out of proportion. I'll only be gone a few days." He lifted his hand from the door and she seized the opportunity, slamming it shut tight. The lock clicked.

Shit. Yeah, he'd been an idiot to let his heart do the talking. His track record was proving once again he had a way of picking women.

Alex glanced at his watch and saw he was twenty minutes behind schedule. Damn, he didn't have time to debate or argue any more. Grabbing his coat and suitcase from the couch, he headed for the door without looking back. His gut clenched, wondering if he could come back.

This is what he got for wanting one more kiss.

* * * *

"Stupid. Stupid. Stupid," Casey grumbled as she stared at herself in the bathroom mirror after hearing the outer hotel room door shut. Alex was gone. Just like that, poof, he was gone.

Grabbing her brush from her purse, she worked the bristles through her hair. Hair that had been caressed and tangled in the throes of lovemaking.

"Arrgh." She tossed the brush down onto the vanity and splashed cold water on the face, trying to forget all the stupid mistakes she'd made in her life.

"Like that's ever going to happen. You'd think I'd learn, but no, I just keep on making one right after the other."

What the hell was the matter with her? Why did she have to be so dumb as to fly off the handle and get all pissy with Alex? It wasn't his fault he had to leave for a few days. She understood where he was coming from— that in order for his business to survive and be successful it was necessary to juggle more than one job at once. She and her business partners strived for the same luck with Studs for Hire.

Then why did she have to act like an idiot? Turning off the faucet, she reached for a towel and scrubbed her face dry. Their night together had been amazing. They'd connected not only physically, but emotionally, she was sure of it. Her weak body proved it.

Alex was everything she'd pictured him to be as a lover—considerate, gentle, yet strong and forthright. He'd made her feel complete.

Completely what? Sexually satisfied? Adored? Loved? Did she dare hope all of the above?

"Oh, God. I've blown it," she said to her reflection. With a deep sigh, she raked her fingers through her hair, mussing up the freshly combed strands. "This is just a bad case of the morning after jitters. It has to be. Calm down." She turned to the shower and cranked the handle to full blast. Steam quickly filled the bathroom.

Or was it deeper than jitters? Was she letting her past step in where it wasn't welcome? Messing up her life, again?

Or had Alex left on an empty promise just like her father had all those years ago? With her past history, Casey was more than a little gun-shy. Frank Burrows had left on a devout promise to return, he'd told her as much as he threw his suitcase into the backseat of his car—claiming he just needed a few days, then he'd be back and all would be right in the Burrows house.

And Casey, in her desperate desire for a normal, loving father, had believed him. It had been Christmas time after all. The season of miracles, of perpetual hope.

Only later would she realize how naive she'd been to take him at his word on that cold, snowy night. She'd stood, her feet freezing in the snow, white fluffy flakes swirling across the yard as she watched his taillights fade to a distant glow down their street, then disappear all together.

After months had turned into years of waiting for his headlights to announce his return, she'd given up and faced the fact he'd lied. He wasn't coming back.

And that's what the scared the hell out of her now. It wasn't the fact that Alex had left. It was the possibility that he might not come back. Men in her life had a habit of promising the world then bailing when things got personal, complex, or when they decided she wasn't good enough. The cycle had started with her father, and had worked its way through a slew of boyfriends.

But Alex wouldn't lie. He wouldn't deliberately deceive her. He wasn't like her father—she wanted so desperately to believe that.

The rational side of her brain told her he would return, that he wouldn't quit the job, forfeit his paycheck, or abandon her. Yet, her father had sacrificed his job, his wife, and five kids for his crazy ideas. If a family wasn't enough to hold a man, how could she expect a set of blueprints and a single night of passion to be?

She tugged loose the bed sheet she'd draped around

herself and stepped under the hot, soothing spray of the shower. Letting her head fall back, the water hit her face and rivulets slipped down her neck, her arms, and legs. All the places Alex had kissed and touched like no man before him had done.

Her heart ached for what had and hadn't been, and the uncertainties that had plagued her life for so many years. She wanted to push them aside and believe in Alex, believe that he would return.

But her father had *promised* to come back, and look what that got her—a lesson in the harsh reality that some men made promises with the intent of breaking them.

Alex had made no promises.

God, she hoped her instincts about him were right, and her logic was wrong.

Chapter Fifteen

Later that morning Casey pulled into Heather's driveway to find it full of minivans plastered with television station and newspaper logos on their sides.

"Looks like Heather's up to her old tricks," Casey mumbled as she braked and looked for a place to park. For the first time that morning, she was thankful Alex wasn't here. He'd have a fit if he could see all the news media.

After some creative driving, she managed to squeeze into a parking spot, cut the engine, and pray her Mazda wouldn't be besieged with door dings.

In spite of her current grumpy mood, Casey was thrilled to see the media crush. She needed a serious distraction. Since her and Alex's little episode bright and early this morning, she'd consumed three caffeine loaded cappuccinos and devoured two large, stop-your-heart, chocolate doughnuts. If she kept this pace up, she'd need someone to pull her off the ceiling today, and pry her into her clothes tomorrow.

Oh, but what a night it had been—she'd burned off plenty of calories to make room for her doughnut indiscretion this morning. Never before in her life had Casey experienced a night of passion like the one she'd shared with Alex.

And she'd blown it.

Another television station van raced up the drive and snuck into a tight space between two others, giving her the continued distraction she so desperately needed. Time to make the most of the situation. Heather's pull with the local media couldn't help but put Studs in the spotlight once more. Exactly what they needed to keep the phones ringing.

She raced up the walk to the front door and entered the now completely refurbished foyer to the sound of distant voices coming down the hall.

"Good morning," Joey the butler said from behind Casey.

"Oh!" Casey spun around to find the tall, dashing man standing right behind her. "Good morning, Joey. You startled me." Casey had been working around the mansion for days now, but she couldn't get used to the butler appearing out of the shadows, then disappearing again. "You need to wear a bell or something so a person knows when you're around."

He cut her a sly smile that suggested he liked it that way. "Sorry about that, miss. May I take your jacket?"

"Uh, that's okay. I'll keep it with me. It's kind of doubling as my purse."

"Ready for another full day of work, I see," Joey said as he took in her chambray shirt, jeans and work boots.

"Always." She smiled and hurried toward the stairs, anxious to get to the Elvis Racing Suite and tidy up a bit in case the television crews wanted a sneak peak.

"Miss Burrows," Joey said, stopping her on the fourth step. She turned around to face the butler.

"Yes?"

"Mrs. Gridmore is most anxious to speak with you. I'll let her know you're here." He walked away before Casey could utter a single word, leaving her no choice but to wait.

She didn't have to wait long. Heather raced into the foyer, an amazing feat while wearing high heels and a chartreuse suit with a skin tight skirt. The yellow greenish color made her red hair flame like fire.

"Casey. Casey. The TV stations are here, and so is the Omaha World Herald. Where's Alex? They all want to interview him."

Oh, shit. So much for avoiding the fact that Alex was on his way to Colorado.

"Uh, he's not here," Casey said, looking down at Heather from her advantage spot on the stairs.

"Why not? He should be. There's so much work to be done."

"He had some business to take care of," Casey said, saying exactly what he'd suggested.

"What? What business?" Her eyes narrowed with suspicion.

"I'm not sure. He…didn't say."

"Call him. Call him right now and tell him to get over here immediately." Heather flung her hands in the air, waving them madly in panic and frustration.

"I can't do that." Well, she could. He was driving down the interstate, probably listening to the radio, humming along. But she wouldn't. Not yet. She'd made a fool of herself earlier and she wasn't ready to swallow her pride quite yet. Besides, she didn't want him thinking she had nothing better to do than pine over him all day long.

"Why not?"

"He said he didn't want to be disturbed," Casey said,

a tinge of panic creeping into her own voice. Cripes. She despised lying, but what choice did she have? They were in too deep with this job to risk Heather throwing a fit and axing them all.

"Argh. When will he be here?" Heather asked, her anger mounting.

Stay cool, Case. The key here is to stay cool. "I'm not sure. He said something about being tied up for…quite a while." Okay. Maybe she wasn't really lying, just stretching the truth a little. Stretching the truth wasn't as bad as lying.

"Of all the rotten timing." Heather circled the floor, shaking her head. "I need him here today. Preferably now. I'm not sure how long I can stall the reporters."

"I'm sorry, Heather. I doubt Alex will make it in at all today. Besides, you know Alex isn't much for publicity. I'm sure I can handle any questions they might have. And I'd be happy to show them the progress we've made on the Elvis Racing Suite. If all goes well, I should be done with those rooms soon."

Heather stopped in her tracks and looked up at Casey, anger now brewing in her eyes. "I want Alex," she demanded, her teeth clenched.

Damn. That's all she needed to deal with—a case of spoiled baby syndrome. Casey's own temper flickered, but she wouldn't let it show. No way would she let it show. First she'd try the, *kill her with kindness* method.

Casey came down the steps and put a comforting arm around Heather. Ever so slowly she steered the distraught woman in the direction of where the reporters and cameras waited.

"Unfortunately, it isn't possible for Alex to be here right now," Casey said in a soothing voice. "But, you're the star of the show anyway, Heather. This is your home. Your Elvis collection. And this was all your idea in the first place. Besides, we both know Alex prefers to work in the background and let his clients shine."

"That's right. This was all my idea." Heather gushed with pride, a huge smile on her face. The tactic was working.

"Yes. And didn't I hear you mention that the Elvis jumpsuit you'd purchased had arrived? You can show it off. Not just anyone in Omaha owns a genuine, authentic Elvis jumpsuit."

"Of course. It's spectacular," Heather said, excitement taking over her anger.

Casey breathed a sigh of relief. "Terrific. Now let's go talk to those reporters."

* * * *

Casey blew past Terri's desk at closing time without so much as a howdy-do, and strode down the hallway. She couldn't handle another day like the last two.

"Hi to you, too," Terri hollered after her, but Casey didn't stop until she reached Syd's office. The door was closed tight, but that didn't stop her. She gave one quick knock then sent the door flinging open. She found Sydnie bent over backward on the desk, Trevor on top. Like two startled rabbits they jerked and scrambled, sending papers and pencils sailing to the floor. Embarrassment filled their eyes.

Sydnie pulled down her shirt and tugged at her bra, shifting things back into their proper place.

"Sorry. I need to talk to you," Casey said, unconcerned she'd found her friend in a compromising position—an almost everyday occurrence as of late. They were in love.

Love. Who the hell needed love? It only made a woman's life a miserable, stinking mess.

"Don't you know how to knock?" Trevor asked sarcastically as he yanked down his T-shirt.

"I did knock," Casey said, striding into the room.

"Then you're supposed to wait until you're invited in, not just blow through the door." Trevor combed his fingers through his disheveled hair.

"Yes, well, this is an office. Save your groping for the bedroom," Casey shot back.

"Okay. Okay." Syd held up her hands to signal an end to the confrontation. "Cool it, you two. Case, obviously you're upset about something. What's up?"

Casey threw up her hands and shot Trevor the best apologetic look she could muster after an exasperating day. "I'm sorry, Trevor. I didn't mean to snap. I'm a little out of sorts."

"A little—" Sydnie's elbow met Trevor's ribs, cutting his comment short. "Uh, apology accepted. Maybe I can help," he gasped from his ribbing.

"I appreciate the offer, but this is a girl problem."

"Say no more. I've got to be going anyway." He turned to Sydnie and gave her a long lingering kiss. "We'll finish this later, beautiful."

"If you insist," Syd said.

Casey's heart clenched. Alex had kissed her like that not so long ago, yet it felt like forever. Now, because of her stupidity, everything in her life, once again, was in a mess.

"I'll see you later at my place for supper?" Syd asked as Trevor headed for the door.

"You know it." He winked and disappeared through the door.

"So what's up with you?" Syd finger-combed her hair and plucked a paperclip out of the curly red strands.

"I've got a problem." Casey planted her hands on her hips.

"So you said." Syd stooped down to pick up her strewn papers and other miscellaneous office supplies scattered about.

"Why don't you do yourself a favor and keep the top of your desk empty? Or do you like picking up all that stuff on a daily basis because you and Trevor can't control your urges?" Casey asked, frustrated and really feeling ready to throw something.

"Okay, let me guess." Syd tossed a handful of pencils down on the desk. "Your problem is you aren't getting any."

Casey's cheeks flamed with heat. She turned away, hoping Syd wouldn't guess the truth.

"Oh. My. God. You *are* getting it," Syd gasped.

Damn. Casey squeezed her eyes shut and counted to ten, searching for patience and strength so she wouldn't take a foray down Looney Road.

"Was," she said with a calm she really didn't feel. "I was getting it. Well, got it, for one night at least," her voice rose a notch.

"One night? Did this, by chance, happen *recently?*"

"Yes. And before you even ask, it was fantastic, mind-blowing, and out-of-this-universe. But none of it matters now because he's been gone for two days. I was the biggest idiot on the planet and now I'm left scrambling to keep things under control."

"Gone? Who's gone? And please don't tell me it's Alex."

Syd cut her eyes to Casey.

Casey cringed. "Okay. I won't."

"Oh, shit. You and Alex did the horizontal mambo and now he's gone? So soon? What happened? Are you okay? What's Heather going to say? Oh, crap. Have you told her?"

Casey threw up her hands in frustration. "Stop. You sound like me now. This is hard enough the way it is."

"Sorry. I had a moment of panic. I think I'm going to need a drink."

"You? What about me? I'm stuck in the middle of this fiasco."

"Okay. You're right. Let's be calm and rational about this. Now, have you told Heather?"

"No. No way." Casey shook her head vehemently as she paced the carpet. "There was a media frenzy at her house yesterday morning and she was insisting that they wanted to interview Alex, and well, I had no choice but to make stuff up as I went, trying to appease Heather yet not reveal too much of Alex's part in all this to the media," Casey gasped. She stopped in her tracks and looked at Syd. "Alex and I had a deal. His name was supposed to be left out of any media hype."

"But Heather spilled the beans," Syd stated.

"Yes. I did a reasonable job of sidestepping their questions about him, though. Hopefully they won't have enough to go on to include him in any of the material. If they do mention his name, he's not going to be happy." Casey turned to the window and watched the fall leaves spiral down to the ground, giving the grass a mishmash splash of color. "And that's one more reason for him to be unhappy with me," she said under her breath.

"Well, we'll just have to keep our fingers crossed they

don't. And if they do, we'll worry about that when the time comes."

"Now if only I could get Heather off my back about Alex's sudden absence. She's driving me crazy."

"Stand strong. Don't tell her anything more than you already have," Syd said.

"I don't intend to." Casey turned away from the window and back to Syd. "The problem is I'm not sure how much longer I can hold her off. She's pestered the hell out of me for two days straight, wondering if I'd heard anything from him, and when he's going to be back. It's amazing I've gotten any work done. Syd."

Casey shook her head. "I can't take this kind of pressure. It's bad enough, the way things ended between Alex and me, but then to be constantly reminded of the fact is embarrassing, depressing and painful."

Ended? Had things really come to an end between them? After two days and still no word from him, she was leaning toward a big fat yes. Oh, how she hated those two little words, *the end*. They meant no second chances, no going back, and she'd heard them way too many times in her life.

"I'm sorry, Casey. I wish I knew what to tell you. As you recall, up until recently, I didn't have the best track record myself in the man department."

"You sure don't have a problem now." Casey arched a brow and nodded toward the desk.

"I finally got lucky."

Lucky? Casey wouldn't mind a little luck with Alex on her side right about now. What did she need to do to find that luck? Nail a horseshoe above her door? Buy a shamrock plant? Carry a rabbit's foot?

"I think you'll just have to grin and bear Heather for

now," Syd said. "If we pretend like nothing is wrong, hopefully she'll lay off and that'll give you some time to work things out with Alex. Then there won't be anything to worry about."

Casey groaned under her breath. Work things out with Alex?

If she were a guy, she wouldn't want to have anything to do with her screwed up way of thinking, either. Yeah, she better do some lucky charm shopping.

"What if we don't work things out? Heather is bound to keep asking questions. I've never been a very good liar. My bag of tricks is empty."

"I know. So, let's kick up productivity. The faster we get the job done, the sooner we'll be out of there."

And the sooner Casey would have no reason to patch things up with Alex. A major ache filled her chest at the thought of never feeling the comfort of his arms around her again, and never knowing the heat, the intense passion of his kisses, of his lovemaking. It had been two days and already it felt like a lifetime ago.

Casey plunked down in an overstuffed chair, feeling tired and defeated. All she really wanted to do was go home and sulk with her dog. To hell with the job. Every stroke of paint, every nail, and every piece of Elvis memorabilia were going to remind her of Alex. The realization hurt more then she could stand.

"You're right, we need to speed up production," Casey managed to say, attempting to put on a brave front. "I'll have Terri line up extra crews."

"I'll talk to Trevor, too. I'm sure he can help a few nights here and there. Terri can handle the office for a while, and I'm between projects. I'll come and work. Do you have all the remodeling details worked out?"

"Yes. And the majority of the needed materials are there, ready and waiting."

"Great. First thing in the morning, we'll hit it hard."

"Sure." Casey forced herself up out of the chair and headed for the door.

"Case," Syd said. Casey stopped, but didn't turn around. "I don't know what happened between you and Alex, and I won't pry. You tell me when you're ready. But maybe you should just pick up the phone and call him. Explain things."

Casey spun around. "Call him? Me? Call him? I was the biggest kind of fool there is and you want me to call him? I'm too embarrassed. I think I need some more time and a pound of chocolate before I can work up the courage."

"Everyone makes mistakes. There's nothing to be embarrassed about. Alex is a reasonable guy. If you explain, I'm sure he'll listen."

"I don't know. That sounds too simple to be plausible. My relationships have never been simple."

"True." Syd nodded her head. "But hey, I've seen the way Alex looks at you. There's something special there. If he's half the man I think he is, he'll hear you out."

"Yeah. Well, I guess that remains to be seen."

"This is no time to be stubborn." Syd shrugged on her coat. "Come on, let's grab Terri and go somewhere for a drink and high fat dinner topped off with that pound of chocolate. I'm sure our indulgence will help us figure out a way for you to make up for your moment of stupidity and get Alex back."

"Gee. Thanks for reiterating my shortcomings."

"You did the same for me, dear friend, and look what it got me," Syd said with a wink.

"That's right. A hot man, regular sex, and no more lonely nights. Speaking of which. Aren't you having a late supper with Trevor tonight? If you go out with us you won't want to eat again."

"Don't worry. The supper date I have planned with Trevor has nothing to do with food." Syd smiled.

"Of course. How silly of me." Casey rolled her eyes. "Then let's get going. You're going to need your energy. And I need a drink."

* * * *

"Something is going on, Rory. I just know it," Heather said as she rushed into the dimly lit, secluded basement room. "Casey has been moping over Alex all week long while he's been gone. I'm afraid they've slept together."

Her friend didn't bother looking up from where he worked with a roll of speaker wire and a bunch of miscellaneous tools under a lamp on a large round table. "Are you listening to me?" she asked.

"Yes, sugar. I heard you. Who do you think slept together?"

Rory turned on his stool, giving her his full attention. "Alex and Casey. Who else would I be talking about?"

Agitated, she crossed her arms and tapped a finger on her sleeve.

"Well." He sighed and took off his black rimmed glasses, setting them on the table. "You've been suspecting something has been going on between your next door neighbor, Leslie, and the software guru on the cul-de-sac for some time. I thought maybe you'd finally gotten definitive proof."

Heather threw up her hands and began pacing around the unfinished room. She hated the drab concrete block walls and the hard gray floor. This room reminded her too much of what her life had been like since Hector died—cold, gloomy and oh, so lonely.

"This is horrible," she ranted. "I'm so mad I could spit. Casey deliberately didn't tell me Alex had gone back to Denver. I should fire her."

"Take it easy, sugar. You can't fire her now. The house is all tore up in the remodel. As much as you hate to admit it, you need her. Just stay calm and it'll be all right."

"No. It won't be all right. This isn't fair, Rory. *I* brought him here." She thumped her chest with her thumb. "If it wasn't for me, they never would have met." She stopped pacing in front of Rory and looked down at him. Tears of anger and frustration stung her eyes. "Alex is supposed to be mine."

"Hey, take it easy." Rory took her hand in his and gently massaged his thumb over her palm, sending tingles of awareness racing through every inch of her body.

Shocked by the unexpected sensation, Heather gasped and pulled her hand away. A flicker of disappointment washed over his face, but she pushed it aside. She and Rory had been friends for years. There wasn't anything more than that between them. Was there?

She turned away, but stole a glance at him over her shoulder. His eyes. There was something different about his eyes—the way he looked at her. Did he desire her? No way. She had to be wrong.

Heather focused on the stark wall in front of her. Rory was an everyday Joe who worked a forty-hour week for the telephone company and helped underprivileged kids at a small downtown theatre. He wasn't her type, and didn't run in her high dollar circles. They'd met simply because of a common interest in Elvis memorabilia. That was it, nothing more.

"Do you know for sure they've slept together?" he asked. Was that curiosity she heard in his voice? Excitement? Hope?

Heather's own mixture of emotions tumbled inside her, making her feel dazed and confused.

"No. But a woman can sense…things," she managed to say around a lump in her throat.

"How?"

"Lovers," she fumbled over the word, "look at each other differently."

"They do?" The ache she heard in his voice made her heart pinch.

"Yes. Like the way a woman brightens when her lover walks into the room. Or the way his breath catches when she flirts with him in their own secret language. The stolen glances they share," she said softly, looking directly at Rory, needing to see if the spark of attraction she'd noticed only a moment before was still there, or if she'd imagined it. "When they're certain…no one else will see."

He smiled at her, a glimmer of tender desire filling his blue eyes. He stood and ever so gently brushed his knuckles against her cheek. The air in the room dissipated.

Oh, God. She hadn't imagined anything. It couldn't be. They couldn't be feeling more than friendship, could they? They shared common interests, knew how to cheer each other up, and knew they could call each other any time, day or night. Those were simply the elements of friendship.

It wasn't sexual attraction. She wouldn't let it be.

Stiffening her resolve, she took a quick step back, breaking the contact.

"Forget the ghost," she said angrily. "I have something else in mind." Turning, she headed for the door, unable to face the truth of what she'd seen on Rory's face.

"Heather," he commanded. She stopped short, surprised by his harsh use of her name. "Don't do something you'll regret."

"Let it go, Rory. I won't lose Alex." Without looking back she fled the room, hating like hell to hurt the one man she could always count on to be there.

Chapter Sixteen

"Done at last," Casey said with a sigh as she hung the final movie poster in the Elvis Racing Suite.

In spite of it being the longest week of her life, she'd managed to accomplish quite a lot, finishing many of the room remodels. The busier she stayed supervising work crews, testing paints and adding the final touches, the less she thought about Alex. Or at least that's what she tried to tell herself. But in reality, Alex was always in the forefront in her mind. She couldn't look at anything Elvis, design sketches, or blue prints without thoughts of Alex intruding and making her feel miserable.

Taking a few steps back, she centered herself in the room to admire her handiwork. The sooner she could get this job finished, the sooner she could put it behind her. "Good. I can chalk another one off the list."

"And you can chalk yourself off the list, too," Heather shouted as she burst into the room.

Casey spun around, feeling like she'd been punched

"You're fired. And without pay." Heather planted her hands on her hips and stared at Casey with contempt.

Casey felt the color drain from her face as if it were being sucked out of her by a high-power shop vac. Crap.

What the hell had happened here? If Heather fired her without pay, where would Casey get the money to pay all of the crews? This couldn't be happening.

"Wait a minute." She shook her head. "I'm confused. We've made great progress on the house. We're ready to start on the party room and finish the museum addition. We should have the entire project wrapped up—"

"You lied to me," Heather snapped. Her high heels tapped on the black and white tiles as she stalked up to Casey, the look of battle etched in her eyes.

"I did no such thing."

"Yes you did. Alex left a week ago and went back to Denver, and before you deny it, I know for a fact he did. Since I couldn't get a straight answer from you, I checked with his secretary."

Casey cringed. She should have known Heather would take it upon herself to call Alex's office. Time for some damage control. Somehow she had to convince Heather that firing her was an extreme measure for the minor offense of Alex crossing the state line.

"Okay, you're right." Casey held up her hands, trying her best to look remorseful. "Alex had to make a quick trip to Denver. Yes, I should have said something, but I didn't because he was only supposed to be gone for a few days. I didn't want you to worry. Besides, everything is under control—"

"A few days to me is two or three," Heather said with enough impatience to crack glass. "He's been gone a week."

"I know, but he's been working with a new client and got delayed. He'll return to Omaha as soon as possible."

"New client? What do you mean new client?" Heather's eyes bulged in her head. Her cheeks reddened.

Great. Heather was going to freak out and not let this drop. She reminded Casey of the stereotypical spoiled little rich girl on the verge of throwing a tantrum.

Casey groaned, debating just how much she should tell Heather to pacify her. If Casey told her just who that client was, Heather might be star-struck enough to let the whole matter drop. On the other hand, her jealousy streak might kick in, making her really go ballistic.

A rock lodged in Casey's stomach. She was walking a dangerous line here. And for the umpteenth time, she berated herself for letting her heart get involved and losing control.

"Alex had a man contact him about building a new home in the Aspen area," Casey said with caution, "and because of the guy's unusual work schedule, he had to meet with Alex this week."

"He can't do that."

"It's not a big deal, Heather. It's not uncommon for architects and contractors to have more than one job going on at the same time. It's business."

"Well, in this case, it is a big deal. Obviously, Alex didn't read his contract close enough," she said, flicking a piece of paper in the air.

Oh, shit. The contract. Casey had completely forgotten about the little, one page contract Heather had insisted upon Alex signing.

"What about the contract?" Casey asked, opting to play dumb and bide some time.

"There's an exclusivity clause in here. He can't work

for anyone else while he's working for me."

Oh, boy. Casey had spaced off the paper as insignificant, and hadn't given it much thought. And apparently, Alex hadn't either. Big mistake. Especially when dealing with a woman like Heather. After all the years of handling Heather and her demands, Casey should have known the widow would make sure her butt was covered in a project of this magnitude.

Heather might put on the blond bimbo persona, but on the inside she was as sharp and shrewd as her late husband. Hector had taught her well.

A second rock joined the first already in Casey's stomach. This is what she got for letting herself veer off the business track. Things had gotten personal with Alex—way too personal, and as a result she'd screwed up royally. And in more ways than one. Not only had she been an idiot with the best man she'd ever known, but put her and her friends' business in jeopardy.

Now she was faced with saving them all. The thought that everything rode on her shoulders made her heart clinch. How could she right a mess of this magnitude when in spite of all of her love and efforts, she couldn't even keep her father from leaving all those years ago?

Casey had no idea, but she wasn't a quitter.

"Heather, you have to understand, this new client is a great opportunity for Alex. He couldn't turn down the job. It would mean a huge financial loss. You wouldn't want Alex to suffer, would you?" she asked, hoping Heather really did have feelings for Alex and they'd be enough to make her see reason.

"I don't care. He's supposed to be working for me. Am I not paying him enough?" She crossed her arms in a huff.

Okay, so maybe Heather really didn't care for Alex. Maybe he was just a handsome diversion from the boredom encompassing her life. But Casey cared for Alex. Heck, more than cared.

She'd fallen in love with him.

Casey squared her shoulders, determined to get through to her client.

"Hey, Heather. You know Hector was a savvy business man. He'd be in complete agreement that Alex shouldn't limit himself to one job at a time. He always said a progressive businessman should be constantly looking ahead if he's going to survive. Hector truly believed those words. His success is proof of it." Casey crossed her fingers and hoped she'd made an impact.

"Well, maybe," Heather said. She began a survey of the bedroom, as if noticing it for the first time, checking out the details that commemorated Elvis' roles as race car drivers in his movies *Spinout, Speedway,* and *Viva Las Vegas.*

The room was painted a crisp white and accented with black and white checkered tile on the floor. A red bedspread with two white racing stripes down one side had been designed to match one of the jackets Elvis had worn in *Speedway,* and yellow and orange throw pillows had been added to complete the Sixties feel.

Dozens of various sized photographs from each movie were clustered in separate galleries around their respective movie posters. And for the final touch to the room, Casey had commissioned a larger-than-life portrait of Elvis, portraying his character in *Speedway,* painted above the bed.

"All right," Heather said, turning away from a collection of movie photos. "I'll cut Alex a break."

A weight lifted from Casey's shoulders. "Terrific! You won't—"

"Under one condition." Heather held up a finger.

Damn. Now what? "And that is?"

"He's back here and on the job within twenty-four hours, personally working on my bedroom. And because I'm impressed by what I see, *if* he makes it, you're no longer fired."

Great. Casey didn't know whether to still feel relieved, or be in panic mode. What Heather was asking for was a mighty big *if*. Especially since Casey's stubborn pride hadn't let her speak to Alex since he'd left. Even if she did call him now and apologize, would it be enough?

"And if he doesn't make it?" she asked, just in case.

"Then I sue him for breach of contract."

Casey's heart tripped in her chest.

"And," Heather continued, "you're still fired without pay."

Now her heart lurched to a stop. That's what she got for asking.

Heather threw her a smug grin and sauntered from the room like a cat who knew there was no way for the mouse to escape the trap that had been set.

Casey had to face it. She was left with no other options now but to call Alex. All week long Syd and Terri had been telling her to do just that, but she'd balked, not yet ready to face her embarrassment, swallow her pride, and admit what a fool she'd been.

But Heather had thrown down the challenge. And time was short.

Casey reached for her cell phone.

* * * *

"As you can see, Hunter, I've chosen cedar trusses for the vaulted ceiling in the great room. They're rustic like you prefer, but are also classic, not to mention stout."

"They look terrific," the actor said as he studied the preliminary plans for his new home from the comforts of an overstuffed chair, his injured leg propped on an ottoman. "This is great, Alex. You've incorporated everything I've asked for. And you've done it fast. I appreciate this."

"No problem. Happy to do it. I'm really excited about the project."

"That makes two of us. I'd really like to take you out to my property tomorrow so you can have a closer look around, get a feel for the terrain."

"Are you sure you're up to it with your leg in a cast?"

"No problem. I'm an *action* star, remember? My fans think I'm invincible and can do anything, like survive a plane crash, a car wreck, and a pulverizing by the bad guy all in a two-hour period," he said with a heavy dose of sarcasm. "Nothing like movie magic."

Alex laughed at Hunter's wit and appreciated his humble, good ol' boy attitude. No wonder he wanted away from the trumped up bullshit of the Hollywood scene when he wasn't working.

"But seriously, I insist on taking you out there so *I* can get out and do something. Boredom is driving me nuts."

"It might be tough for you to get around on those crutches. You mentioned it's rocky out there."

"No problem." Hunter waved off Alex's concern with the empty water bottle he'd been fiddling with. "I've already gotten pretty adept at using the damn things. I'll be fine."

"Okay. If you're sure, tomorrow it is."

The cell phone at Alex's hip buzzed. He checked the caller ID, hoping to let the call go through to his voice mail, but when he saw Casey's name, his breath hitched. He hadn't spoken with her in days. And at the moment he saw her name, he realized once again just how much he'd missed her sultry voice, her subtle spicy scent, and her secret vulnerabilities hidden beneath that smart-mouthed exterior. The phone buzzed again, pulling him from his mini fantasy.

"Uh, can you excuse me a minute, Hunter? I need to take this call."

"Sure. No problem."

Alex left his office and headed for the empty one down the hall where Valerie had done a fair job of running his life and business into the ground.

"Hey, Casey. What's up?" he asked, trying to sound blasé and not let on how he felt—excited, thrilled, and thankful to finally hear from her.

"Alex. I have a…problem here at Heather's. Do you have a second?"

Hmm. No, how are you? No, I've missed you. All business right off the bat. Not a good sign. Apparently she hadn't been missing him as much as he had her.

"Sure." He wanted to say he had way more than a second for her, but refrained. He didn't want to be a dope and ruin his chances of working things out between them before the conversation even got started.

"I'm sorry to bother you. I know you're busy, but we've got a little problem here."

"So you've said. What's this *little* problem?" He laughed, hoping to keep the conversation light, casual.

"Well, it's not really little. It's more like major." Her

voice wavered. She sighed as if she'd had enough and was on the verge of a breakdown.

So much for keeping things light. "Let me take one guess. The problem is Heather."

"BINGO. Alex you have to come back. Pronto." It was obvious Casey was working hard to stay the professional and keep her emotions under control, but her voice didn't lie. She was struggling.

Alex couldn't help hoping he was at least partly responsible for her distress. If so, that meant she'd been missing him. That single thought alone tortured his libido, and his common sense. What he wouldn't give to crawl through the phone right about now.

"Alex?"

"I wasn't planning on heading your way for a couple more days," he said at last, getting his mind back on business.

"But that's too long. You need to be here by tomorrow."

"Tomorrow? I can't. I've got to finish some details with Hunter first."

"Alex, do you remember signing a contract with Heather?"

"Contract?" Alex felt his stomach pitch. "Hell. It was just a one page deal…"

"Did you read it?"

"Yeah, sure."

"Do you remember it having an exclusivity clause?"

His stomach did a nosedive. "Dammit," he grumbled. He braced a hand on the window frame and stared out at the Rocky Mountain landscape shrouded in Denver's daily haze—suddenly feeling as engulfed as the mountain peaks. Now, too late, he remembered the clause.

He'd thought nothing of it at the time of signing the contract, had no clue a major movie star would knock on his door and take him away from the Gridmore job. His business plate had been bare for so long that working for Heather exclusively hadn't even been a worry.

"My thoughts exactly," Casey said. "And you haven't heard the worst of it."

"Do I really want to know?" he quipped, trying not to let Heather and her antics intimidate him.

"Probably not, but it's one of those necessary evil things. Heather is threatening to sue you for breach of contract, and fire me without payment. That means neither you nor I get paid if you aren't back in Omaha in twenty-four hours."

"Real generous of her to give us twenty-four hours to save our butts," he said with a heavy dose of sarcasm.

"She's all heart."

Alex grumbled and raked his fingers through his hair. Although the deal was working out with Hunter, he wouldn't see much in the way of money until the job got underway. And Alex still needed money now to keep him afloat, and make his first, sizeable payment to Western Bank within the week.

"Alex, you have to get back here. I don't want to end up in court over this whole deal. Studs can't afford to take this kind of financial hit."

Alex closed his eyes and prayed for strength. He couldn't take the hit, either. But how could he be in two places at once? He had to be honest with Casey. She was depending on him as much as he was depending upon the deal with Dierks.

"I can't make it back that soon. We're heading out to the job site tomorrow."

"Alex. Heather is serious. She'll sue."

He groaned under his breath. "Can you do something to stall her, bide some extra time?"

"I've been doing that all week. I've run out of ideas."

Alex winced at the hard tone of her voice. He couldn't argue with her there. "I don't—"

"I need you, Alex," Casey said.

His breath caught. She needed him? Like he needed her—in his bed? In his life?

"That is…to save our butts and get this project done," she continued in a rush, as if to clarify that the only need she had for him was work related and nothing more, nothing less.

A wave of disappointment rushed over him. After being gone a week, Casey hadn't said what he'd hoped to hear. What he wanted to hear. Damn, even the impersonal tone of her voice wasn't giving him any hint or indication that she'd missed him.

God, help him. He didn't want to believe they were just a one night stand. And he sure as hell didn't want to compare her to Valerie. But he'd been down this road before. His hand tightened into a fist. Making the same mistake twice wasn't an option in his book.

Yet, his gut nagged at him, argued that Casey was different, that things would be different this time around if they'd both let it happen.

"Look, I'll see what I can do," he said, not sure what that would be.

Deafening silence hung between them for agonizing seconds, then a faint sound of something, like a sigh, whispered through the line.

"Okay," she said at last. "I'll hold off applying for food stamps and unemployment for a few more hours," she quipped. "But I'm not sure I can hold out much longer than that."

Alex heard the forced smile in her voice and in that instant he knew what he had to do.

* * * *

Casey stood in the middle of Heather's stripped bare bedroom, a paint roller in one hand and gallons of Scarlet O'Hara red at her feet ready to be put to use. The white primer coated walls stared back at her, daring her to do something about their starkness.

She stifled a yawn and glanced at her watch. It was nearly midnight on a Friday night and here she was working on someone else's bedroom when other women her age were either out on dates, or at home rocking babies back to sleep.

Casey groaned. She'd been tempted to cozy up with a bowl of popcorn and a good movie, but by keeping her mind focused on work and not on Alex's final words—*I'll see what I can do*, she was at least able to function.

With those six simple words he'd made no promises, no guarantees, but yet left her with enough hope to keep pushing forward. She had to. Besides, the only way sleep was going to come now was if she overdosed on sleeping pills. Everything was at stake—her and her friends' futures, Alex's business, Casey's heart.

Her heart? Yeah, dammit. Her heart. The rate she was going her heart was going to be beat to a pulp, and knowing her luck, charred to boot before this was all over.

"What a fine mess you've gotten yourself into this time, Burrows." She blew a lock of hair out of her eyes and glanced around the room she was responsible for turning into Heather's *Burning Love* suite.

What an irony. Casey's love life teetered on the edge of nonexistence, and she was the one who was supposed to turn this room into a haven for lovers. Damn. Life sucked sometimes.

"Well, this isn't getting it done," she sighed. She bent over to grab the wire handle on a paint can.

"Maybe I can help," a deep voice said from behind her.

Casey's hand froze around the cool metal. Her heart did a triple flip. Alex? Could he really be here? Or was she imagining things?

"Nice view," he said.

Oh, shit. She wasn't imagining anything. And her butt was sticking up in the air in her baggy paint splattered jeans. She stood and spun around. Blood rushed to her head and she wasn't sure if it was from her quick movement, or the fact he hadn't let her down. "You're here? How—?"

"What? No, hello? No, I missed you?" He pushed away from the door frame and shortened the distance between them. He wore his bomber jacket and his usual flannel shirt underneath. Several days' growth of a beard shadowed his chin, making him look tough, sexy, and irresistible as hell.

Casey swallowed hard.

"I'm just…surprised to see you," she managed to say in spite of her racing heart. Beads of perspiration broke out beneath her T-shirt, and it wasn't because the room was hot.

"You didn't think I'd come," he stated, a hard edge to his tone. A muscle ticked at his jaw.

She'd wanted so desperately to believe he would come,

yet, admittedly, she'd had her doubts. "It's just so late. Midnight," she said in lieu of telling the truth. She pointed to her watch, feeling like a silly school girl who didn't have a clue about boys.

"So." He grabbed the handle of the paint roller dangling from her fingers before it fell to the floor. "You said you needed me. I came to find out why."

"I told you. Heather is threatening to sue if—"

"Nah." He shook his head. "I think you need me for more than my expert painting skills." He held up the roller and twirled it between them.

"I…" The word came out sounding like a squeak to her ears. Crap. She needed to get a grip, be the assertive woman she prided herself on being.

"It's been a long week, Case."

"Yes. It has," she said defensively. "One of the longest weeks of my life." She breathed a sigh of relief, glad to get something, no matter how small, off her chest. Every day they'd been apart had been longer than the one before.

"I peeked in at some of the other rooms. Looks like you got a lot done in my absence. You've worked hard."

Because work has been the only thing keeping me sane.

"Just doing my job," she said instead, wanting to remain in control and not let her emotions rule.

"By the paint on your face, I can see that." He lifted his hand and brushed the pad of his thumb over a smudge of primer on her cheek. Casey inhaled sharply, the simple touch as mind-altering as one-hundred proof alcohol.

Her body took charge and leaned forward on its own accord. Alex answered by cupping her cheek in the palm of his hand. Casey's eyes fluttered closed. She could no longer deny the feelings she had for this man. She'd rather die than go through life knowing she'd blown this gift she'd been given.

"Alex." She opened her eyes. "I know I was a dolt the other day. That I overacted. The truth is—"

"Case. It's in the past. Let it go." He dropped his hand and Casey ached from the loss of his touch. No. Not this time. She wasn't going to back down this time and just let him become another hurtful memory.

"No. I can't. The past *is* the problem." She placed her fisted hands on her hips.

"Okay. I'm listening."

"I panicked, Alex. I'm sorry. I have this little problem with men when they realize I'm not perfect. They leave. Including my father. I've been dumped so many times that when you said you had to go to Denver, I thought it was because of me. That I'd failed again and you were leaving because you were disappo—"

He dropped the paint roller and cupped her face in his hands. "Don't say it. Don't ever say it." He captured her mouth with his and kissed her hard, deep, and with more passion than she imagined possible. He smelled of leather and the autumn night.

"So tell me," he said, resting his forehead against hers when the kiss ended. "Was that the kiss of a disappointed man?"

"Hardly," she said, feeling almost star-struck and blissfully happy. Alex had come back to her. He'd told her she wasn't the problem, and even sealed his argument with a searing kiss.

Maybe life didn't suck after all.

He let his hands fall from her shoulders and took a step back. Uh, oh. Maybe she was jumping the gun. Casey held her breath.

"You aren't the only one who's had relationship problems," he said softly.

"Care to share?"

He quirked a brow. "I don't want to bore you."

"I could never find you boring." Casey winked, silently suggesting Alex had plenty of interesting qualities to keep her boredom at bay.

His lips turned up in a smile as he placed a booted foot on the bottom rung of an aluminum ladder. He shook his head and a few strands of his hair brushed over his forehead, giving him that sexy, bad boy look she so desired.

And had missed.

"A few years ago when I was with an established architectural firm, I was introduced to a woman who was VP of marketing for a large window manufacturing company.

"Valerie Turner and I clicked both professionally and personally. We became involved and I quickly discovered she was vivacious and ambitious as hell. I was thinking about starting my own firm, and one night over a few drinks I mentioned my plans. Valerie loved the idea and the next thing I knew I had a business partner. We quit our jobs, set up shop and the rest...well." His jaw tightened, telling Casey he was working hard to keep his emotions in check.

"Things went belly-up?"

"Belly-up is an understatement." Alex laughed with an edge of bitterness to his voice. "We had a good-sized list of contacts from our previous jobs and we hit the ground running. We grew fast. Too fast. We ended up with so many people working for us, I had no clue how large the payroll had become, or how many vendors we'd racked up bills with."

"Let me guess. Valerie was in charge of the finances?"

Alex's brow furrowed as he let out a pent-up breath. "She'd convinced me not worry about the money, to focus on the architectural and construction side of the business. She had a business background, and had held a major position in her last job. I had no reason not to trust her."

"But you found out differently."

"Oh, yeah. I got the shock of my life. I found myself a quarter-of-a-million dollars in debt."

Casey gasped. "What? How can that be? Wasn't there any money coming in?"

"Yes. But it was gone. She'd timed everything perfectly and had been spending money for months." Letting his foot fall to the floor, he walked to the window, braced his arm against the frame, and gazed out into the darkness. "I didn't discover what was going on until *after* I found her in bed with my best lead contractor."

"Oh, Alex." Casey stepped forward, wanting to reach out and touch him, offer comfort for all the pain he'd endured, but the stiffness of his shoulders made her hold back. He'd been wronged by one woman. Would he want comfort from another? "What did you do?"

"I ended the relationship and the partnership on the spot. To my surprise she didn't argue, didn't plead for understanding, or beg for forgiveness. She simply packed her bags and left. For days I went through the motions of just existing. I couldn't believe that in reality, she didn't give a damn about us, or the business." He took a deep breath. "Then my creditors started calling. I began checking the books and it didn't take me long to realize she'd staged the affair for a greater purpose."

"Staged it?"

Alex let his hand fall to his side. He turned and looked at Casey. A mixture of anger, hurt, and regret shrouded his face.

"I was blind, Casey. *So damn blind.* She wanted me to find her in bed with another man."

"Why?" she asked, even though she was beginning to suspect Valerie's motives. But Casey knew Alex needed to say it out loud, not so much for her, but for him.

"The affair was her scapegoat. It was an easy way for her to get out of our relationship, personally and professionally. She knew the breakup would cover her tracks long enough to give her time to disappear."

"And then it'd be too late," Casey said softly.

"Yes. I was flat broke. I didn't even have money to operate with, making it difficult to complete jobs in progress. I had no way to pay the work crews. My credit was soon in shreds, and it didn't take long for my reputation to take the hit."

"But what she did was wrong," Casey said, incredulous. She threw up her hands in disbelief, her temper flaring toward the woman who'd done such horrible things to Alex. "Valerie should be arrested, behind bars."

Alex shook his head. "On paper she really didn't do anything illegal. She'd simply paid herself an exorbitant salary, and all her purchases were categorized as legitimate business expenses. By the time I figured it all out, she was no where to be found. Even if I'd known where she was, I couldn't afford to hire a lawyer and sue."

Casey now fully understood Alex's reluctance to take the job with Studs for Hire and Heather Gridmore. Her heart ached for him and all the injustices he'd been dealt, and ached for what might never be between them. Forgetting a cheating, conniving woman, who'd nearly ruined his reputation in the process, wouldn't be easy for any man. Especially when he had two-hundred and fifty thousand reasons not to forget.

Casey couldn't blame him for wanting nothing more from her than a working relationship. She'd even told herself time and again to keep things strictly on a business level. Maybe one day she'd learn to heed her own advice.

"I'm sorry, Alex. And I'm sorry this job wasn't what you hoped it to be. But we're almost done. If you can stick it out a while longer, we can finish and collect our fees. Then you…can go back to Denver and forget the whole thing." A lump formed in Casey's throat. Her heart threatened to crack in half.

"Forget? Casey, there's no forgetting."

"But—"

He pulled her tight up against his hard body, and his hands slid through her hair, down to her shoulders and down to her back. His fingers burned through the thin fabric of her T-shirt, igniting a blazing fire.

Casey wrapped her arms around his neck and inhaled the tantalizing scent that was uniquely Alex. She wanted to bury herself in his embrace and never let go.

They stumbled backward and Alex pinned her up against the wall. His lips left hers and burned a trail over her cheek. "You said you needed me, Case," he said against her skin. He peppered kisses down to her jaw and to the hollow of her neck. "Tell me. Tell me why you need me."

Casey gasped for air and dug her fingers into the soft

leather of his jacket.

"I don't think I...can live without you, Alex."

Alex broke his kiss from her skin and froze. His eyes gazed deep into hers. Casey's heart pounded so fast she couldn't read the emotions smoldering in their depths. But there was no turning back now. She'd never forgive herself if she didn't tell him the truth.

"No. I need you because I love you, Alex." There, she'd said it. And she was all the stronger for it.

A smile tugged at the corners of his mouth. "That's what I was hoping you'd say." He brushed a lock of hair away from her face. "And you know, even Elvis had to leave the building sometime. What do you say we do the same? I want to show *you* how much I love you."

"Oh, Alex. You've got me *All Shook Up*."

Epilogue

Early December

"My feet are killing me," Terri said as she kicked off her black high heels, joining Casey and Sydnie at the bar in the party room of Heather's mansion.

"Mine, too," Casey said, taking a sip of her colorful, *Blue Hawaii* inspired drink. "And so is my throat. I've never talked so much in one night in my life."

Heather had dedicated the museum wing of her house with major fanfare, and all evening the three partners had given tours and shown off the remodeled rooms in the house to Heather's friends, fellow Elvis fans, and the news media. Even the Mayor of Omaha and the Governor of Nebraska had made it a point to come out and see what all the hoopla was about.

Now, at half-past midnight, the die-hard Elvis fans still danced to one Elvis song after another on the dance floor filling one corner of the massive room.

The cute bartender, dressed like the King, complete with slicked back hair and sideburns, wasted no time in serving Terri one of the many specialty Elvis drinks concocted for the party. Cautiously, Terri climbed up onto a bar stool in her skintight leather skirt.

"Having trouble?" Syd asked.

"I'm not used to dressing like this," Terri whispered so the bartender wouldn't hear. "I feel like I need to be carrying a whip and a pair of handcuffs."

Casey and Sydnie laughed. "I can't believe you just said that," Casey said. "Do you have some secret fantasy we don't know about?" She winked at her friend and gave her a good-hearted nudge.

A rosy blush colored Terri's cheeks. "I'll never tell," she said behind the rim of her glass.

"Oh, yes you will. All we need is a gallon of Rocky Road and you'll be spilling your guts after three spoonfuls. Besides, with these outfits, we all should be having fantasies."

"Yeah, and living them out," Syd said and winked. "Dressed like this I sort of feel like Elvis myself. Trevor's been itching to get his hands on me all night. It was cool of Heather to have these made for us."

"Generous with a motive," Casey said. "It's no accident ours look like Elvis' *1968 Comeback Special* black leather outfit. Heather planned to use us as guides for this party from the start."

"Fine by me. For the first time in months I've actually had men looking at me," Terri said. "It's a heady feeling. Now if I could just find a man, like you two, who wants more than a one night stand."

"You'll find someone," Casey said, suddenly missing Alex. "Just be patient. And speaking of men, have either of you seen our star architect? I feel like we've hardly seen each other tonight." She scanned the crowd for Alex, but only saw a mixture of people mingling in and out of the museum and onto the dance floor, or to the cluster of retro-style sofas and chairs in the center of the room.

"I saw HGTV had him cornered down the hall a few minutes ago," Terri said.

"Well, it's time *I* cornered him," Casey said. She downed the last of her drink. "I'll catch you two later."

"Don't forget to show up for work Monday morning," Syd quipped. "The Bentleys are coming in first thing to discuss their remodel. They're huge Husker fans, so be thinking of some ideas over the weekend."

If the weekend worked out like Casey hoped, she'd be too busy to think about work. "I won't forget," she said over her shoulder. She made her way through the crowd and noticed an early December snow falling outside the large windows encompassing the south wall of the room. A vast coating of white already covered the grounds outside. Maybe, with a little luck, she and Alex would get snowed in together.

Casey left behind the noise of the party and stepped out into the hallway. She checked the various rooms searching for Alex, but he was no where to be found. At last she saw him standing in the dimly lit family room, gazing out the large cathedral style windows overlooking the back deck.

She leaned against the door jamb and crossed her arms, prepared to enjoy the view. She studied his lean form silhouetted by the soft deck lights shining in through the windows. Dressed completely in black, his hair slicked backed in the roguish style reminiscent of Elvis' early days, Alex looked handsome, sexy, and hot. Casey's fingers itched to touch.

Come on snow.

"Looks like immortalizing Elvis in Omaha wasn't such a bad idea after all," she said softly.

Slowly he turned, a smile tugging at his lips.

"In more ways than one," he drawled.

Casey pushed away from the door and walked across the room to where he stood. With each step her heart hitched in anticipation of being with him again. Five days had been way too long.

"I want you to have the piano, Rory," Heather's unexpected voice said from the other side of a partial wall that separated the family room and the kitchen.

Casey and Alex glanced toward the kitchen.

"No thanks," a tall, dark-haired man said. "I don't accept charity." He took a long pull on his bottle of beer and braced a hand on the counter.

Alex clasped Casey's shoulders and guided her back into the shadows.

"It's not charity. If it makes you feel better, think of it as payment for your help. I know Elvis only played it a couple of times, but it's still a—"

"You don't have to buy me, Heather. Look, I have to go. It's late." He set down his beer and turned to leave.

"Then think of it as a gift." Heather put a hand on his arm, stopping him.

"Now what is it you want me to do?" Casey could see his eyes narrow in suspicion. Heather dropped her gaze, and then looked back up at him.

"I want you to stay. I want you to...I just...want you to love me," Heather said softly.

"Love you?"

"Yes. We've been friends a long time, Rory. And I think I've loved you almost as long. I just didn't see it."

The man smiled and caressed Heather's cheek. "That's all you had to say." He leaned in and kissed her.

"That guy has the right idea," Alex whispered into Casey's ear.

"Does he now?"

"You betcha, sweetheart." Without further hesitation, Alex captured her mouth with his. His kiss was gentle, yet intense, passionate. He smelled of leather and the mountains, intoxicating her brain with desire. A moment later they came up for air and Casey noticed the kitchen was now empty. She and Alex were alone once more. And he was all hers.

"Looks like Heather found her man after all."

"Yeah, and it wasn't me." He gave a big smile.

"Are you disappointed?"

"No way. I was holding out for you, sweetheart. Success is mine."

Casey laughed, happiness filling her heart. Alex's eyes darkened, smoldering with promises Casey wanted to personally see that he kept. "And speaking of which, you were right about this job being a good thing. I had more business cards shoved at me tonight than I can count."

"Ah, see. Didn't I tell you, you should listen to me?" She playfully shook a finger at him.

"Not that I recall. But, I did take it upon myself to listen a time or two during the last few months."

"Oh, did you now?"

"In fact, come to think of it, I listened to you a helluva lot."

"Really?"

"Really." He reached into the inside pocket of his leather jacket and pulled out a slim package with a smashed gold bow.

Casey's breath caught. "What's this? Christmas is three weeks away yet."

"It's not for Christmas. This is more like a little

something to…celebrate our success."

"Celebrate. Hmm. You've got me curious."

"So open it."

"You don't have to ask twice." Casey untied the bow and removed the paper. "*Elvis, Aloha from Hawaii* on DVD," she laughed. "You remembered."

"Yep. And I thought you and I could have a little Aloha party," he drawled. Even in the dim light she could see his brown eyes darken with desire. Lifting a lock of hair off her shoulder, he slowly rubbed the strands between his fingers.

Oh, boy. In spite of the party going on down the hall, Casey wanted to strip the leather from his body and have her way with him right here, right now. Terri was right. When a man looked at you like this, it was a heady feeling.

"I'm impressed. You *were* listening," she said, feeling a little breathless. "We talked about this concert way back when we first started this project, before we went to Memphis."

"Before we went to Memphis." He grazed the back of his fingers along her jaw, sending a new wave of searing need rushing through her body.

"Since we listen to each other so well," he said, taking a step closer. "I have a confession to make." Casey's breath died in her throat. He'd already told her that he loved her. Was there something else he hadn't mentioned— like he worked for the CIA, or that he was really married? Was he going to renege on the *I love you?*

"Confession?" Her fingers tightened around the DVD.

"Don't worry, it's nothing earth shattering," he laughed. "Do you remember when you asked me how I knew so much about Elvis?"

She narrowed her eyes. "Yes."

"I used to do Elvis impersonations for a living."

"What?" Suddenly, all of Casey's worries felt lighter than the snow falling outside. "You? An Elvis impersonator? I can't believe it."

"Well, believe it. The King of Rock 'n' Roll helped me pay my way through college. I had such a steady stream of gigs I never had to work a regular job. It was great."

"Whoa. Now I'm really impressed. You must've been good."

"I never got any complaints," he said with a slight drawl. He shrugged and threw her a smile that nailed Elvis to a T.

"Wow. You are good. I knew there was something special about you the moment we met in the airport."

"Why, thank you. Thank you very much," he said, mimicking Elvis one more time. He winked, and their laughter filled the room. "I'm a man of many talents. I bet you never thought I could save damsels in distress *and* portray a legend, did you?"

"Nope. I thought you were just a lowly architect."

They laughed and Casey loved the sound of his deep voice full of happiness. She swore she'd never get tired of the sound.

"There's one more thing," he said.

"More?" Casey's heart fluttered. "Boy, you're full of surprises tonight, aren't you?"

"Maybe." He shrugged. "Open the DVD."

"Okay." She looked down at the DVD case, not sure what he was up to now. For the first time she noticed the plastic wrap had already been removed. Had he put something inside?

She lifted her gaze and saw excitement filling his eyes. Opening the case she noticed a folded slip of light green paper tucked under the clips on the inside lid. The minute she pulled it out of the case she knew she was holding a check. But why would Alex give her money?

She unfolded the check and saw a blur of numbers swimming on the paper. "Alex," she gasped. "What's this?"

"I want to buy into Studs for Hire."

"What?"

"That is if you'll let me," he said.

"Pinch me."

"Pinch you?"

"Yes. Because any minute I'm going to wake up and discover the last few months have been nothing but a wonderful, crazy dream."

"It's not a dream, Casey. In spite of my one failure, I do know a good business venture when I see it. I didn't know for sure how much it would take, but I figured this would be a place to start."

"It's a start all right. But, Alex. Twenty-five thousand dollars? Are you sure? After what you've been through. The financial risks you've already faced—"

"Ssh." He placed a finger on her lips. "*I* have everything under control," he said, quoting one of her favorite phrases. "I took my biggest risk by entrusting you with my heart. If I trust you with that, money is nothing in comparison."

"Hmm. You trust me with your heart, and you're willing to financially commit yourself to my business. Does that mean you plan on sticking around for a while?"

"Like glue that never lets go." He wrapped his arms around her, swallowing her in his embrace. The warmth of him, of his love, seeped into her body and soul, and for the first time in her life, she felt completely whole.

He kissed her again with a promise of what was to come between them tonight, and every night for the rest of their lives. Her heart swelled with happiness knowing Alex would never leave her standing in the freezing cold of a snowy night.

"Besides," he said softly against her lips between kisses. "Elvis taught me there's always more money that can be made."

"Hmm. Is that right?" She traced her tongue along his bottom lip. "Well, do you know what Elvis *taught me?*"

"No." He captured her lips completely for a long, lingering kiss. "Enlighten me."

"That I shouldn't stop myself from falling in love with you. So I didn't. And in case you haven't noticed, I'm an excellent student."

"I've noticed, all right." Alex smiled, leaned back and looked out the window and up at the night sky. "Thanks, Elvis. I owe you one, buddy." He turned his attention back to Casey. "Now, Miss Studs for Hire, let me take you home. On a snowy night like this, I'm in the mood for a fire."

"A little Hawaiian fire?" She winked.

"You know it."

About Sherry James

A native Nebraskan, Sherry James spent her youth riding and writing, and all of those hours spent in the saddle gave her plenty of time to think up a slew of stories. These days she's a wife to an amazing husband, and the mother of two equally amazing kids. She rides when she gets the chance and can't imagine her life without

© copyright Brenda Kranz Photography

horses. A former rodeo queen, and founding member and past president of the Prairieland Romance Writers, she is also a longtime member of Romance Writers of America. She is a multi published nonfiction writer of magazine and newspaper articles, and has been a winner and finalist in many writing competitions. She has written seven romance novels and she is currently working on the third book in her Studs for Hire series.

Write to Sherry at
P.O. Box 5162, Grand Island, NE 68802-5162,
or visit her web site at
www.sherryjames.com

Printed in the United States
95496LV00001B/85-102/A

9 780977 468294